S0-BXW-724

THE ANCESTORS CRY OUT

THE ANCESTORS CRY OUT

Eugenia Lovett West

DOUBLEDAY & COMPANY, INC.
GARDEN CITY, NEW YORK
1979

Library of Congress Cataloging in Publication Data

West, Eugenia Lovett, 1923–
  The ancestors cry out.

  I. Title.
PZ4.W5172An [PS3573.E818]   813'.5'4
ISBN: 0-385-14640-X
Library of Congress Catalog Card Number 78-14686

Copyright © 1979 by Eugenia Lovett West

ALL RIGHTS RESERVED
PRINTED IN THE UNITED STATES OF AMERICA
FIRST EDITION

THE ANCESTORS CRY OUT

CHAPTER 1

You who know only the North do not know
color, do not know light.

LAFCADIO HEARN:
Two years in the French West Indies

No one had come to meet me. I stood alone on the quay while the harbor master talked to the driver who had brought the empty buggy, questioning him in a dialect I could not understand. The message, translated, was that the Thaws sent apologies but there was illness in the household and none of the family could be spared to make the trip into town.

I looked up at the steamer's deck, looming high above, where several of my new shipboard friends were watching; even at this distance, I could see the concern on their faces. Young ladies of nineteen did not travel by themselves in the Caribbean; there would be family, or at least an older chaperone—and certainly they would be met by the host or hostess.

Until that moment my bounding spirits had served me well, but now several unpleasant facts demanded my attention: I was a stranger to the Thaws as well as to the island; it was awkward enough for them to receive me three days before Christmas and now if there was sickness in the house as well—I stared uncertainly at the steamer's white sides. There would be surprise if I marched back up the gangplank but it could be explained, it was still possible.

The moment passed, and the panic. Willing myself to compo-

sure, I walked quickly to the buggy with its perambulator top.
One of the leather buttons on the seat was missing, and I con-
centrated on the torn place as we moved off, listening to the familiar sound of horses' hoofs, and knowing that it was now too
late to turn back.

Once away from the town, the road followed the coast, twisting around hills that rose sharply from the water's edge. I was
startled, at first, by the trees. They did not stand separately,
clean and individual, like my New England oaks and pines, but
battled thickly for footholds, laced together with ropy vines.
Seen from the harbor, the hills had appeared quite brown; there
had been no warning of this uncontrolled green growth that
gave the impression of hidden rot. On the ocean side, however,
the outlook was placid, with long stretches of white reef broken
by clumps of stunted mangroves standing in the shallow water.

During the voyage, the more experienced travelers had
laughed at me as I stood looking at the horizon, hour after hour.
"Don't you ever tire of that sight? You will, before long"—but I
did not believe them. I loved the splendid, dazzling blue. I was
enthralled by this place where the earth and ocean met with no
discernible change of color.

The quay had been fiercely hot, but here a slight breeze lifted
the air and moved the fronds in the cane fields as we passed.
There was no sign of life in the fields; indeed, since leaving
town, I had seen only one elderly woman carrying a basket on
her head, skirts bunched up high for comfort. And then shortly
after came several small boys with fishing poles. They smiled at
me and called out a greeting; the driver flicked the whip in a
friendly way. I was relieved at the good humor; the town was
now far behind us and, unexpectedly, for the first time in my life
my white skin was making me uneasy. I had no knowledge of
these West Indian black people other than what I had read, and
that had mainly been accounts of uprisings and massacres. A
sudden rustling in the bushes made me jump to grip the side of
the buggy; two small black pigs scrambled up out of the ditch,
crossed the road, and disappeared into the undergrowth. I
watched them go, wondering how they could make their way
through the thick tangle, and where they would go at night.

Every noise would be a threat and the smell of decay would rise suffocatingly; there would be swift reprisals for those caught in the blackness.

What nonsense, I chided myself, knowing from experience how quickly my sense of fantasy could get out of hand. What reason for me ever to be alone on this road at night?

As a distraction, I would have talked to the driver, but the fear of not understanding his speech kept me silent. The horses trotted steadily along, dust rising in puffs under their feet, every step bringing me closer to my first meeting with the Thaws. Rather than alarm myself, I would do better to think over my plans, to make certain that I had overlooked nothing before it was too late. There must be no suspicion that, for me, this visit was of desperate importance.

The dream—the nightmare—was the first occurrence in a chain of events that had begun in August, only four months ago, when I was back in Massachusetts. In the dream a man was dying, and the sunlight was hot on his body as he lay in a big bed. I could not understand why no one had shut the jalousies to lessen the heat in the room. His pain was dreadful to see; with every spasm his back arched, lifting him upward as a fish twists to escape the sharp hook. A woman was there—she had evidently sponged him from the basin of water that stood on the table—but now she sat motionless, her head bowed in her hands. For some reason I did not want this man to die and, in my dream, I tried vainly to move forward. Over and over I called to the woman to help him, to ease the pain, but she did not hear. The frightful spasms grew weaker; clearly he was losing his stubborn hold on life. One arm reached out, and dropped heavily

The crash of the overturned lamp woke me and I sat up in bed, gasping from my struggle with the bedclothes; the brilliant sun faded to a square of light from the streetlamp shining on my carpet. But the man and the woman were not strangers; I knew them, and there was a reason for my presence as he died.

As I calmed myself, fetching another lamp, tidying up the broken glass, I tried to explain away the nightmare. My own father had died recently, though not in such an agonizing fashion. A heart attack ended his life, as he sat in his tiny office at the college, preparing next term's lectures on seventeenth-century English poets. "A tragedy," murmured our friends, "and yet it is what we all would choose." Or "fifty-five is too young, but think what he may have been spared." Perhaps. If only we could have had some warning—if only he had left some guidelines. Since the funeral my mother had remained in bed, refusing to accept the truth, and leaving me, the only child, to make the decisions. "Nothing I can do," said the doctor flatly. "Some people work through their grief, driving themselves to exhaustion. Others retreat, as your mother has done; in any case, time is the great healer." Another phrase I began to dislike.

Then came the problem of the future. Much as I had loved my gentle, affectionate father, I suspected that he had made no special provision for us; he was far more interested in obscure poets than bank balances. There would be a pension, I supposed, and of course there was the small trust set up by his father when he was only a small child. We had used it for pleasures beyond the reach of a professor's salary—summer vacations at the mountain hotel, a few rare books.

My grandfather, Daniel Jackson, was a controversial figure in our family. Any childhood fall from grace, willfulness, a wild impulse, a heated word, would be laid at this grandfather's feet: Daniel Jackson's blood showing itself.

He had been a land speculator, the only one of our God-fearing, strait-laced line to leave New England. I sometimes wondered if indeed an inherited trait had set me to longing for travel, to see the cities of the world, the soughs, the deserts. Or was it my own strong sense of fantasy—the childhood dream of becoming a circus rider or a gypsy, and later: "Who is the beautiful, tall girl there, across the room, with the pale gold hair?" asks the young English viscount, while in Vienna the pianist plays for the stranger whose eyes remind him of an etude—grave and green as sea water. I was forever cast as a mermaid in our amateur theatricals; posed on a makeshift rock, I would stare longingly at the far side of the stage. But I had never felt the part. My hardest, never-ending burden had been to hide the sides of my character which so upset my parents; imagination and a hot temper must be painfully concealed behind attention to practical matters. There was a Puritan attitude in our town that looked askance at beauty, and my mother was proud that she had trained me well in all the household arts. No one could say that she had spoiled me. My father, though, saw some of the difficulties ahead.

"I worry about you, Marietta," he had told me, not long before his death. "It's not easy to be a beautiful woman, and you lack experience in the ways of the world. We've sheltered you too much, I'm afraid. You see only what's right in front of you, child —not the subtleties, the hidden difficulties. You're far too trusting and impetuous, Marietta. I can't help but fear for you."

I had protested. "You make me sound like such a silly creature. Is it so wrong to enjoy a little daydreaming and reciting poetry? And I do have a practical side, you know."

"No, no. I'm talking about something quite different from poetry, or imagination. Perhaps naïveté is the right word."

I had not bothered to understand, quite confident that I could make a place for myself in a larger society; yes, as soon as possible I would find an acceptable way to leave this small town and improve my knowledge of the world. But my father's death had put an end to those plans.

I had first seen the name of Thaw as I struggled with the task of sorting my father's papers. Several nights had passed since my nightmare and, happily, there had not been another. But my spirits were sadly low. At one moment, I would be shaken by a despairing wave of loss, followed by indignation that my beloved father could have left such an untidy mess for me to deal with.

"I will never inflict this sort of chaos on my children, if I have any," I muttered, as I sat on the floor of his little study that hot August afternoon. The next term's lectures were in the hands of the English department, but the job of emptying all the desk drawers and cupboards remained; I decided to begin with a small chest that stood in the corner. It had belonged to his mother, I knew, and undoubtedly had not been touched for years. Years? Centuries, I groaned to myself, drawing out packets of frayed, yellowed papers. Perhaps if there were letters they might divert my mother; she still kept to her bed, tightly curled into her world of mourning. My parents had depended on each other far more than I realized, though I had felt like an outsider from time to time, not understanding that they might prefer their collections and reading to sports and theatricals.

The first drawer was filled with essays, several diplomas, a number of prizes; I stared at them with dismay. Fifty-five years, and only these few crumbling remnants of the life of John B. Jackson, I thought, with unwilling recognition of my own mortality. No, there was more, much more: the students who had been brought to an enjoyment of poetry, his child, my children; hastily, I thrust the lot into a large envelope and began on the next drawer, the next packet. The first was a letter, written in a child's precarious hand.

Dearest Mamma,

I miss you and Papa very much. You have been away for so long. Grandmamma is kind to me, but she does not like dogs. It is cold. I have been sleding with Cousin Tom. He says it is hot where you are. I wish I was there. Will you be home at Christmas? I hope so. I think I am going to get a pare of scates.

Your loving son,
John B. Jackon

And underneath, the traditional row of XXX's, which I noted with amusement.

As the pile grew, my father's handwriting became small and neat, and finally, as he entered college, there were no more letters. For his mother had died when he was eighteen, his father when he was seven. Sad, I thought, remembering Shelley's lines:

> O World! O Life! O Time!
> On whose last steps I climb,
>   Trembling at that where I had stood before;
> When will return the glory of your prime?
>   No more—— Oh, never more!

The drawer would not close. I ran my hand over the inside, reached in, and with difficulty extracted a parcel of letters tied with colorless, faded satin ribbon. The first was not in my father's handwriting; it was fine and slanting and troublesome to decipher.

My dearest little Johnny,

I wish you could be here to pull an orange from a tree for your breakfast. Then you and I would go to watch the little pinkneys keep the pigs from running loose in the cane. I know you will be very sad to hear that we are not able to come home for Christmas, but you must be brave and not cry. We must stay here until crop time begins, just after New Year's Day, when the cane is cut. Perhaps next year we will all come back for a visit. Mr. William Thaw has two sons, James is the eldest and then Charles, and then a small daughter but they are older than you and live in England.

We are busy preparing for Christmas at Repose. Every blackie will have a new blue jacket. The women will receive new petticoats and dresses, and the children new white cotton frocks. There will be gifts of candy, salt pork, fish, and sugar. Then, as it is a holiday, the slaves will go to ground, which means that they will go up into the hills to tend their own little plots of land and bring down vegetables to sell at the Sunday market. There will be much singing and dancing and beating on the drums, which have funny names like kitty-katty and shaky-shekie.

Papa and I will picture you wearing your new skates, down at the river, with your mittens and bright red cheeks. We will be thinking of you especially on Christmas Eve as you hang up your stockings, and sing our dear carols. Try to be such a good little boy, and always be helpful to Grandmamma. We love you so much, and miss you. God keep you safe.

Yr. affectionate Mamma

I read this unusual letter with interest; it was undoubtedly from my father's mother—Mrs. Daniel Jackson—as it repeated his mention of skates and of being left behind. It seemed that my grandfather's business interests must have taken him far afield, as far away as the tropics. Quickly, I unfolded the next letter, written in the same difficult hand.

Dearest Mamma,

We were so thankful to receive yr. letter and to know that Johnny is well and not too much of a burden. Who could have thought that we would be here for such a length of time? I confess that I begin to weary of this life that I found so interesting at first. One becomes lethargic in the constant heat, and Daniel is sadly overworked. He and William Thaw rise at five to ride over the plantation, and there is always something amiss: tools are gone, or a slave has run away—"pulled leg," they call it. Can you credit that the horses must be fed right in front of the Great House, otherwise their feed would be scanted?

I know that as William Thaw's partner, Daniel must learn the workings of the estate, but I cannot feel that this is a good undertaking for him. The place is too alien to our upbringing and beliefs. I have been reading the Journal of a former governor's wife, Lady Nugent, and can only agree when she writes:

"There are only three subjects of conversation here: debt, disease, and death."

Indeed, I pray as she did that we may leave this place alive. You would hardly believe how swiftly a man may sicken and die. Only last week we had a dinner guest, a Mr. Eddison of Sylvania plantation. Word came that he died, two days later, of the yellow fever. I could tell you more, but do not wish to alarm you.

Few English—or even American—ladies are in residence, and I sadly miss female companionship. Mrs. Thaw, as you know, lives in London and is replaced here by a good-looking and surprisingly well-educated young woman of color named Martha. I shut my eyes to this sin, which is customary here, as well as an overindulgence in drink and lack of any religious interest.

I visit the estate hospital every morning; this is a separate building, quite well run by an old granny. The new mothers are so grateful for the bits of food I bring, and love their little ones, but how few live beyond a week or so! They sicken and die from the slightest mishap, even a draft seems to bring on the deadly lockjaw. Now that the slave trade is ended, the dwindling number of workers gives great concern. Here at Repose the overseer pays several dollars for each healthy child. But he frowns on

marriage—it is too difficult to break up families at sale time, he
says. I do not care for him. He is a rough, illiterate Scot, and the
two bookkeepers under him do not keep just books, as you might
think. No, their job is to work the Negroes as hard as possible,
which has a coarsening effect on a man. That is another reason
we must leave. It is too difficult for New Englanders like ourselves to tolerate the practice of slavery, even when carried out
in a firm kindly fashion. My endless thanks, dearest Mamma.
Hopefully I will have news of our return in my next letter.

Yr. affectionate daughter
Margaret

I did not put this letter aside immediately, but read it again,
trying to absorb its meaning. If I understood correctly, my
grandfather had become the partner of a Mr. William Thaw on a
large, foreign sugar plantation. I found it odd, to say the least,
that no one in the family had ever talked of this. Scanning the top
of the page, I studied the date on the torn corner. It was faint,
but legible: November 1831. For some reason, 1831 stood out unpleasantly in my mind. I considered this, and then, with a flick of
memory, knew why. The inscription on my grandfather's grave
stone was marked Daniel Frost Jackson—1799 to 1831. I had
stared at it not long ago, kneeling beside the newly dug hole
nearby, trying not to look at the coffin that had been lowered
into the earth.

Did Daniel Jackson return from the plantation in 1831 and
die? I sat on in the study, remembering a conversation with my
father. It had taken place years ago, but now came to me vividly.
I was shelling peas in the garden, while my father worked in one
of the flower beds. It had been hot and after a while he had
come over to sit with me in the shade. Why we had talked about
his childhood I could not recall, but I had been very much surprised to hear that he was only seven years old when his father
died.

"So young, Papa! Was it a sickness?"

"I believe so, but my mother never spoke of it; she never gave
me any details. They were not in this country, I know, because
she came home alone and was very ill for some time. I remember

tiptoeing about the house, trying not to disturb her. His monument that you see in the churchyard was put up quite a bit later. I suppose I was too young to be told very much except that my father had died, and afterward—well, there never seemed to be a proper time to bring it up. She always avoided the subject—it must have been very painful."

"But didn't you *have* to know? Wasn't there someone else you could ask?"

"It does sound odd, I admit. But children were treated differently in those days, kept very firmly in their places. I suppose I felt I had no right to bother anyone, even my grandmother. And don't forget—I hardly knew my father. He was away a great deal, almost a stranger. But I've always been grateful to him with all my heart for setting up the trust fund for me— little as it is. His land investments certainly didn't make him a fortune; my grandmother made that all too clear in the years that we lived with her. Perhaps that's why I became a sober teacher—to live down the reputation of my land-loving adventuresome father."

The clock on the college bell tower was striking six; reluctantly I tied up the packet and put it away for the time being. It was time for my mother's broth and minced chicken. Lucky Daniel Jackson to have escaped from this little town, I thought enviously, as I carefully set silver on the wicker tray, wondering where in the world this place Repose was situated. I could scarcely wait to go on with the unknown thread of family history. But later that evening the family lawyer came to call, and what he told me drove the past completely from my mind:

"I've talked with the bank, Marietta. We've gone over everything very carefully, studied the figures. One thing is clear. Although your father left no serious debts, and believe me, that is a great blessing, your income will be very drastically reduced. In fact, aside from a small pension, you will have to live almost entirely off of the quarterly dividends from your grandfather's trust."

"But that is so *little!* Why, we—"

"I know. It means cutting your expenditures to the bone and

I'm afraid it also means that you must sell this house. That shouldn't be difficult; it has old-fashioned charm that is appealing, even though it is rather small and would need some redoing if you'll forgive my saying so."

"Sell the house! Where should we live?"

"Well, there are some small places on the other side of town, toward the lumbermill. I believe you could maintain yourselves there. In fact, there's one house in particular that my firm is selling for the owner; I could make inquiries for you."

But I was no longer listening; I knew those shabby houses, built close together in a row, the dingy frames outlined in faded paint. I had gone to one at Eastertime with a basket of food from our church. It suddenly became clear to me that our circumstances were not only distressed, as the saying went, they were desperate. I saw our lawyer to the door with a confusion that turned to outrage when his substantial bill arrived in the next mail. I had expected more generosity from my father's friend.

The week progressed drearily. Neighbors still came bringing baked hams, cakes made from family recipes, and chicken, chicken, chicken—even the cat tired of it. I thanked them, knowing that this bounty would soon end. They had done what was customary and kind, but soon our lives would diverge, particularly if we removed ourselves to one of the houses near the mill. If only we had family, blood relations who would feel some responsibility for us. An uncle: "Don't worry about legalities, Marietta. My office will handle those." Or an aunt: "Of course you'll come to us, my dear, until you are settled."

The distinguished president of the small college paid a formal call. He spoke movingly about my father's character and scholarship, and hinted at the possibility of a John Barclay Jackson Chair in English literature. I had to bite my tongue to keep from asking him to increase our tiny pension instead. Perhaps, because of the trust fund, people assumed we had far more money than was the fact.

Hardest to bear, in that endless week, was almost uncontrollable impatience with my mother. She's had her life, I found myself thinking, the life she wanted with Papa—and it was a happy one. But what is there for me except to try to support us as a wretched schoolteacher? I will never be able to leave this town, I will never go to exciting, interesting places!

For days, the valley had been the captive of an August heat wave, and that particular afternoon the air seemed unmoving in the heaviness that comes before the thunder. I took a pitcher of lemonade to my mother's darkened room, and then went to the study. There was no real need to read through all of my grand-mother's letters but I was beginning to feel a bond with her—she too had faced a difficult situation. The folds in the next letter were so thin that I feared it would fall apart and I laid it care-fully on the floor.

Christmas Day, 1831

Dearest Mamma,

This is written in haste to catch the next packet, and to in-form you of our difficulties here. There is talk of a black uprising led by trouble-making Koromantyn slaves—the warrior tribe—in the next Parish, who are spreading rumors that the King and Parliament have granted them their freedom, but that the planters are trying to conceal this news. Did you ever hear of anything so outlandish? I am sorry to say that this has caused great alarm here. We whites are so few, and they so many. If only we had left last month, but always, *always* there is a noose which binds us more and more tightly into the Thaw fortunes.

I well remember the eagerness with which William Thaw sold us the share in the estate after last year's crop failure, but now that his situation is better and the new crop is about to be cut, I think he does not accept our claim on Repose, no matter how legal. I must pity him. He is a tall, hard-working man, beset by worries, and absolutely determined to preserve Repose for his children. But that does not ease our position. At this moment, I would gladly sacrifice our investment, just to be away from this gloomy place. Martha, his mulatto mistress, tells me not to worry, but how is that possible when guns are placed under the loop holes in the living room, to be ready for a slave uprising? And what is even more alarming, yesterday she collected all the table silver so that it could be hidden away. She told me, in a whisper, that William Thaw would put it with his secret treasure, twelve gold chalices of untold worth. She has never seen them, she says, and does not know how he came by them. I suppose they were stolen en route from South America to Spain many years ago. One can only guess, of course. I myself would not care to own gold chalices, no matter how valuable. There is a touch of the irreligious, as if one had robbed an altar. But, it is not my concern! William Thaw is wise to keep them under lock and key, if I read her character correctly. I gave her my amethysts with misgivings, and now wonder if it was the right thing to do, as she tells me she has no idea where they have all been taken. I wonder if I shall ever see them again, uprising or no!

This morning we gave the Christmas presents to the Negroes. I looked for signs of anger or sullenness. Some sweet wine was stolen last night, but that is nothing out of the ordinary. After church—a misery to me as the congregation laughed and chatted among themselves throughout the service—Daniel and I finally had an opportunity to talk. He has at last seen reason, and we will leave at the earliest opportunity. William Thaw and Daniel Jackson cannot possibly be equal partners on Thaw land, and some settlement will have to be made. Mamma, I enclose a paper which Daniel asks that you keep in the safest possible place until we return. What a day that will be! I think of the peaceful orderliness of our old home and town and vow I will never again leave it. Kiss Johnny for me. In haste,

Yr. affectionate daughter
Margaret

Terror seemed to rise from every word set down in my grandmother's delicate hand, spanning the years with startling force. I felt I was there, sitting with her as she wrote of the uprising; I mourned the amethysts, and puzzled over the gold chalices. One more paper; eagerly I picked it up and realized that it was not a letter but an official document inscribed on stiff parchment—the document she had asked her mother to guard so carefully.

There were several paragraphs of surveyor's jargon, east by southeast and the like, which meant nothing to me. But the last portion was clear: William Thaw transferred to Daniel Frost Jackson and his direct heirs the piece of property designated above, located on the estate known as Repose. This in return for the sum of thirty thousand American dollars received by the above William Thaw. At the bottom, William Thaw's signature stood out in heavy ink, followed by the names of two witnesses and the name of a town in the British West Indies.

I studied the paper with great care. "Transferred to Daniel Frost Jackson and his direct heirs!" Until last week that would have been my father, John B. Jackson, but now—

My heart began to beat quickly. I went to the open window and looked out. The garden had never been prettier; orange and yellow lilies were my father's favorites, but I preferred the zinnias—common flowers, but their bold colors pleased me. Soon, strangers would sit in the garden or perhaps they would not care for flowers.

"Try to put the facts in order, Marietta," I said to myself aloud, "consider them like a lawyer. These are not poems, you know, they are facts. Daniel Jackson went to this island. He bought a share of the estate—a large share—thirty thousand dollars must have been a great deal of money then. If my father is correct, Daniel Jackson never returned to this country alive. My grandmother never claimed the property; the deed was left untouched in the drawer for all these years. But if the deed is still valid, if the property still exists—"

Suddenly the room seemed very small, the walls and ceiling drew in upon me. I ran out into the humid air, my mind veering back and forth like an undirected sail. Of course, the deed could be no more than a worthless bit of paper. But if, I thought, if it could be proved that it was valid—and that there was a place called Repose—would I hold the key to our escape from poverty? Might we not be able to keep our house?

Naïve, my father would have said. Harebrained, the lawyer's expression. But to me, this was a challenge born of desperation. If I began to think of the problems, I would tie the deed up in its satin ribbon and never look at it again.

Resisting the impulse to fling open the gate and run to tell of my discovery, I walked sedately to the lilies. Their long heads were beginning to close for the night.

"Come back," I said to them. "Come back and listen to me. It is just possible that I, Marietta Jackson, am an owner of a sugar plantation in the West Indies. A plantation named Repose."

CHAPTER 2

*It is a kind of happiness to know to what extent
we may be unhappy.*

LA ROCHEFOUCAULD: *Maxims, 1665*

The buggy stopped with a jolt that shattered my reflections and
sent me flying across the slippery leather seat. With alarm, I saw
the driver throw the reins to his companion; he jumped down,
ran along the road for several hundred feet, and came to a stop
at the foot of an enormous tree. The giant roots twisted and
curled in a great circle around the trunk. I recognized it as a cottonwood but my small botanical book had omitted to show the
mass of parasitic vines fastened to its limbs, wrapping themselves
tightly around the smooth gray bark.

The tree stood at a small crossroad; two paths met behind,
hardly noticeable unless one looked closely. I wondered if the
driver was having a fit; he ran crazily from one side of the road
to the other, calling out at the top of his voice. It dawned on me
that he was trying to catch something—something hiding behind
the tree—and I watched nervously.

It was astonishing, to say the least, to see a small boy's head
peer around the trunk, a small white boy who darted nimbly
around the driver's outstretched arms and ran to the buggy.
Breathless with laughter, he reached up. I leaned over to open
the door and he jumped in beside me.

"Thank you, thank you very much," he panted. "Quaco is terribly angry. It was funny, wasn't it—Quaco chasing me around the

tree? He has very sharp eyes, you know. I thought nobody could see me, behind the tree."

I couldn't help smiling at him. He was about seven, I decided, the accent was unmistakably British, and I thought him very appealing—a fair-haired, sturdy little boy with hazel eyes set in a wide, freckled face. His clothes were grimy with fresh dirt and the collar of his white sailor suit was torn. I had no idea who he was, no inkling of the importance he would have in my life.

As we moved forward again, the driver launched into a heated litany of complaint, and I found with surprise and relief that I was beginning to understand a few words: the boy, whoever he was, had run away from Louisa; he was bad, very bad, and his grandmother had enough troubles without him acting so bad. My young companion looked downcast and I felt sorry for him. Suddenly his face began to lift and he winked at me. Then, with a smile that showed the gaps in his teeth, and a dramatic gesture, he began to sing loudly, drowning out Quaco's scolding voice:

> "Take him to the gully! Take him to the gully!
>   But bringee back the frock and board
> Oh! massa, massa, me no deadee yet!
>   Take him to the gully—"

The two black men doubled with laughter, shaking so that the buggy swayed and the horses jumped forward in alarm.

"How was that, Quaco? Was it right? Will you teach me another tomorrow?"

"O ki! You bad, Mast' Nicholas. Poor Quaco too mout-a-massy!"

"What does that mean? Mout-a-massy?" I whispered.

"Oh, he says he talks too much. He's been teaching me these songs, you see, while we're riding. Molly knows some of them, too. They make people laugh, especially the blacks. My name is Nicholas Coulter. Are you the lady who's coming to visit?"

"Well, I'm coming to stay at Repose. Is that where you live? My name is Marietta Jackson."

"Yes, that's the one. They were talking about you at luncheon, just today—" This with an inviting, sidelong glance from under his lashes. A sharp child, as well as an appealing one, but I did

not rise to his bait. Coulter, I thought. I knew that name. Mr.
James Thaw, the owner of Repose, had arranged for my trip, but
a Mrs. Coulter, James Thaw's sister, had written to my mother
explaining that while I would be the only guest as the family
gathered at Repose for Christmas, they would do their best to
see that my visit was a happy one. My mother's mind had been
much relieved. I wondered what relation Mrs. Coulter was to
this little boy and answered him in the offhand manner that his
remark deserved.

"Do you have a nickname, or are you always called Nicholas?"

"Mostly Nicholas. Some of my friends call me Nick, and Molly
does, sometimes. She's my sister, my middle sister. She's fifteen
and I'm seven."

"Seven? I thought you were eight, at least."

"Well, I *am* quite big for my age," he replied, pleased at the
compliment, as I hoped he would be.

"Are we close to Repose? Is it far from here?"

"No, not far. Two more hills to go round, and then we can see
the drive." A pause. "Miss—Miss?"

"Marietta."

"Marietta, will you tell them at home that I wasn't at the
cliffs? That I wasn't near the cliffs?" His voice was muffled,
serious.

"Well, how can I, when I don't know? And I don't know
where the cliffs are. Why are you not supposed to go near them?
Are they dangerous?"

Another long pause. Was he uncertain of his answer, or of my
reaction to it?

"Why aren't you allowed to go to the cliffs?" I asked again.
"Does it have something to do with running away?" His expression changed.

"I'm not allowed to go to the cliffs because my father fell off
them," he said in a rush. "He fell off them and was killed."

"Oh, oh, I see." I tried to keep my voice steady, but I was very
much startled. He peered at me anxiously, as though willing me
to understand the connection.

"I'm dreadfully sorry, Nicholas. Was it long ago that this happened?"

"It was in October, just this October." My hands jerked up, and I folded them quickly. Only two months!

"October? I don't see—I thought the family came only at Christmas," I said, and immediately sensed that this was not the response he wanted; he looked away, pulling at the unknotted tie of his blouse.

"We always have done," came the muffled answer, "but he came here in October by himself. He went away all of a sudden, and then—" He stopped and there was silence, as he began to construct a new string of knots on the crumpled tie.

I did not speak; I was greatly disturbed by what he had told me. A family tragedy—still another reason why I might not be welcome. All at once I was discovering that it was one thing to invite oneself to visit from a distance of thousands of miles, and quite another to be within moments of arriving. "We shall make the best of it," they must have said at luncheon. "No manners. What else can you expect from Americans?" The British habit of looking down their noses at the colonials had never failed as a favorite topic of conversation at my mother's sewing circle.

Nicholas was looking at me, expecting an answer, and I considered him, choosing my words with care.

"I think I can understand," I said finally. "Better than most people. Because, you see, my own father died last summer."

"*Your* father?"

"Yes, five months ago. It was very sudden, too, very unexpected. Even now I sometimes wonder if it really happened, but I will tell you something, Nicholas: you'll find that it gets easier, as the time passes."

He stared at me, judging my sincerity.

"How did he die?"

"It was a heart attack. We didn't know he had a weak heart. But it happened in seconds while he was in his office at the college. A friend came to tell us, my mother and myself, and I remember thinking that there must have been a mistake. He was coming home for lunch and then we were going to call on some friends in the next town. It didn't seem possible. Was that how it was with you?"

He nodded, satisfied. For a short time, we were equals in experience. Then, as the buggy rounded another hill, he exclaimed, "Look, Marietta, the gate! And in a minute you can see the house."

Repose, at last. A mansion in the southern style, with pillars rising tall from the porch? Or a Georgian house in the English manner, square, with cornices and pedestals and large-paned windows? In my ignorance, I envisioned neatly laid-out gardens and fine lawns; the stables and outbuildings would be unobtrusive behind high hedges or walls.

The carriage seemed to creep along as I strained my eyes in an effort to see around the curve. How well I remember my first feeling of surprise, almost shock, at the sight of the low, white building atop the conical hill. Far below, a sprawling lot of buildings marched up the slope in disarray. No, it was not what I had expected.

"What are all the other buildings?" I asked quickly, to hide my disappointment.

"Well, the biggest one is the grinding mill," Nicholas informed me importantly, "and the boiling house is the one with the tall chimney. Then right beside it is the trash house for the squeezed-out stalks; they are used to make the fires for the boiling house. Do you see the other houses farther up?"

I nodded. That particular group of houses was made of cut stone, with well-fashioned arches and fine doors—more elegant, I thought, than Repose itself.

"First comes the old hospital and then the bookkeeper's house —no one uses those two anymore—and the last one is where our overseer lives. And right at the bottom, by the gate, is the old slave village. *That's* still full of people, the workers on the place and the cane cutters."

The drive wound upward, like the stripe on a toy top, in shorter and shorter turns, and the horses began to pull and sweat. Suddenly we were above the trees and I could see the great, unbroken sweep of ocean below, azure and green over the reefs, darkening to a deep blue toward the horizon. In the far distance, the waves were tiny, barely flecked with white, but as they rolled in wide, steady lines toward the land, their strength

increased, ending the long voyage across the world with a crashing roar against the rocks. The cliffs were there—high jagged
stretches of limestone, white in the afternoon sun, rising im-
periously from the sea to a narrow plateau of land. One promontory jutted out of the pattern. I could see a large tree and the
outlines of a path leading to the house. Even from the drive, it
was evident that a fall from that height onto the unseen rocks
below would be deadly, and I could understand why Nicholas
was not allowed to go there; a dangerous place if he should venture too close to the edge. One tragedy at the cliffs was more
than enough, I thought, turning my attention to the variety of
trees that now presented themselves for my inspection as the
horses continued to strain upward. A large grove of pimentos,
and beyond them the cassias, not yet in bloom. I recognized the
orange trees my grandmother had mentioned, a giant poinciana,
and many others whose names I longed to know. As my father's
official basket carrier on his horticultural expeditions, I had a
reasonable knowledge in this field, but these exotic trees were
quite beyond my experience, and with growing bewilderment, I
identified an avocado, and then a clump of bananas.

Now the house could be seen directly above. Apprehensively,
I stared at the huge cut-stone arches that made up the ground
floor; a "welcoming arms" stairway led up to a wide verandah
that circled the white upper story, while the gray shingle roof
hung over the whole, like a large garden hat. It seemed a most
unusual house to my New England eyes—open, airy, and so high.
I also noticed a sadly overgrown garden situated on a slope
away from the road, and broken fence posts, signs of inattention
which surprised me. Certainly there were no well-kept lawns
and neat gardens; the place bore the unmistakable stamp of neglect.

With a final pull, the horses, at a light touch of the whip,
hauled us up over the last rise and into the walled courtyard.
Nicholas jumped out, but I hesitated, gathering up my gloves,
searching for a nonexistent object in my handbag—anything to
delay the moment when I must face the Thaws. Untidy masses
of bougainvillaea bordered the yard—so many violent colors—and
there were speckled crotons and spiky red ginger. Two peacocks
stepped toward us with delicate precision, lowering their heads

to search for insects. The male spread his fan, paying not the slightest attention to the common intruders. Nicholas, waiting beside the buggy, began to fidget.

"What's the matter, Marietta? Why aren't you coming? Don't you want to get out?"

"Yes, of course I do. It's just—I can't explain. I just need a moment to catch my breath."

"Catch your—you didn't climb, the horses did! Are you homesick? Already?" He was indeed a perceptive boy.

"No, not homesick. But I don't know your family, and I suppose I am a little nervous, a complete stranger to them."

"Oh. Well. I'll get my granny," he said in a kindly tone. "She always knows what to do for people," but as he spoke, an elderly black woman ran out from behind one of the arches. She was flapping her apron in distress, and began to scold in the same vein as Quaco. "Bad lil boy, how come him do such a ting—him give trouble to Louisa, to him graunee, him too bad, him." I climbed out and stood beside Nicholas, feeling more and more uncomfortable and at a loss as to what to do.

"Very well, Louisa. That's enough, I think, for now." A quiet, firm voice spoke from the verandah above. "Nicholas, go with Louisa and wash up and then come to see me before your supper, dear."

"*There* you are, Granny. I was just going to find you. Marietta is here. She's pretty, and she's homesick. Not at all what Molly said—"

"Yes, well, run along, Nicholas."

"Granny, are you very cross? I didn't go to the cliffs."

"We'll talk later, shall we? No, I'm not cross, darling."

I met Nicholas' grandmother at the top of the wide double stairs. She was as tall as I, with graying hair and a worn, classic beauty of feature made gentle by the warmth of her smile and the kindness in her blue eyes.

"Welcome, my dear, I'm so happy to see you at last. I am Elizabeth Coulter. What a long trip—and I hope they explained at the quay how distressed we were not to meet you. Unfortunately, just at the last minute, Nicholas—" She hesitated.

"It was quite all right," I said, deeply relieved by Mrs.

Coulter's manner. "The man told me that someone was ill. I'm so sorry. I hope it's not one of the family."

"In a way, I'm afraid it is. Yes, Miss Crowell, our old Nanny, who's been with the Coulter children for years, had a dreadful digestive attack last night and it left her very weak. She's not young, and we've been concerned. The doctor has come, and she's more comfortable now, I'm glad to say. But then, just as we were going to meet you, Nicholas disappeared, ran away from Louisa, as you may have gathered, and we have been looking for him all afternoon. Where on earth did you find him?"

"By the cottonwood tree, on the road. I—well, he was very anxious to tell me that he had not been to the cliffs."

"Ah, good. I'm glad of that." A look of relief came into her eyes, a clearer blue than her grandson's.

"He was upset about Nanny, I know; there was a lot of commotion and comings and goings, and poor old Louisa simply cannot manage him. He's a dear boy, but lately he's had these spells of being, well, just plain naughty." Her voice was steady, concealing her loss, the reason for Nicholas' naughtiness. As we talked, she led me down one side of the wide verandah, lined with large pots of maiden hair and baby's tears ferns, and hung with baskets of flowering begonias, orchids, and thunbergia of palest blue throated with yellow.

"I'm putting you in the south wing," she continued, "which is the nursery wing for Nicholas and Molly and Nanny—but last night I moved Nanny into the front spare room, where she can be quiet. Actually, many people prefer this side of the house, away from the noise of the water; it can be rather tiresome." She paused before an open door and motioned me to follow.

The room was large and square, with a high, vaulted ceiling extending to the shingled underside of the roof. I was astonished by the huge four-posted bed which dominated the room; its vast sides were hung with mosquito netting which fastened to the square white canopy; a night stool with several steps was required to reach the expanse of counterpane and pillows. A few pieces of furniture made of dark wood stood on the bare, highly polished floor, and I was pleased to see a bowl of hibiscus on the ornate bureau. Someone had thought to welcome me with flowers, not hostility, and I was grateful.

Mrs. Coulter pulled at the plug of a slatted jalousie to open it wide.

"That's better. And out there, below, are the cane fields. We should be cutting in the next few weeks, so I'm glad you can see them while they're still green. They stretched for miles, as far as the hills, when I was a child, but over the years so much has been let go. You see, since my father's death, no one has really lived at Repose. It's sad to see the place not kept up as it used to be, but a few weeks out of the year is too short a time to accomplish very much. I'm afraid that I've given up trying to turn out the house properly without a year-round staff—it sinks back into dust immediately we've gone." The slightly abandoned look which had puzzled me was now explained.

"I didn't realize that no one lived here, no one at all," I said.

"Not since my father died in 1844, thirty-five years ago. A long time. My brother and I have been in England, you see, though we keep up the tradition of coming here for Christmas. That's why this was the only time you could make the trip. Otherwise the house is closed, with only our old cook as caretaker."

She opened the armoire doors, and went to shake the netting. A cascade of dust drifted out into the light.

"I did tell Cubba to wash it," she said with an apologetic smile. "We still use the nets at night, you know, though yellow fever is rare now, thank the Lord. It was such a scourge to the old-timers—'old-standers,' as we call them—that one still takes precautions. Marietta, may I call you that, my dear? I hope you will forgive us for being in such a state of disarray. We arrived only a few days ago and the entire staff is new, except for Chitty, the old cook. I could weep—just as they'll be trained and settled in, the two months will be over and it's time for us to go back. Now, your maid's name is Cubba, which means she was born on a Wednesday; she undoubtedly has another name, but I don't know it. Cubba is young and she speaks clearly and I'm pleased with her, so far, but you must tell her exactly how you like things done for you. That's most important."

I looked away, biting my lip, perturbed at the thought of having anyone wait on me. "I only hope I can understand her," I murmured. "With Quaco, it was dreadful. I was lost, at least at the beginning. I've never felt so foolish."

"It *is* difficult, I know, but only for a bit. You'll get the hang of it quickly; seventeenth-century English mixed with African. But you might as well recognize one thing right from the start—we are *all* ignorant of what they are saying and thinking, when they wish us to be. On the other hand, they always know all about us down to the least detail. It's uncanny. Of course, the houses are so open; one cannot avoid talking in front of the servants as one does at home—they are everywhere! Now, what more can I do for you before I go back to Nanny? We dine at seven, which is late in this part of the world, but coming here as we do for such a short time we keep to our English customs. It will be just family—my brother James Thaw, my son's widow—Mrs. Gerald Coulter—and Molly, her younger daughter. At the last moment our governess could not come—another blow—as the children will get sadly behind in their lessons and she could have been pressed into looking after Nicholas while Nanny is ill. We shall manage, of course, but you must overlook a little confusion here and there. I'll send Cubba to help you unpack, as soon as she gets back from an errand to the village. So, will you be all right now?" She smiled reassuringly and went to the door, her lavender dress rustling as she walked. I would always associate Mrs. Coulter with pale, soft dresses and a scent of verbena.

"Oh, thank you. I have everything I could possibly need, and the room is lovely. But, Mrs. Coulter, I had no idea I had come at such a difficult time. There *must* be something I can do—perhaps help to look after Nicholas while his nurse, I mean, Nanny—is ill. We became friends, I think, this afternoon. I believe I could get on with him."

"How kind of you, and after this afternoon I may well accept your offer. You can't imagine—we turned this place upside down. Poor old Louisa. Perhaps with someone as young and pretty as you he might behave better. And Molly is too young to take all the responsibility. Fifteen is such an up-and-down age; she's a good-hearted child, and I hope you and she will be friends, too. My older granddaughter is considered to be rather a beauty, and

I suspect Molly often goes out of her way to invite comparisons. But a beautiful older sister can be far more trying than a beautiful friend."

"Fifteen," I said, pleased. "I remember myself at fifteen. I was dreadful, the skinniest girl in town. I shall certainly try to make friends with her, Mrs. Coulter."

"Good. Then we'll see you at seven. No one will disturb you until then except Cubba; you will want to rest after such a long day."

After she had gone, I took off my bonnet and went to the open window, flanked on either side by the jalousies. To my left, below the orange trees, a small stream ran downhill to the stone aqueduct and water wheel. Cattle grazed in pens above the banks—ribby, cream-colored animals with long curved horns and large flat hoofs. A peaceful scene, pleasantly joined by the cane fields that swept out to a border of small hills.

A low murmur of voices, mixed with high-pitched laughter, rose from under the arches; a sound that went on as continuously as the stream, I soon learned. The number of servants at Repose astounded me—the only servant I had ever known was a silent maid-of-all-work who kept to her place behind the kitchen door. It would have astounded me even more to know how quickly I would become accustomed to these faces that, as Mrs. Coulter said, were everywhere.

As I stood there, absorbing the new atmosphere, I reflected once again on the events that had led me here. Unbelievably, only four months had passed since my visit to the British Consulate in Boston. With surprisingly little difficulty, I had learned that a James Thaw was the present owner of Repose and I obtained his London address. The letter had required far more effort; I must have filled an entire copy book with attempts to achieve the credibility of a young lady with a valid claim, rather than a troublesome imposter. In the end, I wrote that while sorting out family papers after my father's death, I had come upon an inventory of my grandmother's possessions. It seemed that some jewelry, including a cherished amethyst set, had been left at his estate, Repose, in the West Indies. I would be most

obliged if he could give me any information about this. I gave
the year of my grandparents' visit and a few other details. No
mention that I knew of a slave uprising, hidden gold chalices,
the fact that my grandmother had returned alone—and certainly
not that I now had in my possession a deed which might entitle
me to a large share of the property.

Some weeks were to pass before I heard from Mr. Thaw.
Often, I debated the wisdom of my course. Should I have gone
immediately to our lawyer and allowed him to take charge of the
matter? A legal communication could not be ignored, particularly if it dealt with land rather than jewelry. After all, forty-
eight years was a long time, and James Thaw had been in England. But the lawyer's large fee for the small services rendered
his old friend still rankled; I dared not risk more bills on what
might amount to nothing. No harm could come of one letter, and
I told no one about my discovery.

The letter postmarked London arrived on a morning in early
autumn. There was a feeling of change in the air that suited the
occasion. Leaves had lost their summer strength and hung from
the trees with a spent, weary look. Before long, strangers would
walk through our house, opening doors and peering into cupboards, murmuring about additions, renovations. My mother rose
late and did a few household chores as if in a trance. Sometimes
I would find her standing quite still, holding a book or piece of
china in her hand; she knew that we must leave the house but
left any further decision to me. I could not bring myself to tell
her of the mill houses; cowardice on my part, I knew, but I was
delaying until the last possible moment.

Running to my room with the letter, I seated myself carefully,
having read somewhere that one should always sit down in moments of crisis. My greatest fear—that I should hear nothing at
all—was now ended; the matter would go forward, one way or
another. I studied the address, the handwriting, the quality of
the paper before finally tearing open the envelope.

The letter was courteous—and overwhelming. I read and
reread it several times with shaking hands. The Repose records
of 1831 noted the visit of Mr. and Mrs. Daniel Jackson, and of
Mr. Jackson's death from yellow fever, shortly before leaving the

island. The overseer had been instructed to make a thorough
search of all the old, closed-up storerooms. A box marked "Property of Mrs. Daniel Jackson" had been located. Mr. James Thaw
very much regretted the oversight, but since his father's death no
one had used the storerooms, or known of Mrs. Jackson. He
would be delighted to settle the matter, but the only time that I
could come to Repose to settle my claim would be at Christmas,
when the family would be in residence. If I could manage this—
and a letter of credit for traveling expenses was enclosed, with
further expressions of regret.

If I could manage! I stared at the letter of credit and then
again at the letter. At the least, I had expected delays and legalities, certainly not such an invitation. I could hardly believe my
good luck. So they brought back the buried valuables, I thought,
and my grandmother's jewelry was put aside, for some reason.
Perhaps William Thaw had wanted nothing more to do with the
Jacksons.

As I stood now by the window at Repose, night seemed to rise
from the ground, first darkening the fields and woods, then
creeping toward the hills. There was no lingering sunset; color
was swiftly replaced by blackness, and the afternoon air by a
heavy languor that pressed against my face. As if to atone for the
absence of color, the fragrances thrust boldly upward: angel's
trumpets and night jasmine. I did not recognize them, but drew
in deep breaths of the heady scents. The birds were silent, and
multitudes of invisible tree toads asserted themselves in the
nightly change of precedence. But again, I was conscious of an
unhealthy presence; I had felt it in the afternoon, looking at the
twisting mass of foliage along the road, almost as if the land
were conveying a message: admire my beauty, but for those who
intrude upon me, there is danger.

Uneasily, I thought of William Thaw, dead these many years.
How angry the sight of another Jackson at Repose would have
made him. I was not at all certain of my next move; I would
have to feel my way with caution. The document was meticu-
lously sewn into the lining of my undergarment case though I
had pondered long whether to leave it behind or bring it with

me. If I should need to produce the evidence, I argued, it would be close at hand. But if not, no one would be the wiser.

The maid Cubba arrived in a rush, carrying hot water. Clucking at the darkened room, she hurried to light the oil lamp, saying that she had been in the village fetching herbs for Missie Nanny. Cubba was young and plump; her round bottom filled out the white skirt and swayed as she moved about, unpacking my valises and hanging the dresses in the armoire. I was soon to learn that the smiles could change quickly to a stubborn expression, the underlip pushed out in protest. The voice that now chattered softly could be sharp and strident. But, as Mrs. Coulter said, she was eager to please and bade me rest myself on the big bed. I lay, half dozing, listening to the unfamiliar noises: Nicholas' footsteps in the hall, the background singing of the tree toads.

"Missie sleep now," came Cubba's voice through my weariness. "I come back in time to help him dress for dinner."

I was glad to be alone again, to review the impressions of the day—the warmth, colors, sounds, smells—and particularly the inhabitants at Repose. My hardest task was still to be faced: the meeting with the redoubtable James Thaw. He was the head of the family, the one with whom I must contend; the others were merely bystanders. Nicholas—a friendly little boy, and Mrs. Coulter—a lovely, gentle lady.

I realize now that it was Elizabeth Coulter's sheer goodness that led me to assume, naïvely, that no evil could exist in her presence, no harm come to those under her protection.

CHAPTER 3

It is a great ability to be able to conceal one's ability.

LA ROCHEFOUCAULD: *Maxims, 1665*

"Welcome, welcome to Repose, Miss Jackson." A small, white-haired gentleman stepped forward to greet me, and I did my utmost to hide my surprise. This was no towering figure, with stern face and intimidating manner. Over the months, James Thaw had grown to gigantic and ridiculous proportions in my mind. I must have stammered nervously, for the expression in his eyes, which were small and close-set and a deeper blue than his sister's, changed from sharpness to affability. Probably he too harbored misconceptions and was expecting an older, more seasoned Miss Jackson—the unknown lady who had come at such an inopportune time and to whom he must "do the agreeable."

"Not too tired from your journey, I hope? I find the trip from London more and more wearing, but then, I suppose that's one of the penalties one pays for growing ancient—something that needn't concern a young lady." His voice was fussy and precise; the white linen suit showed not a crease or wrinkle. I suspected that he was rather a dandy, and probably a bit of a martinet.

"Thank you, but I'm not at all tired. The trip was pleasant, and it is such a surprise to be warm in December. I do thank you for bringing me here, sir. It was truly kind of you." I could almost sense his relief as I spoke: an extremely pretty girl, knows enough to call me "sir," provincial clothes. Intelligent? Probably not.

He began to look about with annoyance. "We must go in to dinner. You have met my sister, I believe," as Mrs. Coulter joined us at the door to the dining room. Her evening dress was of finely patterned light silk, with lace collar and cuffs. "Elizabeth, my dear," James Thaw asked in a querulous tone, "where is Serena? It's past seven."

"I know, James, and I've just been in to see her. She's not feeling quite herself, and will have her dinner alone."

Serena? The widow, Nicholas' mother, I decided.

James Thaw looked alarmed. "Not—not Nanny's trouble, I hope?" From his expression I gathered that illness was of concern to him, and the idea of contagion quite appalling.

"No, no, James. Nothing like that. It's just—" And her voice trailed off with a significance that he seemed to understand.

"And Molly? Is she not to grace us with her presence tonight?"

"Yes, my dear, she's just dressing. And James, don't be annoyed with her. She has done her best to help, and it's been a most difficult day. Perhaps we should go in now." I added a footnote to my list: attaches great importance to punctuality.

James Thaw offered me his arm, motioning to his sister to precede us. As he seated me in the high-backed, ornate chair, I could have laughed aloud with relief. The dreaded moment was over, and I could see nothing in the least frightening about this rather self-important little man.

I had not understood what Mrs. Coulter meant by bringing English customs with them until we sat down to dinner, but now as I looked about, I wondered if any London table could have been more impressive. Light from the high, branched candelabra shone down on the white cloth, creating reflections in the fine green and gold china and in the heavy, cut glass. A huge epergne stood in the center of the table, supporting glass dishes filled with nuts, candies, and fruits. A butler, wearing white gloves and followed by two white-capped maids, came forward with the soup.

These were puzzling contrasts that had not seemed possible in my small experience. Broken fence railings and white-gloved butlers; unweeded gardens and damask tablecloths. I must open my mind, I said to myself, and try not to make quick judgments.

The conversation began with several polite questions from Mr.
Thaw, but he soon turned it to his particular interests, the old
plantation customs. I began to sense a wish on his part to recapture past glories.

"Breakfast used to be at five-thirty," he told me, "so that the
planters could do their work before the heat of the day. Second
breakfast, as they called it, was around eleven and would be the
equivalent of our luncheon—soup, fish, pepperpot, rather light.
Dinner around five. I believe some planters still keep to those
hours, but most people follow the English customs to quite an
extraordinary degree. Everything English is much admired and
imitated. London fashions may take their time in arriving, but
arrive they will, eventually, and be painstakingly copied."

Exactly the same in America, I reflected. The most admired
style was to drink English tea, wear English shoes, and subscribe
to English periodicals, whereas French shoes and French maga-
zines—my thoughts were interrupted by the loud sound of running feet on the verandah. Our forks wavered in midair. A young
girl entered with a pounding rush and plumped into her seat
with a force that shook the candles. Mr. Thaw winced, and Mrs.
Coulter spoke quickly.

"Ah, here you are, Molly. Do make your apologies to your
great-uncle, my dear. And this is Miss Jackson. My granddaughter, Molly Coulter."

Molly's resemblance to Nicholas was strong—the same thick,
fair hair and open face. She'll be very handsome, I judged, when
she sheds a considerable amount of weight and learns to move
gracefully.

"Sorry, Granny. Very sorry, Uncle James. Jilly had a thorn in
her paw and I was trying to get it out. I had no idea of the
time."

"That dog! She is beginning to run our lives!"

Mrs. Coulter intervened. "But she's such an affectionate little
thing, James. Really a blessing to have her appear just now.
Nicholas is so taken with her and she keeps him amused."

"Well, where was she this afternoon, may I ask? No, I'm grateful to Jilly, I suppose, but I fully expect to find her sitting in the

living room receiving our guests, one of these days. And you know as well as I, Elizabeth, that it doesn't do to become attached to these ginger dogs; there is such a flood of tears when we go and they are left behind."

"I do know, all too well. But this year—she's such a diversion, she takes his mind off—"

"Don't misunderstand me, my dear. I'm not forbidding him the dog. The boy needs every entertainment we can produce for him at this time." I sensed that James Thaw was very fond of Nicholas. On the other hand, if Jilly had been Molly's dog—

Soup was followed by a joint, roast potatoes, Yorkshire pudding, and a number of vegetables.

"Granny, when does Pamela's ship get in?" asked Molly, pouring large amounts of gravy over her potatoes.

"At four o'clock the day after tomorrow, if it's on time, and I do pray that it will be. Otherwise we will have to delay Christmas Eve dinner. Such an awkward time, the day before Christmas. I would think that earlier in the week or later would suit people better; but perhaps there are reasons. James, I've sent Quaco with a message to Dr. Barrows, asking him to come again this evening. I'm not happy about Nanny—she seems weaker tonight. And I think it might be wise for him to look in on Serena."

"Of course. I'm sorry to hear this. Poor Nanny, what an inconvenience. Pamela's ship arrives the day after tomorrow? Why not send Molly for her? You will exhaust yourself with nursing, and all the preparations for Christmas as well." He turned to me. "Pamela, I should explain to you, is another of my great-nieces, Molly's older sister. She was delayed, and could not come with us."

"I see." I also noticed that there was no question of James Thaw's meeting the boat.

"I'll go," said Molly bluntly. "But it was silly of Pamela to stay behind just to go to some fancy castle for a visit. Wouldn't they have asked her another time?"

James looked at her sharply. "Of course, Molly, you can't be expected to understand that Pamela had no choice in the matter. An invitation like that is almost a royal command. Your sister is very fortunate to have an entrée into those circles; it will be a great help to her when the Season begins."

"Oh pother the Season." Molly clearly did not share her great-uncle's feelings. "Well, she can entertain Mother with gossip, and invitation lists and all that nonsense; we'll never hear the end of this wretched Season."

"Don't be too hasty, Molly," said her grandmother, smiling. "You may be begging for a Season, you know, in no time at all."

"Sorry, Uncle James." She grinned in Nicholas' disarming way. "I didn't mean to be rude, but can you honestly see me gliding gracefully around the floor, followed by a pack of admirers? Can you?" We all laughed. I knew that I would enjoy Molly.

A savoury followed the sweet fruit pudding. So many courses! I was glad when Mrs. Coulter finally rose and led us into the next room for coffee. I had not been in the main living room, and looked about with interest. Here, too, the ceiling rose high up to the shingled roof; the polished floor, patterned in a variety of woods, was bare except for a worn turkey carpet in the center. There were a number of sofas in the Chippendale style, with badly split upholstery along the sides and front. But the chairs were beautifully carved from mahogany, as were the numerous tables on which stood oil lamps and candles encased in hurricane shades. An old spinet was half hidden in one corner, and several oil portraits, so cracked that their subjects were almost unrecognizable as to gender, hung askew on the walls.

"My father, William Thaw, the founder of Repose, painted by some itinerant artist," said James, following my glance. But I was no longer looking at the portraits. Above them, in the shadows, I had seen the loop holes, so vividly described by my grandmother. Perhaps it was in this room that she had given her beloved amethysts to Martha and learned about William Thaw's mysterious gold chalices. The portraits would have been clear, then, and the upholstery fresh and gold-colored. Perhaps she had sat in this chair, looking up at the odd holes in the wall, then glancing with fear at the guns standing below, ready for use against a rush of maddened slaves. She could not know that her husband would soon be dead of yellow fever. I remembered her words: "Always, always there is a noose which binds us more and more tightly into the Thaw fortunes—" A noose. Suddenly, my hand was at my throat with an unconscious gesture; a look of fright must have passed over my face, for when I dropped my hand I saw that James Thaw was staring at me with concern.

I smiled, trying to hide my agitation. Who was to be feared? Certainly not Molly or Mrs. Coulter or this kindly, if self-important man. "The slits in the wall," I said. "What are they?"

"The loop holes? They were used for the guns, in the old days, in case of attack from the slaves. You'll find that most of the Great Houses are built on hills, like the old castles. But luckily Repose has escaped that sort of trouble, in the past, at least." He rose from his chair and took cards from a table drawer.

"Now, whose turn is it to play with me tonight?" The question was more of a command; I wondered if the change of subject had been deliberate.

Mrs. Coulter stood up. I could see that she was very tired.

"I think I shall sit with Nanny for a while, until Dr. Barrows comes. Tomorrow we really must find a proper nurse and someone who can help with Nicholas. The maids have more than enough to do, as it is. I hate to call on Agnes Shepheard again, James, but perhaps she can spare a girl for a few days."

"Granny, you know that would be useless," Molly broke in. "He'll twist a new girl around his little finger. Crikey, I never thought I would long for Miss Despard and our lessons. And you know what is so truly dreadful is the way we took Nanny for granted. I never knew how much she did for us until today; she has always been hurrying about, doing whatever was needed."

"Well, my dear, you'll appreciate her more when she has recovered—we all will."

"Mrs. Coulter," I said hesitantly, "I meant it when I said I would love to help with Nicholas. I would feel much happier if I could be useful, and I really do think I could manage him."

"And I can spell her," Molly interrupted. "We could take turns keeping an eye on him. Wouldn't that be better than getting in a new girl?"

Mrs. Coulter considered. "Yes, it would be, at that. It's a pity he has to be watched so closely; ordinarily he's such an easy child, in spite of his high spirits, but just now—" She stopped, abruptly.

"You should tell her, Granny. If she's to help look after him she should know the reason why he's running away."

"Please don't interrupt me, Molly dear. It's not mannerly." Mrs. Coulter turned to me; the expression on her face was sad, yet controlled. "Marietta, as you know after this afternoon, we are desperately worried about Nicholas' compulsion to go to the cliffs. You see, my son, his father, was killed there two months ago. For some reason that we don't yet understand, he was trying to scale the cliffs from the rocks below, and partway up, the rope must have given way and he fell. It was a frightful blow to us, but we've—accepted it, the fact that he's gone. All but Nicholas. He seems to have a compulsion to go to the cliffs. He won't say why, but twice now we've found him standing right on the edge. He's such a little boy—the only son—" Mrs. Coulter's voice wavered.

"So you see, I'm sure, why someone has to be with him all day?" She steadied herself, but there was a drawn look on her fine, even-featured face.

"I do understand, Mrs. Coulter. We did talk about it, Nicholas and I, in the buggy this afternoon. Until then I had no idea that you had had this tragedy. I want to help in any way that I can, and I would do my best, you may be sure of that."

James Thaw had seated himself at the card table and was mixing the cards impatiently.

"Well, Elizabeth, Miss Jackson—may I call you Marietta—has made you an extraordinarily kind offer, and I think you should accept it without any further hesitation. Now, who is to be my partner? Molly?"

The big, fair-haired girl made a wry face. "You know I'm hopeless, Uncle James. I keep forgetting what's been played."

"Cards are excellent training for the mind. Piquet is not a difficult game, but you must pay attention."

"Oh, is it piquet?" I asked. "I used to play with my father. It was one of his favorite games, that and backgammon."

"There! Now you have a new partner, Uncles James. Will you take my place, Marietta? Please?"

"If you like. You are probably being modest and play far better than I, Molly, but I'll try."

"Oh what an angel! Now I can finish Jilly's paw." She ran from the room and the candles shook.

I thought that Molly's eagerness to quit the game might provoke her uncle, but perhaps he too felt a certain relief. I picked up the first hand with trepidation; I would be pitting my brains against Mr. Thaw's, and it required all my concentration to think only of the cards and not of the larger issue between us. We played several hands, and I did my best to give him a good game, but the fatigue of the day was beginning to dull my mind. For whatever reason, I felt that his thoughts too were elsewhere. Finally he laid down his hand.

"Pique and re-pique, and that's enough for tonight. Thank you, Marietta, you play well. Beauty and card sense are a rare combination in a woman; they don't often go together, in my experience. Now, shall we plan to meet tomorrow morning to conduct our business? I find that it's best to do these things right away, clear the decks, so to speak."

"Yes, of course. And thank you again, Mr. Thaw, for inviting me here. I've never traveled much, and it's quite overwhelming; the trees and the flowers are so different from anything I've ever seen before."

"It's an interesting part of the world, I must agree. And tomorrow I will try to take time to tell you more about our history and customs. But you must be anxious to get to your bed, so now I shall wish you a good night's sleep, after all your new experiences. Until tomorrow, then." He directed me to the inside hallway that led to my room, and I slipped along the passageway, longing to climb at last into the big, soft bed.

But inside the room, Molly was waiting, her feet propped up on the rung of a long leather chair by the window.

"Just creolizing—relaxing, that is. Did you win?"

"Oh no, I'm afraid not. I was tired, and he plays a very subtle game, your uncle. He's cautious most of the time, then suddenly he takes a wild gamble and catches one off guard."

"Well, perhaps it was more diplomatic to lose, actually. He doesn't like opposition, our Great-uncle James."

There was no mistaking the antagonism in her voice; I hesitated, torn between reticence and curiosity.

"What do you mean?" She looked doubtful, debating, no doubt, between loyalty and the need to unburden herself.

"It's no good pretending," she said at last. "This show of the happy family gathering together for Christmas is making me positively sick."

I turned from the dressing table where I was taking the pins from my hair and stared.

"Whatever do you mean? I thought that the Thaws and the Coulters loved this place, that it meant a great deal to them."

"You've just come. You couldn't possibly understand what I'm talking about. But you will, after you've been here awhile. Oh, if only people wouldn't be such hypocrites! If they'd only come right out and say that we're here because of the money."

"The *money!*"

"Yes, the money! Well, I can see that I'll have to explain it all to you, and it won't be Great-uncle James's version. He would like us to believe that Great-grandfather Thaw was a fine gentleman; the truth is, he was a real hurry-come-up, as they say. But he came over here and worked hard and made Repose one of the finest plantations on the island. My great-grandmother was much more of a lady, I guess. But she hated it here and went back to London to live, taking the children with her. Losing the children was a real blow to Great-grandfather; he couldn't bear the thought that no one would love Repose as he did, and that no one wanted to live here. So he arranged that anyone who wanted a share in the yearly profits must come to Repose for Christmas. Actually be here. Blackmail! That's the fine, old family tradition."

"You mean—" I tried to express the thought delicately and failed. "You mean that if you don't come you get no money, no money at all for the year?"

"Exactly. A dead hand over us all, the way he arranged it. And the sad part is that I do love Repose—the place and the people and the fun of the trip in the winter. It's the money part of it,

Marietta. There's something about the money that makes people behave so badly. And this year it's bound to be far worse, because with Father gone we need the money more than ever. Nobody will say this out loud to me, naturally, but I know it's true. And Father kept us all on an even keel, he was like Granny, kind and understanding about people, and he could jolly us all along, which she can't. All the fun is gone, since he died." She shifted violently in the chair.

I brushed at my hair absently, ignoring the tangles.

"But Molly, isn't there some way to change William Thaw's rule? Especially after what happened to your father?"

"There is. I know it could have been done, but Uncle James insisted that we come. Even Pamela begged him—she's his favorite and she doesn't often beg—but he wouldn't hear of it. So here we are, my mother in a state, Nicholas in a dither over the cliffs, Nanny sick—oh, it's going to be a fine Christmas, a dandy." Privately, I could see her point. To come so soon to the place where Gerald Coulter had met with such a dreadful accident seemed difficult, to say the least. But it would not help to dwell on the subject.

"Your sister Pamela. How old is she?"

"Eighteen, three years older than I am. But you wouldn't know we were sisters. She's dark and thin and beautiful, and very sought after. Men fall at her feet—and she hardly says a word! That will never happen to me. I'm such a clumsy creature, and I'm fat." There was an undertone of bitterness in her laugh.

"Nonsense," I said cheerfully, remembering the gravy. "You don't have to be fat, you know. Anyhow, it's almost worse to be thin. You should have seen me when I was fifteen—skin and bones, a real fright."

"I don't believe it. Your hair must have been gorgeous, and faces don't change. But I meant to tell you, Marietta, to be careful of the sun, with your pale skin."

"I will, and the mosquitoes are making a feast of me. But"—returning to the more interesting subject of the Thaws—"perhaps this Christmas won't be as bad as you expect."

"Hah! It's worse, with Nanny so sick. I've never known her to be sick before. She's always been bustling about, every day since

I can remember. Nothing, absolutely nothing, gets by Nanny, which is a bore sometimes, but today, without her, was simply dreadful. And my mother—you haven't met my mother. I might as well tell you, though I'm not supposed to know—she takes laudanum. Since Father's death she takes a great deal of it. I think she is almost an addict." The last words were spoken in a hushed tone.

"But surely—" I stopped, remembering the look that had passed between Mr. Thaw and Mrs. Coulter before dinner.

"Oh, I suppose she must have taken drops before he died, lots of ladies do, but now it's much, much worse. We depended on him, all of us. I can't explain but it's as though the foundations of the house had been knocked out from under us. I wish you could have seen him, Marietta. He was tall, like Granny, with fair hair like Nicholas and me. Mother and Pamela are dark. He never raised his voice that I remember, but when he told you to do something, you did it. And there was always a joke, hidden under the serious side. I suppose he might have appeared to be a serious person to strangers, but underneath he was fun, he loved to tease."

"Molly, I *know*—" The tears in my voice were as loud as a shout.

"Yes, you do," she said in surprise. "Yes, I'd forgotten. Nicholas told me. I'm sorry to let down like this, to someone I've just met, but there's no one to talk to."

"I don't mind—in fact, it makes me feel better. That awful saying 'misery loves company'—it's true. But what do you think is in Nicholas' head when he goes to the cliffs? You don't think he's trying—to kill himself?"

Molly frowned, concentrating. "No, I don't. Most of the time he's perfectly all right. And then something comes over him, as though he can't believe that Father is dead. As though he must go and find him. He seems to be looking for something. When I ask him, he won't say a word, and he used to tell me everything. And the strange part is, I feel the same way. I keep asking myself why Father should have come here in October. He never did before, never. No one did. And then to fall, climbing the cliffs. Why, if you could have heard him forever telling us to keep away from the cliffs. It doesn't make sense, that's the hardest part. It just doesn't make sense!" She flung herself back in the chair with a despairing gesture.

I sat motionless, trying to understand Molly's outburst. There were sharp undercurrents at Repose that I had not noticed earlier.

"It does seem hard, that you should have to come back," I said at last. "But are you right in blaming your Great-uncle James? Perhaps he really had no choice."

"Well, he's the head of the family. Coming here at Christmas is a custom, not a legal thing anymore. But he controls all our money now. We couldn't afford to disobey him. We need the money from Repose."

"He talks as though he loves Repose, perhaps that's the reason. Perhaps he couldn't bear not to be here at Christmas."

"I doubt that. He doesn't love it enough to live here and run the place properly. Every year it's a little more run down, and there's a little less money. No, he likes his life in London and his precious collection of china far better than Repose."

"Is he married? No one has spoken of a Mrs. Thaw."

"No, he never married. No children. My father would have inherited Repose; he was beginning to be concerned about it, the way Great-uncle James was handling the estate. I think he wanted to have a hand in it, but was not allowed. I just don't understand old men, do you? Why he hangs on just for the look of the thing, as though he might lose his title as head of the family. Title! I think that's one reason he's so fond of Pamela—she might even marry a title! He's a snob."

"You shouldn't speak that way," I felt compelled to say.

"I know, but it's the truth. The Thaws have come a long way since old William, and now the hopes rest on Pamela. I wonder how you and Pamela will get on. Goodness, two raving beauties under the same roof, one dark, one fair. A man would have a frightful time choosing—"

"Nonsense, Molly. It's just for a short time, anyhow. Don't try to set us against each other right from the start."

The room, I noticed, was becoming warm and airless. The sash window was shut, and I went to open it.

"No wonder it's hot. Why on earth would anyone shut the window on such a warm night."

Molly laughed. "Cubba did. The blacks hate night air, you know. They're afraid the evil spirits will get in."

"What do you mean, evil spirits?"

"Well, there's Old Hige, for one. The living hag woman who takes off her skin and wanders about in a ball of fire, sucking the blood of sleeping people—"

"Oh, Molly!"

"And then there are the duppies, thousands of them. Chitty, our cook, can tell you about the duppies."

"*Duppies?*"

"The shadow of a dead person. After three days it rises from the grave and begins to exist as a duppy. It can be harmless and wander around and play tricks on people, or it can be enslaved by an obeahman, a sort of witch doctor, and used for all sorts of ghastly things."

"Do you mean to say that Cubba believes this? That she would shut the window to keep out the duppies?"

"Of course she would. They're real, to her. Let's say that a man has been murdered and is being carried in his coffin to the grave. His friends will ask the body which way it wants to go, and when they come to the house of the murderer, the body absolutely will not pass it. The friends will tug and pull, sometimes the coffin falls off their backs. Did you notice the big cottonwood tree on the road, the one with all the roots?"

"Yes, that's where I met Nicholas."

"Well, let me warn you, Marietta. Never go by that tree alone at night, because that's a home of the duppies—they live in cottonwood trees."

"Thank you so much! I don't plan to go by that tree at night, but it isn't because of spirits. I don't give one pin for spirits. The road would scare me to death in the dark, I admit, but not because of ghosts. I like air, and I'm going to keep the window open at night, no matter what Cubba thinks." I yawned, suddenly overcome with weariness.

"Oh, I *am* sorry! I've stayed much too long, keeping you up when you wanted to go to bed. I really came in to see about Nicholas. Shall I take him in the morning, so that you can sleep?"

"Yes, I think the morning *would* be best; Mr. Thaw wants to see me, and I'll have my turn in the afternoon."

"That's settled then." She rose from the chair and stretched. "Sleep well, Marietta. I'm very glad you're here. I only wish— well, my room is down the hall, across from Nicholas. If Old Hige pops in, just scream and I'll hear you."

I laughed and shut the door firmly behind her. Flinging off my clothes, I dropped them on the floor—a thing I would never have done at home. Molly—what a funny girl, I thought. Does she exaggerate about the spirits? Perhaps it's partly to take her mind from larger troubles.

Once again I was drawn to the window. There was a quality in the air that stirred the blood—and the imagination. I stood quietly, letting fragments of Shelley's verse wander in my head.

> I arise from dreams of thee
>   In the first sweet sleep of night,
> When the winds are breathing low
>   And the stars are shining bright:
> I arise from dreams of thee,
>   And a spirit in my feet
> Has led me—who knows how?
>   To thy chamber-window, sweet!

Reluctantly, I turned away—"the first sweet sleep of night"— and noticed two tiny lights below on the road; they wavered, disappeared, and then shone out again. A carriage on the winding curves, I decided, and after a time I could hear the sound of horses' hoofs on the stones. Who would come at this time of night, I asked myself, and remembered Mrs. Coulter's words. The doctor, for Nanny. Hopefully she would be better in the morning, for everyone's peace of mind. Digestive upsets were unpleasant, but certainly not uncommon.

I turned down the wick of my lamp and was about to climb the steps into the huge bed, when a sudden impulse sent me back to the window. Reaching up, I quickly pulled down the open sash.

There might be mosquitoes and bugs; no sense in letting them in, I rationalized, and returned to the bed.

The pillows were soft, and the sheets smooth and cool—yet I could not settle myself. The picture of the living room as it must have looked to my grandmother and as I had seen it tonight was strangely clear and haunting. And I had been frightened; even now a shadow of the sudden terror was still with me.

I lay awake for some time. It was her fear, I reasoned, and the sight of the loop holes that made me clutch at my throat. Flights of fancy were amusing and I thoroughly enjoyed them, but always in their proper place. They should not be allowed to dictate one's actions, ever. I did not like what had happened to me after dinner, and I should have resisted the impulse to close the window. For the practical side of my nature insisted that nothing on earth should lead a rational person into a situation beyond his control.

CHAPTER 4

Great cry and little wool.
ENGLISH PHRASE

The strips of early morning sun, tentatively reaching into the room, were not pale, as my own wood aconites or daffodils, but a rich, golden shade. I had slept lightly for some time and then, pulling up the coverlet against the chill, had fallen into a deep sleep, unconscious of disturbance in the house.

It was quiet. I had no idea of the hour, and I waited peacefully for signs that others were awake and stirring. A tap at the door, and Cubba's face peered around at me.

"Good morning, Cubba. Is it late? What time is it?"

"Six-thirty, Missie. I brings you tea now." She came in with a tray, which she placed carefully on the bedside table. A teapot and strainer, a flowered cup with a mended handle that looked very old, and a porcelain plate with three small biscuits. I regarded them doubtfully. In spite of the heavy dinner, I was hungry.

"Is this my breakfast?"

"Oh no, Missie, this is just you tea. Breakfast later on the verandah. Bad news, Missie. Him died in the night, Missie Nanny."

I pulled myself up in bed.

"She died? Nanny died?" Cubba nodded. There was a furtive look of excitement in her eyes that belied the solemn mouth.

"Doctor come, and then him better, but still not too fine.

Louisa she got to sleep. When wake, Missie Nanny quite dead."

"Oh, my heavens!" I sat still, absorbing this bad news. Nicholas would be more upset than ever, and poor Mrs. Coulter—this was truly a misfortune, a calamity. Molly had been right, after all. This Christmas had all the signs of a disaster.

"Is there anything I can do, Cubba? Where is Mrs. Coulter?"

"She sleeping now. They service to be at church this afternoon. Missie Nanny to be buried there, not at Repose. This graveyard full long ago. Not room for any body more."

"Yes—well, where is Master Nicholas?"

"Him with Missie Molly. Him say to let you sleep. I come back later with hot water. Oh ki! Bad dog!"

She shook her apron at a small brown dog wriggling around the door. With a running leap she landed on my bed and began to burrow under the sheet, digging about to make a nest at my feet.

"Oh look—look at her! No, it's all right, I love dogs. This is Jilly, Master Nicholas' dog?"

"Yes, Missie, him named Jilly. When I come, him just a yard dog, not to set foot in the house. And Mast' James still no want him in the house. But God A'mity, to keep him out. And lil Mast' Nicholas do love him so much."

As if aware that we were talking about her, Jilly now emerged and gave us a sharp stare. She—for Cubba's "him" applied to both sexes—was a comical little dog, tan with a coarse black ruff around her neck and black markings on her face. Her dark terrier eyes protruded, and there was a questioning wrinkle between them as she looked at us, trying to fathom the words. Then her gaze fell on the biscuits, and I felt her body tense, gathering for a surprise attack.

"No you don't," I said, hugging her tightly. She licked my chin and settled down beside me, one eye still on the biscuits, waiting her moment.

"Too smart," said Cubba, picking up the clothes I had so carelessly flung on the floor. "Him always follow the trays, that ginger dog Jilly."

I poured myself a cup of tea—tea, before breakfast! It was delicious, clear and hot. I sipped it slowly, thinking about Nanny, whom I had never met, and could not mourn, but I knew all too well the gloom and confusion that come with death to a household.

Later, when I walked along the verandah to breakfast, I found Mrs. Coulter alone at the table. She was pale, and the corners of her eyes pulled down in weariness, but she welcomed me to her side with a smile.

"I hope you slept well, my dear, and weren't disturbed by the comings and goings."

"No, I didn't know a thing until Cubba brought in my tea. I'm so very, very sorry. It was sudden?"

"Yes, mercifully. Louisa called me around three, that strange hour of low ebb, when so many slip away. Dr. Barrows had given her a strong powder; she wasn't in much pain, thank heavens. But I still can't believe that she isn't here with us this morning—bustling about—such a sharp vital person for her age, and a twinkle behind the brusque manner. I'm sure she would not have hesitated to scold me, if she had thought it necessary. And such a strength to us all, after my son's death. Well, it's a blow, a dreadfully sad blow, but we must keep going along as normally as possible; it's what she would have wanted, especially for Nicholas. One finds it's the only way. Marietta, my brother still wants to see you this morning, though of course he's upset, as we all are. Then, if you don't mind, I'll leave you in charge of Nicholas while we go to the service and burial this afternoon. I've had a long talk with him; he and Molly have both cried and feel better. You'll be amazed how easily children are distracted from grief, and I'm sure it's not callousness. They feel the loss, but differently. Somehow it does not interfere with their pleasures."

"I've noticed that, and I understand. After my father died, I often felt so guilty when I found myself enjoying something; and yet it was what he would have wanted."

"Exactly. I keep forgetting that you have been through this same sorrow, and recently. You are being a great help already, and I do appreciate it, my dear. Now, I must hurry along— there's so much to do. We're very informal at breakfast, as you can see. Just ask Charmian or Thomas for more coffee, or anything else you want."

A round table covered with a flowered linen cloth had been placed at one end of the verandah, outside the dining room. Wicker chairs with faded chintz seats stood on the worn tiles that I later learned had been brought as ballast in the old sailing ships. Above my head, a tiny hummingbird darted in and out of the thunbergia, and I could hear Charmian singing a hymn under her breath as she polished the dining-room floor with coconut-husk pads.

At nine o'clock the sun was already hot, and I moved into the shade, eating the mango that Charmian had brought, gazing out at the tranquil water.

> While birds, and butterflies, and flowers
> Make all one band of paramours—

Nearby, a coconut fell with a tiny thud, startling the small lizard who had been lying motionless on the rail. He began blowing out his throat and changing color from dark green to yellow. Subdued voices rose from under the arches, and the butler, Thomas, now in shirt sleeves, crossed the courtyard to speak to the boy who was cutting back oleanders at the entrance. Something about his manner enraged the peacock, who screamed for his companion, and led her away from the interlopers.

I could not overcome the feeling that I and all the household should be in mourning, but death seemed to come and go far more easily here, with none of the trappings we were accustomed to at home: the black crepe on the door, lowered blinds, hushed voices. Trappings that served the living, after all. A small black bird hopped on the tile by my chair. Staring at me with a round, yellow eye, he seized a crumb of fallen toast, and then, seeing no harm in me, he proceeded to move around the table making a good meal. Thomas, now in his coat, appeared to pull back my chair.

"Kling kling," he said, pointing to the bird. "Make noise like kling kling."

"Thank you, Thomas," I said regally, reflecting that at home I would be washing up the breakfast dishes. "Can you tell me where I can find Mr. Thaw?"

"In his room, at end of verandah."

"Would you ask him if he will see Miss Jackson now?"

I waited for his return, my mind drifting, trying to memorize forever the look of the vast, cloudless sky. I should buy a little sketch book; I could never recapture the astonishing blues, but perhaps the flowers could be copied. Belatedly, with a touch of guilt, I thought of my mother and how she would have benefitted from the sun. It had seemed heartless to leave her alone at Christmas, but neighbors and friends had promised to stand by—and, in all honesty, the only person whom she truly missed was my father.

"Ah, good morning," came James Thaw's voice close beside me, and I jumped. "What a pity to start your visit in such a sad way. I think we had better proceed with our talk, though, as I shall be busy later with funeral arrangements and letters. Nanny had almost no relatives and none here, of course, but they must be informed that in this climate one has to be buried immediately. We are going to miss her sadly, such a sharp, bright little woman, but that's the way of it. We cannot choose the time and place. Shall we go to my sitting room?"

This was a man's room, clearly, and I guessed that it had once been his father's. A terrestial globe stood on a table by the window, and the huge desk was covered with papers. I noticed that the legs of the desk were placed in glass dishes filled with oil.

"To keep out the ants," said Mr. Thaw, following my look. "And the papers are my holiday penance. The Repose bills are paid once a year when I am here; a Herculean task, I assure you. Now, over on this table, I've collected all that was in the box marked with your grandmother's name. It's difficult to be accurate, after all these years, and that is why I was anxious that you should come and see these things for yourself, rather than my shipping them to you."

I twisted my hands behind my back. Now that the actual moment had come, I found, to my dismay, that I was trembling. I stared at the collection; it was interesting, and clearly of some value. Several silver boxes, a carved jade ring and brooch, a bracelet and necklace of brilliants, several tortoise combs, and two cameos. But there was no set of amethysts. I stood uncertainly, not knowing what to say, or what my next move in this obscure game should be.

"Well?"

"They're—very pretty."

"Yes, and I think the jade may be rather fine. I should take it to an expert when you get home; you might find that it's of some value. The silver boxes are nice, but more on the sentimental side. I'll have everything wrapped and put into little boxes for you, easy to carry back. Well, so the matter is settled at last! I suppose no one ever looked at the shelf after my father died. That particular storeroom had been locked for years."

As he talked, my mind worked desperately. It was clear that he felt that his responsibilities toward the Jackson family were now over. I might never have another opportunity to ask questions.

"I'm very happy to have all this, Mr. Thaw," I began, "but there is one more thing. In my grandmother's letter—her list, that is—she mentioned a favorite amethyst set. And there are no amethysts here. Do you know—do you have any idea what might have become of that set?"

James Thaw's benign expression became slightly wary. "An amethyst set? I'm afraid I know nothing about that, Miss Jackson. I had the overseer go through the guest book and then through the entire house, where he was lucky enough to find these things. After all this time, I thought it rather a miracle. But if you're not satisfied, perhaps you would want to make a search of the house yourself."

"Oh, no, no! There's no need for that," I answered quickly, annoyed to feel the color rising in my face. "It's just that she was so positive about the amethysts."

"And what else was on her list, if I may ask, anything else that is missing?"

I was silent, trapped in my own snare. There was no list, of course, and, in her letter, she had mentioned only the amethysts. To go further along this tricky path might be a grave mistake. The jewelry was of little importance, compared to the land. The land was my real objective. I must not be diverted from that end. I swallowed hard and tried to speak lightly.

"Oh, after all these years, how can one be sure of anything? You've gone to a lot of trouble and I'm very grateful. My mother and I will be happy to have these pretty things, and if the jade is valuable, that will be all the better."

But somehow, under the politeness, I had the impression that I was being dismissed, fobbed off too quickly, and I continued to talk.

"Strange though," I said, "that she should have left all these things behind. It has always been a mystery in our family as to how my grandfather died. She never spoke of it, apparently. In fact, until you wrote that he had yellow fever, we didn't even know that."

James Thaw regarded me with raised eyebrows. "Mystery? How odd. I don't see why any mystery should have been made. Mind you, I was in England and know nothing of what happened here at the time. But I was under the impression that my father had had American guests, and that one of them died of the fever just before leaving the island. There is a law—'the sun may not rise twice upon the dead'—so he must have been buried here, either at Repose or in the churchyard. You may want to have a look, for family interest. But there was no mystery as far as I know. Death from the fever was a sadly common thing in those days. It was a great mercy when it suddenly stopped, no one knows quite why."

I couldn't help but be disappointed in the interview, which I had anticipated for so long and which now had resulted in a few trinkets and a rather final dismissal of the Jackson family. In all fairness, I told myself, James Thaw had been thousands of miles away at the time; he could not be expected to know any of the details. And his father, it seemed, had never told him of the short-lived partnership. Had they never found the chalices, I wondered. Were the amethysts still hidden with the gold? But I dared not overplay my hand by asking further questions.

Perhaps James Thaw sensed my frustration, for he motioned me to sit in the Spanish leather chair, and settled himself behind the desk.

"Before we finish our business and I go back to these endless bills, tell me a little about your present situation, Marietta. From your letter and from what you say about the jade, I deduce that there are financial complications. Is it the will? That can be a tedious matter, if it is not in order." I hesitated, unwilling to reveal the state of our poverty.

"Or other legal questions? If I can advise, I should be very glad to do what I can. I've acquired a certain amount of legal knowledge over the years."

I assured him that the legalities seemed to be in order, and after a few more polite questions he rose, saying that he must apply himself to his correspondence.

"Perhaps you'd like to borrow my father's estate books for a while," he added. "I promised that I'd tell you about the plantation, and reading them is really more instructive than anything I can say. Take them out to the verandah. Thomas can bring them back when you've finished."

The books were heavy and worn. I settled myself in a wicker rocking chair, away from the sun, and began to examine them with interest.

The Hospital Book: "Cudjoe began a course of bark. Suspect him of malingering—"

The Dispute Book: "Jug-Betty today accused Lorelia of biting her hand. Gave both extra tasks in the kitchen—"

The Estate Journal: complicated entries of slave histories, cattle pedigrees, cane experiments, and prices on shipments and insurance.

I turned to the pages marked 1831—the fateful year. Rats in the cane appeared to be a major disaster, and I was studying the amount of losses in amazement when I became aware of Mrs. Coulter's voice, around the corner. It was sharply distressed, not her usual gentle tone.

"But that is impossible, Dr. Barrows! I can't believe what you are saying! Are you quite sure?"

"No, Mrs. Coulter, as I said, I'm not at all sure. But it is my obligation to tell you that I can't rule out poison as cause of death." I leaned forward; his voice was low, and he spoke in an undertone.

"But Nanny, of all people—and who could possibly do such a thing? We have only family here and one guest who arrived yesterday, long after the attack, and the servants of course."

"Yes, the servants. I was coming to that. Are they all well known to you? I mean, have they worked here for some time?" A pause. I remembered Mrs. Coulter's remarks, at our first meeting.

"No, no, as a matter of fact, they are all new to us, except the cook, who is caretaker. It's quite difficult to find ones who will come only for the holidays. Usually the old-timers will oblige, but this year we were unlucky, for some reason. Really, Dr. Barrows, what earthly sense would it make to poison Nanny? They could not have held a grudge against her; they hardly knew her!"

"Hmmmm—not a grudge, perhaps, but it comes to my mind that Miss Crowell was a pretty sharp old lady, with a sharp tongue. I've heard her lacing out dogs, children, and servants over the years. Now, she may have caught one of these new ones thieving, given him a real scolding, or even frightened him, and then was paid back. I've ruled out corrosive sublimate but there are, as you well know, any number of native poisons. Deadly poisons."

I felt a touch of cold sweat on my neck as I absorbed the doctor's words.

"What am I to do, then?" Mrs. Coulter's voice was lower, but still filled with distress. "Should I dismiss them all? I've never had to deal with this kind of situation; it would be almost impossible to find others so close to Christmas, but far better that than to have a poisoner in the house."

"No, no, I don't think that is necessary. In the first place, poison is only a possible factor, as I said; the real cause of death was heart failure, of course. And in my experience, if you had a real poisoner on your hands, the other servants would be quick to tell you; they'd be afraid for themselves. You may well find that the culprit, if there is one, will disappear on his own account. He probably didn't mean to kill Miss Crowell, just pay her back, and now is terrified. And by the way, speaking of hearts, I wouldn't upset your brother with this. We don't want him starting Christmas with one of his spasms. I'm going to list heart failure as cause of death, brought on by acute indigestion which, after all, may be the whole truth of the matter."

"Yes, well, there's nothing that can be done now. I know you did your best, Dr. Barrows, but it has all been a shock, and now this news! Nanny has been so close to us, and the mere thought of her going in this way seems so terribly wrong, so senseless."

"I know, and I don't like to worry you, but on the other hand—"

"Quite. I understand, and I'll keep it entirely to myself. Shall we go to Mrs. Gerald now?"

Their footsteps sounded on the tile as they went away into the house. I was alone again, fervently wishing that I had not overheard the unpleasant conversation. It would be impossible not to study the friendly black faces and wonder if there was a poisoner among them.

Mrs. Gerald Coulter—Serena—appeared at luncheon. The dining room was dim, the jalousies drawn against the heat; I tried not to stare at her, Molly had hinted at an addiction to drugs, and I had never, to my knowledge, met a person who took drugs. She was dark-eyed—the children must have inherited their fairness from their father—and I thought her quite beautiful apart from the droop of her mouth and the shadows under her eyes. Nicholas and Molly seemed pleased to see her at the table and anxious to bring her out of the sadness into which she had withdrawn.

"We rode in the direction of the caves this morning, Mother," said Molly. "Do you remember when we went there last year? What a good time we had?"

"Let's go tomorrow, Granny," Nicholas chimed in. "We'll play hide-and-seek. You'll come won't you, Mother?"

"No, Nicholas. You know I would not be up to it." The tone implied that he should not have asked; he hunched his shoulders and looked down at his plate.

Mrs. Coulter tried to ease the rebuff. "But Nicholas, tomorrow is the day before Christmas. Had you forgotten? And we still have all the decorating to do. I'm going to need your help here, darling."

There was a long silence as Charmian and Thomas removed the soufflé plates and began to pass the salad. No one mentioned Nanny, or the service, but the atmosphere was strained and unhappy. Finally, James Thaw turned to me and asked if I had found the estate books interesting. I was quick to reply.

"Oh! Very interesting indeed. They gave me such a vivid feeling of the place, and I learned so much about sugar cane. But what a difficult life. One catastrophe after another! At one point, almost everything except the Great House seemed to have burned down. But the book didn't say what caused the fire."

"No, my father was very touchy on that subject." Mr. Thaw glanced around to see that Thomas and Charmian were out of the room and continued:

"It was the slave rebellion of 1831, one of the most dreadful times in the island's history. Most of the neighboring Great Houses went up in flames that night, but even though this house was spared, my father was very angry. He blamed it all on the missionaries."

"The missionaries?"

"Yes—you see, Marietta, by that time, the great era of sugar was over. Prices had fallen as other countries competed with us; the slave trade had been abolished years before, and the slaves who were here knew that they were going to be freed. The missionaries told them so—those do-good Baptists, Moravians, and what-nots who came to bring Christianity and ended by bringing ruin to the slaves as well as the planters."

I was astounded. The blood of New England abolitionists ran strongly in my veins and in my education. Nothing in the world was more horrible than slavery, I had assumed, and only good could come of its demise.

In spite of the fact that James Thaw was beginning to breathe heavily, I pressed on.

"I'm sorry, but I don't quite understand what you mean by ruin. I can see why freedom would ruin the planters—but the slaves?"

"Very simple. In my father's day, the blacks were fed, clothed,

and cared for all of their lives; a far better life it was than that of
a coal miner in the Midlands. When the Proclamation of Freedom did come in 1834, what happened to them? Half ran off to
their little plots in the hills, others lounged about on the roads
higgling rum and sugar stolen from their masters; some of those
trained to a trade stayed on the estates, but few cared to cut
cane. Oh no, they were now too fine to cut cane."

"But someone must have done the work, surely?"

"Yes, laborers imported from India, at a fearful cost. The old
estates, those that hadn't been burned, were sold out one by one.
The absentee owners couldn't afford them; they accepted com-
pensation from the British Government for the loss of slaves and
sold the places to their trustees and lawyers, mostly for a song.
Repose is one of the few that has stayed in one family. One out
of hundreds!" He stopped, and I asked no more questions, fear-
ing to make him really ill.

Again, silence at the table; dessert was passed.

"Oh, good! Spotted-dog pudding!" said Nicholas. Molly took a
large helping, and I saw her mother's eyes close in disgust.

"Did you and Marietta have a successful morning?" asked
Mrs. Coulter, with a glance at her brother; his breathing was
easy again.

"I believe we did. We went over all her treasures, and some
day after Christmas we'll pack them up for her. I think the jade
may prove to be particularly valuable—"

Everyone jumped as Serena Coulter's fork crashed from her
hand onto the china plate.

"*Her* things? Her treasures? Why should anything in this
house belong to *her?*" I felt Nicholas stiffen in his seat.

Mrs. Coulter spoke soothingly. "We talked about it at lunch
yesterday, my dear. Don't you remember? Marietta has come for
a few trinkets that belonged to her grandmother, that somehow
had been forgotten all these years."

"Uncle James said 'treasures,' not 'trinkets'!" She turned to
him, dark eyes flashing, her face quivering. "So we've come to
this, have we, Uncle James? This girl, a perfect stranger, goes off
with all our valuables, claiming that they belonged to her grand-

mother. What is this family coming to! There will be nothing left for Nicholas—for any of us!"

She might as well have called me a thief. The hot blood rose up my neck and into my face; I tried not to meet anyone's eye, but that was impossible. Molly's face was shocked, and she looked at me imploringly. Mrs. Coulter seemed stunned. We all waited for James Thaw to speak. Finally he rose from his seat.

"Serena, Miss Jackson is a guest in this house and I do not think we should expose her to our family problems. If you have— any suggestions—I wish that you would come to me. All things considered, I think you owe me that courtesy." The mention of courtesy may have reached Serena, or perhaps she remembered her dependence on James Thaw. She looked about in a confused way, as if she had already forgotten what the outburst was about.

"I'm—I'm not myself," she muttered, pushing back her chair. "Forgive me, Miss Jackson. I'm not myself. Molly—" A pale and shaken Molly was already beside her, a hand on her arm, leading her mother from the room. Nicholas, in answer to his grand-mother's nod, excused himself and ran out.

It was my first experience of an unpleasant family scene. I sat, my face still scarlet, trying to persuade myself that there had been nothing personal in this extraordinary attack. Molly had tried to prepare me, but I wondered if Serena Coulter was seriously deranged.

James Thaw's face had flushed to an unhealthy color. "It's in-excusable," he exclaimed bitterly, "after all I've done for her, for the family!"

"Don't excite yourself, James." Mrs. Coulter, the peacemaker. "It's so bad for you. Do try to forgive her, Marietta. It's the upset about Nanny as well as her husband, and we must try to put this—this unfortunate outburst—out of our heads. Dreadful, but these things happen when one is under a great deal of strain. James, I do wish you would rest before we leave for church. I think I will lie down for a while, and Marietta, perhaps you'd take Nicholas for a walk, away from the house, so that he won't see us start off. He loves to play in the stream."

"Elizabeth. Have you told Marietta about Anna Thaw? Have you warned her?"

Mrs. Coulter looked flustered. "No, James, I haven't. I didn't think it was necessary, at this time."

"My dear, you know that it is. It is most necessary, if she is to be left with Nicholas." He sighed and rubbed his hand over his forehead. His linen suit was immaculate; he must have changed it at least once since breakfast.

"James, I think you should put this off until later, after what has just happened. It seems rather too much—"

"You must allow me, Elizabeth, to use my judgment in this matter. We will all be away for several hours. She must know about Anna, otherwise how is she to take the responsibility?"

"Very well. But, I do beg you to leave yourself time for a siesta—it will be a trying afternoon. Marietta, I apologize again for my daughter-in-law; this really had nothing to do with you."

"I do understand, Mrs. Coulter. Losing her husband, and now Nanny, it's bound to be upsetting. Please don't worry." But I sounded more forgiving than I felt. It would be hard, if not impossible, to forget that she had accused me of robbing the family.

As we returned to the sitting room, I wondered who Anna Thaw might be. My confidante, Molly, had not mentioned other Thaws in the neighborhood. Again, I found myself facing James Thaw across the big desk.

"Well, the skeletons are falling out of the cupboard, I'm afraid," he began, "but it's only fair to make you aware of them. You see, the property that adjoins Repose belonged to my younger brother Charles, who died some years ago. His widow, Anna Thaw, lives there now. You are never, under any circumstances, to set foot on that land."

My consternation must have showed in my face. What land? Where? "Of course, Mr. Thaw, if you wish it. But how will I know the boundaries? I might, by mistake—"

"You must stay on this side of the stream. Nicholas knows this. He is the reason for my great concern; I have told him never to go into the woods beyond the stream, though I have not given him the reason. I must explain to you that my brother's widow is a woman of color. My father was very strict in his views on marriage, and he disinherited Charles after his marriage. He forbade the two families to speak, and he would have taken back the land if it had not already been legally settled on Charles, this younger son whom he hoped to keep on the island."

"A family feud," I murmured. There had been mention of two brothers in the letters, I remembered.

"Anna Thaw is a dangerous woman, Marietta. It is common knowledge that she knows obeah and witchcraft, and she has great power over the blacks because of this knowledge. But worse than that"—and he looked at me piercingly, his small blue eyes intent—"I now believe that she is actively working to destroy this branch of the Thaw family. Gerald is gone—and his death has never been understood. Nicholas is next in line to inherit. Nothing must happen to him. I rely on you to be on your guard, Marietta, against this woman while you are in charge of him."

It was an unhappy story but I had no reason to be alarmed, and I assured Mr. Thaw that I would take care to see that Nicholas did not cross the stream. Anna Thaw did not seem like a tangible threat; there was no probability that we should meet. Possibly my mind was still on the acute embarrassment I had felt at lunch. Although Mrs. Coulter had assured me that Serena's vicious words were not really directed at me, I was not so certain. As I left the sitting room, I was far more fearful of Serena Coulter than of Anna Thaw.

CHAPTER 5

Let dogs delight to bark and bite,
For God hath made them so.

ISAAC WATTS:
Divine Songs for Children, 1715

Nicholas was delighted to conduct my first tour around the Repose estate. Flushed with importance, he began with the ground floor, behind the arches.

"Do you see the conch?"—pointing to a large shell that hung on the wall—"That's the alarm bell. One long shell blow, and everyone comes running from miles."

Shell blow. What an odd expression, I thought. How could the sound of a shell be heard for miles?

"How do you know, Nicholas?" I asked, skeptically.

"The shell blow is for danger. It's a call for help. If you don't believe me, ask anyone."

"I believe you."

We continued to the kitchen house, where I averted my eyes from the squalid collection of pots and pans, marveling that Chitty could conjure up endless courses from the primitive stove. A large tree with glossy leaves stood by the kitchen door; I had thought it a horse chestnut, but Nicholas corrected me, saying that it was a breadfruit tree and had been brought by Captain Cook, from, from—he hesitated.

"Tahiti," I finished, adding in a schoolmarmish way that it was not this tree but its forebear that Captain Cook had brought.

As we passed the servants' quarters and started down the drive, Jilly bounded ahead, looking like a miniature doe with her soft tan underside and stiff little flag of a tail.

Nicholas had pointed out the hospital, bookkeeper's and overseer's houses as we had arrived; now we passed the blacksmith's shop, the carpenter's shop, and the cooperage on our way to the old slave village at the foot of the hill, near the stream.

Several women in long white Mother Hubbard dresses and madras bandannas were drawing water from the well; they stopped to greet us with warm smiles and polite discussion about my hair.

"So white, that. Most like my graunee's." Jilly squeezed under a broken slat and sent a bare-bottomed baby and a number of hens scuttling to safety.

I looked about with considerable interest. Although I had not felt qualified to debate the merits of slavery with James Thaw, I had my own opinion, drawn partly from Harriet Beecher Stowe, and also from the fact that many of the older men in our town had suffered grievously to abolish slavery. I had seldom met a black person, let alone walked in a black village, and I was curious to observe their way of living.

The village was only partially occupied; the wattled, thatched-roof houses were set between sweet-smelling hedges, each with its fenced-in plot. Through the open windows, I could see leisurely activity in the tiny rooms furnished with beds and tables, and hear voices calling, or raised in song. The friendliness shown me, a white stranger, was touching.

Slowly, we wandered back past the aqueduct to the fields where the animals were kept, stopping to give a banana to Nicholas' dusty pony.

"I've learned the first verse, Quaco," he told the driver, who was leading out horses for the big carriage. "Listen to me!

> "Peter, Peter was a black boy
> Peter him pull foot one day—"

"That right, Mast' Nicholas. But Quaco busy now, you go long, you."

"What on earth is that?" I asked, to catch his attention. "That big stone square below the garden?"

"Oh, you mean the barbecue? That's where we dry the coffee beans. If it rains, we have to run out and pick them all up."

"You mean the coffee I had this morning is grown here at Repose?"

"Well, of course it is. Don't you grow your own coffee in America? What shall we do now? Would you rather go to the graveyard or the garden?"

I had seen the garden from a distance, a ruin of weeds, where a few roses had raised thorny stalks and struggled to present a few limp blooms to the tropic sun. There was a far more pressing reason to go to the graveyard.

"How many Thaws can you count, Nicholas?" I asked, as we entered the walled enclosure, where the logwood grew wild against the borders. I wanted a few quiet moments to walk about unobserved. He was off in a flash, mumbling to himself as he wove in and around the stones. It was not a large place, and I soon found what I was seeking. The name was sadly eroded; it would have been impossible to decipher if one had not been looking for it.

——KSON
DIED DECEMBER 28, 1831

A small and insignificant stone compared to the gray marble monument in the churchyard at home. This is my grandfather's real grave, I thought solemnly. This is the place where he is buried. As I stared at the remnant of his name, I hoped that Daniel Jackson could know that the last of his line was mourning him. Quietly, I went to the wall and picked a small flower, placing it beside the stone.

"Only three Thaws," shouted Nicholas, "but a lot of other names, and five dogs, I think. Look at this, Marietta. Wouldn't you say that Brownie was a dog?" I went over to the marker.

"Brownie, a Faithful Pet," I read. "There's no date. Maybe your grandmother remembers Brownie."

"I have a capital idea! Can Jilly be buried here too? She's a faithful pet, except she still loves her food more than me."

"I wouldn't worry about burying Jilly, just yet. Do you want to play at the stream now?"

"Yes—and Marietta, Nanny *always* lets me take off my shoes and stockings." He had forgotten, for a moment, that she had gone. "Look, a firefly! When it rains they'll all come out, like a sky full of dancing stars!" I smiled at him, pretending to show interest in the dull little bug, but my thoughts were back at the insignificant worn stone. I was acutely aware of my pulse, the even flow of my breath, the delight of being alive; for a part of me lay in the hillside, buried in alien land.

At the edge of the stream, I established myself on a rock and put up my parasol. Even my coolest summer dress was warm over the chemise and heavy petticoat. Soon Nicholas' middy was wet and stained, but I was glad to see him absorbed in a private game, building a small dam of twigs, intent on his work. A wave of affection for him swept me, and a real concern. How could he keep his happy and friendly nature, I worried, with all the upheavals in his life—his father dead, his mother unstable, and now Nanny gone. He was too young to face these troubles; no wonder he ran away.

My eyes began to close, in the quiet afternoon sun. What a paradise this place would be, I mused, without people. Flower of light. I tried to remember more of Ben Jonson's poem.

> It was the plant and flower of Light.
> In small proportions we just beauties see:
> And in short measures life may perfect be.

No, to be entirely alone might be dull; I could imagine sharing this world with one other person. He should be dark, in contrast to my fairness, with a quiet manner and quick sense of humor. And he must be kind and sensitive; I disliked rough, abrupt men, perhaps because of my father's gentle nature. We would travel continuously, to the out-of-the-way places in the world, explore and linger if we chose. How he could support this taste for travel did not concern me just now.

"Marietta, have you seen Jilly?" I jumped, startled from my daydreams.

"No, not for a few minutes. Wouldn't she stay with us?"

"Yes, except when that dog—oh dear, oh, blast!" He was pulling on his long stockings, fumbling with his laces. "She's gone to find that big dog, the one she hates. Whenever she sees him—and he's so much bigger. I should have been watching her, away from the house."

I stood up, looking about. "Call her. Maybe she hasn't gone far." But even as I opened my mouth, the distant sounds of terrier shrieks broke the hour's peace.

"I knew it! There. Over there!" In a second Nicholas was off, crossing the bridge, running down the path that led to the woods —the woods that had been so strictly forbidden by his great-uncle.

"Nicholas! Stop! Come back!" I called, but nothing on earth could have held him. Throwing down my parasol, I flew after him, holding up my long skirts. As I neared the woods I could see the narrow path he must have taken. "Nicholas, wait!" But he was out of sight.

I stumbled along in the green undergrowth, my thin summer shoes slipping on the roots. Moisture was running down my back, and I felt that the dark trees were closing in, separating me from air and light. Somewhere ahead I heard Nicholas cry out sharply. Sheer fright lifted my feet and I ran even faster toward the sound of Jilly's wild barking.

Suddenly I was in the daylight again; Nicholas was ahead of me, running through a field of guinea grass. Fierce, deep snarls now mingled with Jilly's screeches.

Oh God, I thought, the blood drumming in my ears, he's going to get into the middle of the fight. What shall I do? "Nicholas, wait!"

The field ended at a dry-stone wall. I ran through the gate and in the direction of a low shed. I could not see the dogs, but suddenly a man's shouts rose above the noise of the fighting. As I turned the corner, I could see, in a dreadful picture, that he was holding off the bigger dog with a pitchfork. Nicholas had thrown himself on the ground beside a small brown body. The tears blinded my eyes and I brushed at them frantically, but as I came closer I could see that Jilly was not dead. Although bleeding from her hindquarters and shoulder, she was struggling to get up, the light of battle still strong in her popping, dark eyes. Of the two, Nicholas appeared most damaged. He was crying loudly, his hands covered with blood.

"You've been bitten," I gasped.

"No, he's all right. The dogs didn't touch him," called the man, who had managed to get a rope around the big dog's neck and was tying him to a post. This one, too, was not ready to abandon the fight, and hurled himself forward with frantic snarls.

I pulled myself to my feet; my hair had fallen about my shoulders and my face streamed with tears.

"Oh, thank you, thank God you were here," I stammered. "I have never been so frightened in my entire life! One moment she was with us, and then she was gone and we could hear her yelling—I'm so sorry, but thank you."

I wiped my eyes, took a deep breath, and looked at our rescuer. He was a little taller than I, and slender; his dark eyes regarded me with amusement and sympathy.

"Well, these dogs do seem to have declared war to the death," he said pleasantly. "But yours is much smaller, and off her own turf. I'm glad it wasn't worse. The more she bleeds, the cleaner the punctures will be, you know, but we'd better go to the house and have a good look. I don't think he got to any vital spots."

Nicholas stood up, snuffling and rubbing his face. In addition to the blood on his hands, there was a nasty trickle down his leg.

"Oh, you *have* hurt yourself," I said. He looked down.

"I tripped in the woods. I didn't feel it until now." He suddenly looked pale, under the freckles. The stranger was lifting Jilly carefully, trying to steady the bleeding hind leg. His suit will be ruined, I thought remorsefully. We followed him past the outbuildings and over the rough grass toward a small, one-storied house, a gory little procession, Jilly now whining dismally. But even in the confusion I took note of the garden, as we straggled up to the trellised front door. The well-tended masses of canna lilies, hibiscus, heliconia were cleverly arranged and mingled with plants whose shapes were unfamiliar. Gardeners were generally kindly people, I told myself; we would be well cared for.

"I think we'd better go through into the scullery," said our host. "We won't make such a mess in there. And I'll tend to this little rascal outside. She's not a pretty sight for a young lady." He led us into the house and disappeared.

I looked about the little room with interest. Shelves covered with bottles of preserves lined the walls; dried roots and vegetables hung from the ceiling. It reminded me of storybook illustrations, everything small and tidy and ready for use.

"Who is he, Nicholas?" I asked. "Do you know him?" I took hold of the pump handle and began to draw water for the basin.

"Well of course I know him! He's my cousin. His name is Stephen Thaw and he comes here to visit his grandmother, Miss Anna."

I let go of the handle; it flew up, almost hitting me in the eye. This was the land—the house—where Nicholas must never set foot, and where, according to James Thaw, his very life was in danger! My heart began to pound in slow, heavy strokes. After the first alarm, I had utterly forgotten about Anna Thaw. Now, by a frightful mischance, we were in her house.

I leaned against the stone sink, trying to collect myself. There had been no sign of anyone else.

"Nicholas," I said urgently, in a whisper. "You do know that you are not supposed to be here, don't you? That we'll be in terrible trouble. You know that?" He nodded, suddenly grave.

"Uncle James won't let us come here, but I don't know why. I like Stephen." His voice seemed to echo loudly.

"Hush, Nicholas, now listen. We must go—quickly! Right out the door and around the shed to the field. Don't argue with me, just come!" I took his hand and began to pull at him.

"But I can't leave Jilly!" His voice rose in a maddening whine.

"Never mind. We'll send for her later." But as I tried to move him, I could hear footsteps in the house, coming toward us. I dropped his arm and turned, bracing myself against the sink, hands outstretched to protect him.

The woman who stood in the doorway was thin to the point of emaciation, and her head, with its cropped white hair, was held high. If James Thaw had not told me of her mixed blood, I should not have guessed it. She must have seen my dismay, known the reason for it. Even Nicholas was round-eyed and silent. She regarded us with penetrating cold eyes and I had the feeling that she was deciding how to receive us. Outside, we could hear her grandson talking to Jilly.

"I've looked at your dog," she said in a low voice with a singular accent. "She'll do." Then, motioning Nicholas to a stool, she began to examine his leg. I stood by as she covered the cut with ointment from a small jar, and I prayed that it was harmless.

"Infection sets in quickly here," she said to me severely. "You must keep this covered until the scab forms." So she did not plan to keep us prisoners.

"Yes, yes, I will," I whispered, pinning up my hair as best I could. My first hour of responsibility was over and I had disobeyed my most important order. Now I was in a panic to leave, so that we might get home before the carriage returned and we were viewed in our torn and bloody condition.

Anna Thaw was regarding me with a long, searching look. "You're not a Thaw," she said, and my hands jerked up.

"No, no, I'm not. My name is Marietta Jackson. I arrived yesterday, for Christmas."

"Daniel Jackson's granddaughter." I stared at her, shocked. "How—did you know? Did you know my grandfather?"

"I knew of him." She opened the door, motioning me outside. For a second, I had an overwhelming desire to ask this strange woman about my grandfather—what exactly she knew of Daniel Jackson. But I was far too shaken to prolong the conversation.

"Thank you," I muttered instead. "Thank you for your help. I'm very grateful and so is Nicholas." My fingers tightened on his arm.

"Yes, thank you very much," he echoed. He was still pale, whether from the accident or fear of Anna I did not know.

"We must start back," I chattered stupidly; "they will be waiting for us, waiting tea for us."

"Why, no," said Anna Thaw coolly. "They won't have returned from church. Tell me, Miss Jackson, what brings you to Repose?"

My nerves almost gave way. Yet it did not occur to me to evade the question.

"I—I came to collect the jewelry my grandmother left here, years ago. Mr. Thaw invited me to come."

"And how long do you stay?"

"Just a short visit—three weeks or so." My knees were trembling. Why these questions? For what purpose? I shoved Nicholas forward. But Anna Thaw had not done with me.

"Three weeks is a long time," she said evenly. "May I offer you some advice? In your place, Miss Jackson, I would leave on the next steamer." And before I could answer, she had gone into the other room.

"Leave Repose?" This was a clear warning, one that I would have heeded had I not been so demoralized. As it was, I scarcely heard the words. My immediate need was to return Nicholas safely home, and I hurried from the house.

Stephen Thaw had finished doctoring Jilly; she was already working off the bandage on her hind quarters. James Thaw had not mentioned a grandson and I wondered if he too was considered a threat; he seemed a particularly attractive young man, in my opinion.

"I'll carry her for you," he said now. "She's heavy, for such a small dog, and a dead weight at the moment." We started back across the field; Jilly, the cause of the whole misadventure, lay in a towel, rolling her eyes at us. As we neared the woods I began to feel calmer; Nicholas walked ahead, scuffing the grass with his good leg. I glanced up at Stephen Thaw and smiled.

"I do thank you again, so much. How I ran when I heard your dog. I didn't know what I was going to do!"

"Yes, it must have been very frightening. So you are staying at Repose. Are you enjoying your visit, Miss Jackson?"

"Very much. It's a beautiful place, this island. And you—are you visiting your grandmother?"

"Yes, I come over from time to time to see her. She's alone otherwise. My parents live in Italy—have done for years. She's an eccentric old girl, but she puts me up and leaves me to my writing, which is exactly what I want."

"You're a writer? On what subject?"

"Historical novels, two books, moderately successful. I used this island for background in the last one. And for fun, I collect more Annansy stories."

"Annansy?"

"A folk-tale creature who came here from Africa in the shape of a spider. He spends his time outwitting his friends, often in a devious way, I'm sorry to say. The stories are incredibly involved with characters like Bredda Tiger, Bredda Monkey; the only one who can fool Annansy is Sister Peel-head Fowl."

"Peel-head Fowl! What a lovely name."

"People know I'm collecting these stories, and often a stranger will come to me with a new one—and get a shilling or two for his pains. On the serious side, though, I do research on island history, and that takes me from one end to the other—a fascinating place it is. I hope you will be here long enough to become acquainted."

"I shall have to read it. There are history books at Repose, I'm sure."

"Oh yes, undoubtedly. James Thaw is a student of sorts." Was there a note of bitterness in his voice? I decided to pursue the thought.

"Just this noon, as a matter of fact, he was saying that emancipation had ruined the sugar trade; he blamed the missionaries for this. Do you think that was true?"

"Two sides to everything, you know. Some planters were so terrified at their loss of control that they went to extremes; they charged exorbitant rents for the village shacks and even tore them down. Then they tried to contract for more Africans, and that didn't work. In the end, it was Indian coolies who worked the cane fields, a strange twist for an economy founded on African slave labor. But I have a theory that much stronger attempts should have been made, at the start, to colonize the island with white immigrants—Scots, Irish, English. With more subsidies, they might have done well. As it was, they came mostly as overseers or bookkeepers, far down the social scale. And they left their mark in ways that I won't go into. Yes, the slave economy has exacted a terrible price, as you in your country know to your sorrow. And where, in America, do you live?" He smiled at me, with a look of appreciative interest.

"A small New England town, near Boston. My father was a professor of English at the college there. This has been my first chance to travel outside the United States, and I'm trying to learn all that I can—so thank you for the history lesson, Mr. Thaw."

"You are very welcome. I hope that we may have more, but I'm sure, by now, you have heard of the family feud between the two branches of Thaws. My great-grandfather started it; three generations later, it all becomes rather ridiculous. In fact, the young Coulters and I are good friends. I often see them in London where I live when I'm not traveling. But here—well, I just stay clear of Repose." He shrugged his shoulders with a wry, amused look.

"It seems a pity, to me."

"There's no point in being bitter—bitterness is so corrosive; I'd rather spend my time in more constructive ways. I must admit, though, that I am frustrated at the moment. I would like very much to see you again, Miss Jackson, and I don't know how to arrange it. Do you have any plans for tomorrow?"

I tried to keep my face calm, and my voice even. This attractive man—a writer, a traveler—wanted to see me again. "I really don't know. I may be needed to look after Nicholas." I glanced ahead to Nicholas, hoping he could not hear us. "Or I might go with Molly to meet her sister at the steamer."

"Well, I think I shall go into town tomorrow afternoon, and perhaps with any luck we may be able to have another lesson. Now, I had better leave you. Here's the little fighter. I'm grateful to her for being so ferocious, otherwise we might not have met."

I took Jilly from him; our hands touched briefly.

"I'm the one who is grateful," I murmured. "I can't imagine what I should have done if you hadn't separated them, if you hadn't been there."

"The will of Allah. Keep an eye on your dog, Nicholas," he called. "I have a feeling she'll be back as soon as she can run again, to finish off the job."

"I will, and thank you, Stephen, thank you very much. Did you know that Nanny is dead?" Nicholas asked, looking back at us.

"Yes, old boy, I did and I was very sorry to hear it."

"Pamela doesn't know—she won't know until tomorrow. Marietta is looking after me now, and Molly."

"Well, you're in good hands, I can see that. And you're getting to be a young man, not a little boy."

"Yes, I am. Good-bye, Stephen."

We started back through the woods, which now seemed far less menacing. The endless stretch was, in fact, only a short walk.

"Marietta?"

"Yes?"

"Do we have to tell them about this afternoon?"

"Someone will notice Jilly's bites and your knee. We'll have to explain."

"I don't see why. I'll keep her in my room and Uncle James won't see her. We can tell Molly what happened. She won't care —she doesn't care a scrap about the family feud and neither does Pamela. Besides, they think Stephen is handsome and—it sounds like Rome."

"Romantic?"

"Yes, that's the word. He comes to see us in London. That is, he comes to see Pamela."

So, in spite of his grandfather, they are allowed to see him, I reflected, deeply relieved that Stephen Thaw was not considered an outcast. Then, turning to the immediate problem, I told myself firmly that it was not my fault that the dog had run away. I had not deliberately disobeyed James Thaw's orders; hopefully, no harm had been done, and I would take great care in the future. Should I make a report to James Thaw and no doubt upset him? With a twinge of bad conscience, I said to Nicholas:

"All right, we won't speak of it except to Molly. But if anyone asks questions, no lies. Agreed?"

"Agreed. You're a good sort, Marietta. I'm glad you came to Repose. Will you stay, now that Nanny's gone? I'm going to miss her but having you would help very much"—with a wheedling look from the hazel eyes.

"You're buttering me up, Nicholas! I wish I could stay with you, but we've got the rest of my visit. There must be many more things that you can show me." His face brightened.

"Oh, yes, lots of things. Look! The horses aren't in the field. We're in luck—they aren't back!"

"We're in luck," I echoed. Above us, the Great House loomed
peacefully, touched by the last of the afternoon sun.

Cubba was in my room, putting away clothes. She jumped when
I appeared, dirty and disheveled, and the underlip shot out.

"Don't worry, Cubba," I said quickly. "Jilly got into a fight,
but it's all right—except that Master Nicholas and I have some
very dirty clothes. Cubba, would you please put that nightdress
in the second drawer where it was before?" I had noticed this
morning that she had a way of shifting my clothes, which was irritating.

The girl was not in her former good humor. She gave me a
look which was almost sullen, and muttered something under her
breath. I tried to imitate Mrs. Coulter's firm, kindly manner.

"Thank you, Cubba. When you're done here, would you go to
Master Nicholas and see to his things?" Hopefully the flash of
bad temper would soon be over. Perhaps with Nanny gone, she
had more work to do.

I went to Nicholas' room and found him scrubbing his face
and hands with unusual vigor, as if to ease his conscience. Jilly,
ensconced once more in a basket by his bed, was fast asleep,
breathing heavily.

"What shall we do now?" I asked. "Something clean and sedate, don't you think? Like reading, or a game?"

"Shall we go on with the tour? Shall I show you the inside of
the house? There are some funny little rooms down below behind the arches. You haven't seen those yet."

"If you like." I was delighted with the idea, for the fortune in
gold was still on my mind. I tried to recall phrases in my grandmother's letter: "twelve ancient gold chalices of untold worth—
how William Thaw came by them Martha does not know." My
grandmother had suspected that they were stolen en route to
Spain from South America. Perhaps, I reasoned, they were left
by Spaniards fleeing the island when it was conquered by the
British. Gold chalices, I mused. Would they be tall, over a foot
high? With handles? The gold shining or dulled with age? My
Congregationalist grandparent had felt uneasy about them, as
though they were heathen instruments of worship. I, on the other

hand, was deeply curious. I would certainly keep my eyes open.

Some of the storerooms were so dark that Nicholas had to light a candle. I peered up and down the dusty shelves, but could find no amethysts or Spanish gold, nothing more than odd bits of china and glass, cracked basins, and a few toys which the termites had reduced to little more than heaps of dust. My hands ached to make order of these long-neglected rooms, to sweep out the dirt and open them to the sunlight.

We completed the rounds with a quick look at the upper bedrooms: Mrs. Coulter's, large and airy, and the front spare room where Nanny had died. It was clean and orderly, but I could not hold back a shiver.

"You do like Repose, don't you, Marietta?" asked Nicholas, anxiously, as we returned to our wing. "Uncle James says that someday it will all belong to me. Did you know that? And then you can come and stay as long as you like. You could even live here. Would you like that, Marietta?"

The innocence of this request caught me off guard; my throat tightened. Nicholas, the heir, asking *me* to live at Repose. I felt most uncomfortable.

"Wouldn't you like to live at Repose?" he insisted.

"Of course. Of course I would." I ruffled his hair, realizing suddenly how both he and Repose had endeared themselves to me in this short time—twisting around my heart like cottonwood roots. This afternoon I had met a writer, an interesting and charming man with dark eyes and a sensitive smile. "I would like very much to see you again, Miss Jackson, and I don't know how to arrange it. Do you have any plans for tomorrow?" How gently he had carried Jilly, how kind he had been to Nicholas.

Again my grandmother's words, written in her slanting hand, came into my mind: "But there is always a noose which draws us more and more tightly into the Thaw fortunes."

That was quite different, I told myself firmly. I could understand my grandmother's feelings about Repose, far better than when I sat in the study reading the letter so many weeks ago. But where she had failed, I would succeed.

CHAPTER 6

Time and chance reveal all secrets.

MARY DE LA RIVIERE:
The New Atlantis, II, 1709

The dream came to me again in the night, with an even greater urgency, as though compelling me to take heed. The man lay in the four-poster bed, twisting in agony. The woman sat helplessly by his side, unable to relieve his pain, and again I woke, gasping with my efforts to reach them. However, I was closer than before. As I sat up, drenched with sweat, I recognized the jalousies that had been left open so heedlessly, allowing the sun to fall on the face of the dying man. They were the same jalousies that flanked every window at Repose. Oddly enough, I was not frightened. I only wished that I knew why these suffering people continued to interrupt my sleep.

I rose and went to the window. It was early—so early that mist covered the cane fields and village like thin, white smoke. The colors were soft at this hour: fawn, dove gray, with faint streaks of rose in the sky. Even the birds were subdued. There were no tentative calls to be heard, the nightingale was silent. A lizard joined me by the sill, listening attentively to the papery sound of wind in the coconut palm.

> Radiant sister of the Day
> Awake! arise! and come away!
> To the wild woods and the plains
> And the pools where winter rains

Image all their roof of leaves,—
Awake! arise! and come away!

Of all the poets, Shelley could best catch my mood.

Dressing quickly, I tiptoed along the verandah unobserved; even the servants were not up and stirring as I picked my way across the wet grass. I would go to the cliffs before Nicholas was awake—a perfect place to watch the great leap of sun from the ocean. There was excitement in this secret, early morning expedition; I picked up my skirts and ran, feeling the blood race, the heart speed in rhythm with my steps. I could be as gay and carefree and silly as I liked, before the responsibilities of the day began.

My steps brought me across the lawn to the path that led to the promontory and the cliffs. I stopped, leaving a safe distance between my feet and the eroding strip of rock that marked the beginning of the jagged limestone.

From this angle I could see the ledges far below that formed a shallow base and were connected to the shore by a long, flat strip of rock. A man with a rope could begin to scale the cliffs only at that point, I realized. And then fall back onto the rocks, or the submerged coral, split into pieces. For a moment I stared down, trying not to imagine the rope loosening, the second of disbelief before the impact. Then, with an effort, I raised my eyes and looked out over the water.

The waves reflected the soft, muted sky; there was a sense of expectancy, the moment when the hall is hushed, waiting for the conductor to walk out onto the stage and raise his baton. I watched the delicate infusion of pink into the gray, the imperceptibly growing dawn—a scene that would become part of my private collection of beauty—a remembrance to be brought out from time to time for inner delight.

The sharp sound of falling stone broke the enchantment. Instinctively, I moved back into the shadow of the single tall tree that stood like a watchtower on the narrow strip of land. I had thought I was alone, in the growing light. More stones clattered on the rocks below as I stood, pressing myself against the rough bark, uncertain as to what I should do.

Then, far to the left, a man's head appeared, emerging slowly as he climbed; there must have been a path which I had not noticed, leading down to the flat strip of rock. He pulled himself up over the ledge and stood motionless, looking out over the water.

From the safety of the tree, I studied this unexpected arrival at the cliffs. He was one of the tallest men I had ever seen, the broad shoulders outlined against the light. When he turned his head, the profile reminded me of a famous coin: the nose jutting out from the strong cheekbones, eyes set deeply in the rugged face. He was in riding clothes, hands thrust into the pockets of his coat, dust thick on the boots as though he had come from a distance. I should have gone forward then, and made my presence known. But for some reason, I was reluctant to face him and so I stayed in the shadow of the tree, watching.

He stood without moving for a while, and then began to pace along the cliff as though making a measurement. From time to time he would pause, go to the edge and then step back, eyes narrowed, working on some problem known only to himself. Once he muttered words I could not hear, and I had the impression that he was angry.

My position was becoming more and more uncomfortable as the minutes passed. I prayed that he would go away; I had no wish to be discovered spying on him.

The wind may have moved my white skirt, or perhaps he sensed that someone was there. Suddenly he turned and stared at me, and his expression grew stern. I came forward slowly, and tried to return his look without flinching.

"Who are you? What are you doing here?" His eyes were blue, the voice very cold. I felt my temper begin to rise; yet I knew I was at fault.

"My name is Marietta Jackson," I said, standing before him, the color coming to my face. "I—I woke up early and came out because it was so beautiful—the early morning. Then you came; I was looking at the water when you climbed up and I didn't—I didn't feel that I could disturb you. You seemed to be very—occupied." How chilling blue eyes can be, I thought, trying to avoid his gaze, feeling like a child caught in a sly act. I looked

nervously at his hands, strong and long-fingered, and yet I did
not think he would hurt me physically; he seemed very much in
control.

"You woke early and came out to see the dawn. Delightful.
But then, why did you run behind the tree? Why stand there
watching me all this time? I would have been glad to make your
acquaintance in the customary way. I take it that you are staying
at Repose. A friend of Molly's?"

By now my temper was barely manageable. He was being al-
together too harsh about my innocent though misguided behavior. And there was something so demeaning about being taken
for a fifteen-year-old—

"I told you I was sorry. I should have come forward, but you
startled me; you suddenly appeared up from the edge. I didn't
know who you were—and I'm not a friend of Molly's—I mean, I
am not her guest here. Mr. James Thaw invited me to come."
The answer surprised him; his dark eyebrows lifted. James Thaw
had few guests, I suspected.

"I should introduce myself, it seems. My name is Philip
Coulter."

"Coulter? Then you are one of the family?"

"My mother is James Thaw's sister." I must have gaped at
him. No one had told me that Mrs. Coulter had another son. Perhaps he was the black sheep whose name was never mentioned;
he was here on some devious errand and would disappear and
that was why he was angry at being seen. My thoughts must
have crossed my face in quick succession.

"I'm a perfectly respectable captain in the Northumberland
Fusiliers," he said grimly. "You haven't heard of me because
they think I'm in India—and because I haven't been back here
for years."

"Well, why didn't you—"

"Come straight to the house. What am I doing at the cliffs at
this ungodly hour? Well, Miss Jackson, is it? At the risk of being
rude may I say that this is my own personal business? I'd be
much obliged if you would not run back and babble the news. I
will arrive at luncheon today and"—he paused, looking at me
severely—"I would very much like to surprise my mother."

At this, my thoughts became more confused than ever. Why indeed had he been pacing about in that strange fashion? Why arrive unexpectedly? And why should he require an explanation of my behavior when his was far more questionable?

I drew myself up to my full height. "Mr. Coulter—Captain," I said, drawing out the words. "If you think that I shall concern myself with anything you do, you are quite mistaken. I have no interest whatsoever in when you arrive at Repose."

Pleased with the choice of cutting phrases, I turned, head held high, and walked with slow dignity across the field and into the courtyard. It was only when I was out of his sight that I ran up the stairs and down the verandah to my room, breathless with rage. He needn't have been so rude, I fumed. He needn't have treated me like a naughty schoolgirl. How odd that gentle Mrs. Coulter should have such a curt and unmannerly son. It was not hard to imagine him as an officer in India, tall and arrogant, ordering his men about, but I wished that he had stayed with them, thousands of miles away.

Perhaps I *will* go to Mrs. Coulter and tell her that he is here, I said to myself, knowing very well that I would not.

We were joined, that noon, by Mrs. Shepheard—the Agnes Shepheard of whom Mrs. Coulter spoke with affection, and to whom she turned for help in household crises. As they talked, I was reminded of our banker's wife—brusque, sharp-tongued, and supremely kind. My father had called her "the undertaker's assistant" because she was always the first to appear at a house of mourning, but I and many others had good reason to be grateful. I could see that Mrs. Shepheard, too, liked nothing better than a good solid crisis, particularly one with which she could deal singlehandedly. Yesterday, she had been a pillar of strength with arrangements for Nanny, and today a new, though far less tragic, disaster had occurred: Thomas, the butler, had left in the night, taking his belongings, leaving no message. No one, not even the other servants, realized until breakfast that he was gone.

I watched Mrs. Coulter's face as she talked to Agnes Shepheard, remembering Dr. Barrow's words: "You may find that the culprit, if there is one, will disappear on his own account."

Thomas had been little more to me than a pleasant young man who wore white gloves when he passed the plates, but I felt very much relieved, and I suspected that the feeling was shared by Mrs. Coulter. Nothing could alter the sad fact of Nanny's death. But if she had been poisoned, the culprit was out of the house; it would not happen again.

"So frustratin', just before Christmas," Mrs. Shepheard was saying. "I suppose he suddenly found he had pressing holiday obligations and was ashamed to face you, as well he might be. Well, I think I can put my hand on someone else—Tilford, who is my head yard boy's brother. He's helped out with big parties and he always needs money. Better than nothing. I'll get in touch with him, and send him right up, maybe this afternoon, and you, Charmian"—she turned and gave the handsome young girl a knowing look—"don't you go bothering him or I'll send you back to the hills to look after your children. Your mother must be getting tired of them. A new one every year. Shame on you." I caught my breath and looked at Charmian. She broke out into a fit of giggling, hiding her face. Old Louisa too was shaking with laughter, and I thought she would drop the soup tureen.

"No, missus, I not bother Tilford," and the two removed the plates, laughing softly.

We were midway through the curried beef, and still no sign of Philip Coulter. Serena had appeared for luncheon. I had not seen her since yesterday and dreaded the next meeting, but she gave no impression of remembering her outburst or of having met me. She sat silently, taking morsels of food from her plate, while Mrs. Shepheard entertained us.

"I'm constantly homesick for England," she said, addressing Serena kindly, "and nobody will believe me. Why, I'm lucky if Major allows me to go over for a few weeks out of the year, just long enough to cool coppers before I'm dragged back. He doesn't seem to realize that I need a vacation from my responsibilities, all the entertaining he insists that I do."

"Come, come, Agnes," said James Thaw, smiling. "You must admit that you enjoy every second of it. It's the breath of life to you, entertaining. You should have lived in the days of the trunk fleet. The trunk fleet," he went on, turning to me, "was one of the great sights in my father's time. In those days friends and relatives would come, *en famille*, for a visit of at least several weeks. The servants would go ahead, in the early morning, carrying the baggage. Quite an unforgettable spectacle, this long line of men and women, marching single file, each with a tin box or band box balanced on the head. And the excitement when the family finally arrived—the dinners, the festivities. I look around me now and I can scarcely believe those times existed."

Suddenly my attention was drawn to the sound of horses' hoofs in the courtyard, and the voice of Quaco's young son, coming forward from his cool place under the arches where he usually waited, sucking on a piece of cane, to take a visitor's horse. Then came the footsteps on the verandah. I held my breath. For an instant I had a vision: I knew what was about to happen.

Mrs. Coulter was the first to see the tall figure in the doorway. Her face was transformed from tired gentleness to glowing delight.

"Philip! My dear! Oh, what a surprise! We thought you were in India—I sent all your Christmas parcels there. Why didn't you let us know? But it doesn't matter—I can hardly believe my eyes!" She had risen and was reaching up to kiss him.

I glanced at James Thaw. For some reason he was frowning, and I wondered why he did not share his sister's pleasure. Molly and Nicholas were wide-eyed with excitement. Nicholas ran from his seat and seized his uncle's hand.

"Uncle Philip! The last time you were home you promised you would teach me to shoot. I'm almost eight, now. Will you, Uncle Philip?" Uncle Philip looked almost genial as he swung the boy up, ruffling his hair.

"Almost eight? Yes, you've grown a lot, young Nicholas. We'll talk about shooting later, let me speak to the others. Uncle James, I hope you're not too surprised to see me at Repose after all this time. Fact is, I've just been appointed A.D.C. to the governor. Came straight from India, granted a week's leave before I start. Good to see you, Mrs. Shepheard. Major not here? Hello, Molly." He looked at me questioningly.

"Well, Philip, you are indeed an unexpected arrival," said James Thaw. His tone was pleasant enough, but I noticed that he used the word "unexpected" rather than "welcome." "Aide to the governor—quite an honor. May I introduce our guest for the holidays, Miss Marietta Jackson?" He gave no explanation for my presence. We bowed politely; I thought I detected a hint of curiosity in the captain's eyes, and I raised my chin in an aloof manner.

Mrs. Coulter was clearly overjoyed. "Charmian, lay another place here beside me. Philip, this is the most wonderful Christmas present you could give me, to come this particular year. It makes all the difference. And what extraordinary luck to be A.D.C. How did it happen? Why didn't you write?"

"I came as fast as any letter. I think they needed me for the polo matches, and I was dispatched in a hurry."

"Major will be delighted," boomed Agnes Shepheard. "You were always one of his most promising pupils on the field. But don't underestimate your brains. Captain, at your age? Your father would be proud of you, and don't you forget it." She turned to James Thaw. "Well, James, wonders will never cease, eh? I imagine you thought he had washed his hands of Repose. What is it—eight, nine years? Well, I can't think of a better time for him to return. Great good luck to be posted here, I call it. And just before Christmas, too."

Mr. Thaw's lips compressed into a thin line, and he paused before answering. "Yes, just before Christmas. Naturally, I must welcome any member of the family. It was my father's wish."

No one spoke; his meaning was clear. Philip Coulter had arrived just in time to share in the yearly profits. It remained for Molly to put the thought into words.

"But he *is* here, Uncle James. There's plenty of money to go round, isn't there?" And as all heads turned, her face grew scarlet.

"Spoken like a Thaw, Molly," exclaimed Mrs. Shepheard. "Don't spoil the homecoming by looking like a thundercloud, James. The prodigal son, you know," and she led the conversation onto the subject of polo. But the damage had been done. Mrs. Coulter's eyes showed the hurt, and the captain no longer smiled. His expression was closed and hard, as I had seen it at the cliffs. If James had not been his relative—his mother's brother

—I wondered what he might have said. This was not a man to trifle with; his curt words still stung me, and I studied his face surreptitiously as he talked to his mother, discussing the new appointment. The even features were hers, though cast in a strong, aggressive mold, and the eyes were the same clear blue. Molly had mentioned a grandfather, a soldier killed in a frontier skirmish many years ago, long before she was born. Perhaps the darker hair and great height came from him, as well as the career in soldiering. I had read with interest of British army life— the regimental pride, the jealous traditions, the personal servants, the luxury of everyday existence. At home, a friend's brother had joined the army—little was said about it, as though he had demeaned himself. What a contrast to this British arrogance, I mused, with the scorn of everything military that often pervades academic circles. No, I did not care for the military, American or British.

There had been no chance to discuss Stephen Thaw with Molly, my chief source of information. But I had thought about him constantly, reliving the meeting, recalling the smile, the warm expression of his eyes. I tried to tell myself firmly that I did not mind if I could not go to town this afternoon. Undoubtedly, Mrs. Coulter would need me here on account of the wretched captain.

"Molly," she said, pouring coffee after luncheon, "I do think you had better go to meet Pamela, after all. I have so much to do, and I want to spend a little time with Philip. Marietta, will you go with Molly? I shall give you my shopping list, rather a long one, I'm afraid, so many things I should have done earlier. Nicholas can stay here and help me with the decorations."

"Of course, Mrs. Coulter, I'd be happy to go." Under the prim demeanor, my heart was beginning to beat quickly. I could see Philip Coulter's assessing stare; no doubt he was trying to place me: governess, companion to Molly? Not many guests came to Repose, I suspected.

Molly chattered beside me, as we proceeded to town in the buggy. "I could have swooned, positively swooned when I said that awful bit about the money. I didn't mean to, the words just popped out. I do wonder, though, why Uncle James was so rude to Philip. We call him Philip, at least Pamela and I do as he's not yet thirty, years younger than my father. It is odd that he managed to get here, just at this time. For years he's refused to take any money from Repose! If he was in business, he might have had reverses but it can't be that, and we are forever hearing what a brilliant success he is, what a great future. Don't you think he's handsome, Marietta? We saw him parade once, when we were little, riding in front of his men with his sword raised—it made me cry, I was so proud."

"He certainly is commanding. Is he close to your family?"

Molly considered. "Well, he's been away so much that we don't know him very well. But he and Father were fond of each other, very. They wrote back and forth, and I'm sure it was a dreadful blow to him when Father died—he could not get here for the burial, of course. None of us could. Did you know there's to be a memorial service next Sunday? Granny is giving the church a new altar cloth in his memory. She had it made by the best needlewomen in London, all in greens and dark reds."

"She's wonderful, really, your grandmother. A stranger would have no idea what she's been through. She never thinks of herself, does she?"

"No, and I don't know how she manages to keep her temper, no matter how irritating we are, all of us. She's always been this way, calm and understanding, never criticizing—and I love the way she looks, don't you? Good people often look so untidy, as if they don't care about their clothes. I'm so glad that Philip is here, because this will make her happy. But I'm afraid my mother—" She stopped abruptly, but I could tell that only a slight nudge was needed.

"What about your mother?" Molly glanced at me unhappily.

"I hate to remind you of yesterday, Marietta, how she accused you of taking things from Repose. But I'm afraid she's been this way since Father died. She's convinced that Nicholas will lose Repose, that people are plotting against him, the eldest son of the eldest son. I know it's ridiculous, but you wait and see if she won't read all sorts of sinister things into Philip's visit. He's next in line, you see, after Nicholas. If anything should happen to Nicholas, he will inherit Repose."

I sat quietly, assembling my scattered thoughts. First Anna was the threat, now perhaps Philip. On the surface, it *was* ridiculous and yet what had he been doing so mysteriously this morning, the pacing and measuring?

"Oh, bosh," I said sharply, "I know one can never be certain of people when there's property involved, but he really doesn't seem the kind to do in his little nephew."

"*I* didn't say that he would, Marietta! It's Mother. She's going to be more difficult now that he's here. I feel as if we're walking a tightrope—one little mistake and we'll all fall off."

Poor Molly. I tried to think of comforting words. A happy-go-lucky girl of fifteen should not have to shoulder these burdens. So many opposing forces were rising from under the surface at Repose—rather like a tug of war, with Nicholas as the prize. I gazed out at the road, searching for words, noticing how fast we had traveled toward town—or perhaps I was beginning to know the road, and to lose my uneasiness about it.

Suddenly, I clutched Molly's arm. Two large birds stood at the side of the road, snatching at the remains of a bloody animal carcass. They were hideous birds, with mottled red caps, and feathers covered with dust. One of them raised his head as we approached; a fierce eye seemed to single me out for attention. Then they both waddled into the bushes, leaving their ghastly meal until we had gone.

"What are those disgusting creatures, Molly?" My voice was shaking. One bird had looked straight at me, with a conscious menace. If I had not been in the buggy, I would have cried out in fright.

"Oh, those are only turkey vultures, John Crows, we call them. Now don't tell me that they frightened you, Marietta. I didn't know you were so nervous. Nasty-looking, I admit, but they clean up all the dead things that lie around. Surely you have vultures in America?"

"Yes, of course. But I never saw one so close, and eating. And not in the least afraid. Molly, did Nicholas tell you about yesterday afternoon?" I wanted to wipe the sight of the filthy bird from my mind and talk—at last—of Stephen.

"Did he not! If Uncle James ever finds out! What was she like, Miss Anna? I've only seen her in the distance, once, and she didn't seem so terrible. Rather old and thin."

"She wasn't terrible, but she is frightening, I must admit; her eyes look right through you. I had the feeling that she knew exactly what I was thinking—everything about me—" I stopped. What had Anna told me? To leave on the next steamer? Strange words, but of course Anna Thaw was undeniably a strange woman.

"We met Stephen Thaw," I went on quickly. "He was very pleasant, I thought, and thank heavens he was there to save Jilly. He said he was a writer. Have you read any of his books? What is he like?"

"Oh, Stephen! He's handsome, isn't he? He comes to see Pamela, but I don't think he notices me. I see pictures of him in the weeklies, going this place and that. He's quite well known."

"He told me that he lives in London. Does he live with his parents?"

"No, they spend most of the time in Italy. They left the island years ago, when Stephen was a baby. I suppose they wanted nothing to do with the family feud, and perhaps they were ashamed that Miss Anna has a little bit of color in her blood. Such nonsense. Lots of people here—oh, look, Marietta, the parrots! Aren't they beautiful?" And I watched the flight of brilliant green birds which flew across our path, soaring then settling in a huge lignum vitae tree, lost in the blue flowers that tipped the branches.

We passed the last open fields of cane and came to the outskirts of town, with its clusters of tumble-down shacks; the yards, fenced with broken boards and wire, pressed closely against each other. An old woman was sitting in the dust by the roadside, surrounded by wilting vegetables and mangoes. Quaco shook his head as she gestured wildly at us, pointing to her little market, urging us to buy.

As we neared the center of town, the streets became wider and the shops larger, with arcades and stories above, and dirty water running green in the deep gutters. The main square was crowded and dusty; the statue in the center, standing on its grassless plot, had a forlorn dignity, but there was much to admire as we circled about, vying for a hitching post. The court house was particularly fine, a handsome building of cut stone, with porticos and a long row of windows on each floor. I wondered if we would find Stephen in the holiday throng, for he and I had set no time or place to meet.

The haberdashery was connected with Miss Charlotte's Couture, and while Molly tried on the latest fashion in bonnets from Martinique, I struggled with Mrs. Coulter's lengthy list: osnaburg for trousers and dresses, madras for bandannas, black alpaca, red alpaca—the Indian woman behind the counter moved slowly, pulling down bolts of material and cutting with endless deliberation. The precious time was passing; I went to Molly and suggested that she go out and tell Quaco that we would be delayed—perhaps she and Stephen might see one another on the street.

When I finally emerged, my stratagem had been successful; they were standing by the buggy, and Quaco took my packages. "Good afternoon, Miss Jackson," said Stephen, bowing over my hand. "What good luck to meet you here today. I hear that Jilly is mending nicely. No ill effects at all. Molly, how long is it since I've seen you? You're getting to be as pretty as Pamela—she will have to look to her laurels in a year or so." It was a nice compliment, and Molly flushed with pleasure. "I expect you're here to meet the steamer," he continued. "If you've done with your errands, let me take you around the corner to the hotel and give you a cool drink. We can see the harbor from the verandah, and watch the ship come in. No need to wait on the quay, you know."

It was a pretty view of the boats and the fishermen, paddling their hollow canoes. We sipped limeades and talked about Christmas. I confessed that I was slightly homesick for candles in the windows, wreaths on the doors, and the crunch of snow underfoot as I trudged about with the carollers.

"I can't believe Christmas will be tomorrow; at home, we spend weeks getting ready; the whole town is in a turmoil."

Stephen laughed and looked at me with quick sympathy. "What can we do about this, Molly?"

"I don't know. I've never been anyplace else for Christmas. But we could sing carols tonight. Nicholas knows a few—and we will have decorations, Marietta. Oh yes, and the drums will begin to beat tonight. You don't have that at home, I'm sure."

"Drums? You mean native drums—all night? Are you sure this isn't more of Old Hige?" I turned to Stephen. "Molly has been telling me the wildest tales about duppies and obeah and witchcraft. You don't believe in obeah, do you? What is obeah anyhow?"

"Well, it was brought from Africa on the slave ships. Voodoo came too, but it did not take hold here as it did in Haiti. Now what you have to remember is that the obeahman, the descendant of the witch doctor, keeps his hold through the other fellow's belief in his powers. For instance, Molly has wronged you, and you want revenge. You will go to the obeahman, carrying a piece of her clothing. For money or payment of some sort, the obeahman will make a spell against Molly, using chicken feathers, bones, nail parings, herbs—to name a few of the materials. Now, when Molly realizes that a spell has been laid on her, she will probably do one of two things—she'll lie down and die of fright, or she'll go to another more powerful obeahman who will put a counter-spell on you. Do you see how it works?"

"Well, I suppose so. But I do think one would have to be extremely ignorant to believe such nonsense. Where do you find this obeahman, by the way? Does he have a shop in the square where he sells these spells?"

"Don't be too scornful, young lady. You might find yourself at the mercy of obeah one day. No, he practices in the hills, as obeah is illegal, and has been for some time."

"Then, why isn't he in jail?" We were all smiling.

"Ah, you still don't understand, I see. Would you bring a case against an obeahman, knowing that he might put a fatal spell on you? You would have to be very brave. In all seriousness, obeah is extremely important to these people, and many times it is a substitute for the law."

"Well," I said at last, "I'm a newcomer, and I suppose I must believe you. After all, we have ladies who tell fortunes at the church fairs."

I hadn't meant to be amusing. Finally, Molly stopped laughing and jumped up, knocking over her glass.

"Lawks, there's the steamer coming in! It's only a quarter to four. Are you coming, Stephen? I'm sure Pamela would love to see you!" She ran down the steps to summon Quaco.

Stephen took my hand and looked at me intently. "I'll see you at church tomorrow," he said in a low voice, "and perhaps I can contrive something for the afternoon. Do you know your Shakespeare?

> "Being your slave, what should I do but tend
> Upon the hours and times of your desire?
> I have no precious time at all to spend
> Nor services to do, till you require!"

He dropped my hand as Molly came back. I could not speak for fear my voice would betray me; a wave of excitement had left me dizzy and shaking. I turned and climbed into the buggy, hoping that Molly would not notice my agitation. But she was sharp, Molly.

"You like Stephen, don't you?" she asked, as we went toward the quay.

I was hearing Stephen's voice reciting Shakespeare. "What? Of course," I stammered, "of course I like him—"

"Well, he most certainly likes you, Marietta. You should have seen his face, looking at you. He thinks you're beautiful. What was he saying, while I was getting Quaco? So serious! I do believe he's falling for you, Marietta."

"Don't be silly. We've barely met, and besides—"

"What difference does that make? Don't you believe in love at first sight? I hope Pamela won't be jealous; that would be a great pity."

"Whyever? He's her cousin, after all, not that there's any reason to be jealous."

"He's an attractive man—she wants them all to herself. Why, Marietta Jackson, you're blushing. Don't tell me you like him, too!"

"Haven't I just said that I like him? He's very charming. Really, Molly, you are worse than a penny novel. You'll have us eloping if you go on this way."

"Ha!" said Molly happily.

The first sight of Pamela Coulter left me with feelings of surprise and relief. I had been bracing myself for an incomparable beauty; this girl was shorter than I, with gray eyes and brown hair, nothing so out of the ordinary. But, as I carefully observed her in the buggy, I began to feel her fascination. Where my slimness had strength in it, hers was delicate and melting. Her eyes slanted upward at the corners, giving them an oriental inscrutability; one could not guess what she was thinking. She spoke slowly, with a drawn-out deliberation and in a tone so low that I had to lean forward to hear her. That, of course, was part of the secret, I told myself—complete attention from the audience.

Molly gabbled along with the news of Philip and Nanny, while I sat silently, feeling more and more the interloper, the American who had thrust herself into the family's Christmas holiday. Pamela's manners were perfect; yet Molly was not her usual forthright self, and I began to wonder if indeed my hair had a rather suspect candy-box prettiness. I had never before thought of my looks as a weapon, but Pamela Coulter—and I searched my mind for the exact word—Pamela Coulter had a subtle, enigmatic quality that outranked mere beauty. I regarded her uneasily. She might be the femme fatale of London, but where Stephen Thaw was concerned, I would not withdraw meekly from the lists.

CHAPTER 7

Children and fools have merry lives.
JOHN RAY: *English Proverbs, 1670*

In our absence the entire household at Repose had worked in high gear. As the buggy rolled to a stop, Nicholas came dancing out.

"Pamela, Marietta, come and see what I've done!" He scarcely paused to greet his eldest sister in his impatience to show us the changes.

Clusters of red akee fruits decorated the living-room paintings, while plants hung with large orange balls stood in the corners.

"Quaco brought them from the fields. They have a very pretty name, Marietta—'cockroach poison!'" There were Japanese lanterns on the verandah, and a lopsided tree, covered with old-fashioned ornaments, stood by the front door. Repose was ready for Christmas.

Serena Coulter emerged from her room, and greeted her daughter with surprising warmth. I hoped that they could occupy themselves with gossip of dressmaking and parties, and that I would see as little of them as possible. To give Pamela her due, she kissed her mother delicately, but with evident tenderness.

Supervising Nicholas and his efforts had obviously tired Mrs. Coulter; I removed him to my room to help me wrap the small presents I had bought, and also to receive some instruction.

"We'll do 'Silent Night' and 'O Little Town of Bethlehem' first, shall we? I want you to pretend that you're all wrapped up in a muffler, and that you've been walking from house to house in the snow."

"Will I get money, like John Canoe?"

"Don't be greedy. Not in our town you wouldn't. You would sing to shut-ins and old people for love. What is John Canoe?"

"You'll see later. I'm not going to spoil the surprise. This is my special night, isn't it? Because my name is Nicholas?"

"Of course, it is. Will you hang up your stocking and leave milk and cookies for St. Nicholas?"

"Oh, I always hang up my stocking. But I've never left milk and cookies. Is that what American children do? Where do they leave them?"

"Near the fireplace, usually. So he can find them when he comes down the chimney."

Nicholas considered this. "There's no chimney here. But let's have them anyhow. I'll eat some myself and take the rest to Jilly for her Christmas treat. The new butler is here."

"Oh?"

"His name isn't Tilford, it's Hazard. He looks as if he has Indian blood, Uncle Philip says. American Indian, that is. I have a picture of one at home, with feathers and war paint. Do you think Hazard will do a war dance, Marietta? Shall I ask him if he will?"

"No, I shouldn't, not until he's been here longer, anyhow. Now hurry and change into your dark-blue serge. It's almost time for the party."

The silver bells and tiny gold angels on the table gleamed prettily in the candlelight, as we gathered for the Christmas Eve dinner. Even Serena looked agreeable. There was a general desire, I felt, to make the evening a happy one for Nicholas. He was delighted to be dining with the grown-ups, and there were favors, and silly hats, and the usual succession of rich, heavy courses.

I glanced curiously at the new butler. The young Negro had a thin face and high cheekbones, but he would never have been taken for an Indian at home. It occurred to me that in this short time, I too had become used to servants as part of the background. They had no existence except as Charmian who waited on the table, Cubba who looked after my clothes, and now Hazard who had come from Mrs. Shepheard's to take Thomas's place, the new butler with a slightly Indian look. I looked at him again, disturbed that I could so easily slide into indifference toward human beings, black or white, and yet I could not pass judgment. I was beginning to appreciate—though not accept—the great historical differences between this island's culture and mine.

The port, carefully decanted by James Thaw, was ceremoniously poured, with instructions to Hazard to go clockwise around the table for luck. We toasted the Queen, God bless her, and then, in my honor, the President of the United States.

"Do you remember the marzipan cake, James?" asked Mrs. Coulter. "Our mamma," she told us, "loved marzipan cake, and once she was determined to have one sent from London for our Christmas. Well, after enormous trouble and expense, it arrived and the marzipan had all gone moldy. To please her, we pretended to eat it but we couldn't. Most of it went to the dogs, and they wouldn't touch it, either. She found them sniffing at the pieces, and oh dear, she *was* angry!"

"And of course you remember the annual holiday party," her brother went on. "The men celebrated so heartily that they always ended up asleep in Father's sitting room. It was a rare undertaking to get them home in time for Christmas."

"Oh, James, that was only old Mr. Taylor. We girls amused ourselves very well. There was a swing under the poinciana; we would swing for hours, and sometimes we would play blind man's bluff. Later on, there would be music, and cards. So many people lived here then, one could always get up a party. This was when we were very young, of course. After that, we spent most of the time in London."

"Speaking of music," said Molly, "Marietta and I have decided that what we need tonight is some nice old-fashioned Christmas carols, and we will lead the rest of you. Pamela, you'll sing, won't you? Philip, will you sing?"

Captain Coulter, dressed in formal dark clothes, seemed even more austere. Throughout the meal he had been quite silent,

twirling the stem of his wine glass, exchanging a few words with
his mother and with Pamela on his right. His glance at me, as we
sat down, had been assessing, rather than curious; undoubtedly
Mrs. Coulter had explained my situation while I was away. I still
felt uncomfortable in his presence. Although he was courteous to
Serena, and affectionate to his mother and the children, I could
not forget his incivility when we met; he had treated me far too
harshly. Unlikely *he* would ever quote Shakespeare, or make a
girl feel clever and beguiling.

"Silent Night" went well, and was applauded by the small audience. My voice soared above the others, and I wished that
Stephen could have been there; our recital was proving a success.

"Now 'O Little Town of Bethlehem,'" I whispered to Nicholas. He shook his head, with a look in his eye that should
have warned me. "I want to sing by myself, Marietta," he said
in my ear. Then, "Ladies and gentlemen," he announced with
gusto, "I shall now sing by myself." He placed his hand over his
heart and stared solemnly above our heads. We sat expectantly,
waiting for the carol.

> "God Almighty make me free!
>   Buckra in this country no make we free!
> What Negor for to do? What Negor for to do?
> Take by force! Take by force!
> To be sure, to be sure, to be sure!"

With a hop and a skip he opened his mouth to begin the next
verse. I saw the expression on James Thaw's face.

> "O Little Town of Bethlehem,
> How still we see thee lie,"

I sang, motioning Molly to join in. James could not explode in
the midst of the carol. We continued loudly, and just as we were
floundering into the third verse, Hazard came from the dining
room and spoke in a low voice to Mrs. Coulter. This apparently
was the signal Nicholas had been expecting. He jumped up and
rushed out onto the verandah calling, "John Canoe is here!
Come out, everyone! John Canoe is here!"

In the light of torches carried by the villagers, the group of strolling mummers stood waiting for the lords and ladies of the household. The dozen or so men were brilliantly costumed in striped pantaloons and fancy jackets. But their hats were the most extraordinary part of the outfit. They looked like boats— great boats filled with all manner of odd passengers: men, horses, tiny ships, puppets gleaming with bits of ribbon and tinsel.

The entertainers capered and somersaulted and sang; they juggled, mimed, and jousted, supported by an ecstatic audience that shrieked and stamped.

"What custom is this?" I asked Mr. Thaw, trying to picture our pastor at this Christmas Eve rite.

"The name John Canoe comes, we think, from the French 'l'inconnu' but we don't know much else about him except that he is a familiar sight at Christmas and New Year. I believe each group has a sponsor who pays for the clothes and probably gets more than his original money back in donations." Descending the stairs, he pressed silver into the hand of the man with the largest hat.

There were loud expressions of good will, and heart-felt wishes for a good cane crop; then the entire group disappeared into the darkness, and we could hear the laughter and shouting as they went back down the drive.

"Well, that's over for another year," said James Thaw, as we returned to the living room. "Now the drums will begin. In the old days there would have been an ox roast and a huge celebration. Why, I couldn't close my eyes all night when I was Nicholas' age on account of the noise. They believe that the spirit goes back to Africa for eternal feasts with the ancestors, so of course the sound must be loud enough for the ancestors to hear."

The festive mood of the evening ended abruptly with the departure of John Canoe. After Nicholas had hung his stocking, I wished everyone good night, and went down the hall to my room, happy to escape the nightly game of piquet. As I left, I could hear Mrs. Coulter instructing Hazard to put out the candles with great care, and to place buckets of water near the tree.

Just what Papa used to say, I remembered, trying to ignore a
creeping homesickness. Perhaps it was because Pamela and
Philip made me feel uncomfortable, or perhaps I missed, more
than I realized, our simple family celebrations, marked with
love for one another, and for Jesus at the time of His birth. John
Canoe did not provide the religious celebration I associated
with Christmas Eve.

I *must* not be so provincial, I told myself. This was, after all,
the opportunity I had longed for: the chance to venture beyond
my tidy life and test myself in the deeper waters. I should be
confident that if a few difficulties presented themselves I could
avoid the pitfalls. A number of worries had already been re-
solved. I could do nothing more about the land, at the moment;
the poisoner was gone; Nicholas, through my carelessness, had
not been harmed by Anna Thaw. Why, then, these vague misgivings?

I opened the door to my room and was surprised to find
Cubba there at this hour, laying out my nightdress. She jumped
when she saw me, the underlip shot out, and she mumbled ex-
cuses; she was later than usual, she said, because of John Canoe.

"Will you have a celebration yourselves tonight, Cubba? All of
you and the new butler?"

The eyes rolled angrily. "Him not nyam with us," she said
hotly. "No one know that neger." There was a note of real
hatred in her voice and I felt sorry for Hazard. Perhaps the high-
cheekboned Indian look made him an outsider, but this was
none of my affair, and I was annoyed with Cubba. She continued
to rearrange my things although I repeatedly asked her not to.
Tonight the writing case was on the wrong side of the table, but
as she could not read, there would have been no reason for her
to go through my half-written letters.

"I'll finish, Cubba," I said. "Merry Christmas."

I brushed my hair slowly, absently parting the long, pale strands.
What an extraordinary day it had been, beginning at the cliffs
and the meeting with arrogant Captain Philip Coulter. He had
redeemed himself slightly, in my opinion, by his obvious affection for his mother, who could scarcely take her eyes off the

tall son whom she had not seen for over a year. "It makes all the difference," I had overheard her saying to Pamela, "it is really too good to be true to have him posted here. I only hope James will let him help with Repose. Your great-uncle's heart isn't what it should be, you know."

Separating the thick hair, I began making a braid for the night, more comfortable in the heat than letting it fall loosely over the pillow. Still, I mused, there was no excuse for his rudeness. Perhaps he didn't like the idea of an outsider at Repose. Or perhaps—he didn't like me! From now on I would take care to keep clear of him. I would not let him upset me with that cold blue look, and that towering way.

Having neatly disposed of Captain Philip Coulter, I happily turned my thoughts to Stephen Thaw. How quick he was to grasp ideas, how humorous and how kind; the compliment to Molly, comparing her to Pamela, was the very best way to bolster her self-confidence. And his voice, reciting poetry—

I studied myself in the mirror. There was a softness in my expression, a sweetness that I had not seen before. "To wait upon my desires" he had said, his eyes looking into mine. I relived the words we had spoken since we met so unexpectedly, standing over Nicholas and Jilly.

The drums were beginning to beat softly, a rhythmic, soothing sound with none of the fury described by James Thaw; there were no echoes of voodoo, black magic in the hills, no suggestion of wild orgies.

"Well, I hope the ancestors will be pleased with these quiet, well-behaved children," I said to myself as I turned down the wick on my table lamp, and clambered up into the great, enfolding bed.

Cockroach-poison decorations, John Canoe mummers, duppies in the night, native drums, even this huge bed—surely I was as far from my ancestors, this Christmas Eve, as any of the people down in the village. I could not drum out my longings as they did, but I lay there wishing that I could see into the future. Marietta Jackson Thaw. Mrs. Stephen Thaw. The names sounded well together, and I smiled in the darkness. Marietta, you are leaping ahead, I told myself. You are embroidering a

picture that hardly exists. But it was no use. I began to compose
a letter to my mother: "We met at a dog fight, of all things, so I
cannot say that it was love at first sight. But two days later we
realized that we were deeply attracted to each other . . . he
is planning to visit us. . . . Mother, I am unbelievably
happy . . ."

CHAPTER 8

*For if "faint and forced the laughter," and if
sadness follows after,
We are richer by one mocking Christmas past.*

RUDYARD KIPLING: *Christmas in India, 1886*

"Joy to the World!" sang Nicholas, tugging at my shoulder. I turned over, pushing him away.

"Too early. Much, much too early."

"I *knew* you would say that! You've overslept, Marietta. Breakfast is almost ready, and Granny needs you to give out the presents."

"Oh my heavens! Go away and let me dress and—Merry Christmas, Nicholas!"

The people of Repose were arriving, walking slowly up the hill, laughing and talking among themselves; the children and women wore spotless white dresses, beaten clean on the rocks and ironed in the crowded houses. We hurriedly finished breakfast, and James Thaw went to the bottom of the steps to greet them, a delaying tactic while Mrs. Coulter marshaled her forces on the verandah. Hazard and the maids brought out the great piles of presents and she assigned us our duties.

"Nicholas, you and Molly give out candy. Pamela, you and Marietta do the children's clothes, and Philip, I want you to help me with the grown-ups. Try to count heads, everyone, so that we end up even."

There were wide smiles, lowered eyes, and whispered thanks from the children as we passed out the frocks and jackets, judging the sizes as best we could. Pamela worked quickly and efficiently; she had done this since she was Nicholas' age; I assisted her.

"We *are* going to run short," she said after a while. "Philip, count the children, will you? How many are left?"

"More than you have clothes for. Quite a few must have been adopted for the day."

"Yes, but I don't know which. Should I ask Morris?"

"I doubt very much if that would help. He doesn't seem to know any of them by name."

"I'm afraid you're right. He seems utterly useless, even worse than last year."

She glanced with controlled irritation at a slender man standing near James at the bottom of the steps. I had not seen him before, and I wondered who he was. His face was a curious color, neither dark nor white, and was topped with odd reddish hair. It was impossible to guess his age, he could have been elderly, or a youngish man who had been ill, for there was a sickly look to him.

"Who is he?" I asked. "I have never seen him before."

Pamela's face was expressionless. "His name is Morris. He's the overseer."

"Oh, then he must live in the nicest stone house. Nicholas pointed it out. Is he new? Is that why he doesn't know the people?"

Pamela stared past me without answering. I turned away, annoyed at myself for asking questions, feeling that once again I had been gauche.

Philip cleared his throat, giving Pamela an inscrutable look.

"No, Miss Jackson, he isn't new. He's lived here all his life. The fact of the matter is—Morris is my grandfather's son by his mulatto mistress. He is my Uncle James's half brother."

I bent over the clothes, trying to hide my startled expression. What a country! And then came the thought: how could James Thaw look down on Stephen's grandmother when his own half brother had far more color than Anna? I took another quick look at Morris. For an overseer he certainly kept out of sight. What work did he do? But then, I reflected, which group would he belong to? He could not drum and dance with the blacks, nor would he be welcome at the Repose dinner table, the illegitimate son. As the piles of gifts dwindled, and the ceremony ended, I found myself studying Morris Thaw as he departed with the last of the villagers. I wondered if he ever set foot in the Great House, and if he was secretly—or openly—bitter at the irony of his position. But in the ensuing scramble to get ready for church, all curiosity about Morris Thaw vanished.

"I can't find my prayer book," wailed Molly, while Nicholas somehow managed to sit on a croton and stain his white suit, which then had to be changed.

"I can't stand blue serge," he protested. "It's too scratchy. I won't be able to sit still, I know I won't, so you might as well not be cross when I wiggle."

Even the larger carriage proved to be a squeeze, and Nicholas was forced to sit on his mother's skirt, crushing it into wrinkles. She looked vacant and ill. I was surprised that she would accompany us, but Molly had told me that she was seeking help from the spirit world and perhaps God fell into that category. Philip's big chestnut horse snatched at the bit, impatient to be off.

"We're going to be late," said the captain impatiently; I could see that he disliked the confusion attendant on moving a number of females. "Nicholas, get out and I'll take you up in front of me." Nicholas' face brightened, and in seconds they were off at a fast pace, which upset Serena even more than the damage to her dress.

"You shouldn't have allowed it," she said pointedly to James. "There might be an accident." Nobody vouchsafed a reply and she subsided, the dark eyes anxious as the precious son and heir disappeared down the road with his uncle.

The church was built of stone, in a fine English Georgian manner. Inside, shining native mahogany had been used extensively for walls, pews, beams, and as framework for the large, open windows. We arrived just as the choir was forming, and were hastily ushered to an empty pew far down the aisle that must have been reserved for the Thaw family. The church was almost filled, and I doubted that I should see Stephen.

"Once in Royal David's City," I sang, glancing about surreptitiously. Soon I found him, only two pews ahead on the other side of the aisle. With a great lift of heart, I stared at his back, slim yet strong. I especially liked his neck, I decided, before kneeling for the prayer, and as the service proceeded, my mind departed from the church. We were in Italy on a long visit to his parents, and then en route to Arabia where he would acquire background for the newest book; the house in London had been closed for the time being. It was a relationship like that of Robert Browning and Elizabeth Barrett—tender and close. I did not write, but devoted myself to creating an atmosphere in which his wonderful talent could flourish. Molly nudged me sharply.

"You're talking out loud," she whispered. Beside me, Nicholas was holding back laughter. I looked at him severely, and gazed up at the plaque above us.

> In Memory of John Alexander Whitehorn
> Who Served God and His Fellow Man
> And Gave His Life for His Country

I read it several times, considerably impressed. There were a number of these plaques on the wall, honoring soldiers who had died for their country. Perhaps I should not dismiss an army career so lightly, I concluded, glancing along the pew to Philip Coulter. To devote one's life to serving a country in peace or in war—there was a nobility in this that could not be denied.

The sermon was over and we were rising for the last hymn. My heart began to beat faster, anticipating the moment when Stephen Thaw would turn, his eyes would light in recognition, his mouth twist into the captivating smile.

The surge of people into the aisle blocked him from my sight; friends and neighbors stood in leisurely groups, greeting each other on Christmas Day, exchanging news of families. I finally pushed ahead and made my way to the front door. He was waiting at the bottom of the steps, and his expression changed when he saw me. We greeted one another discreetly though he held my hand a few seconds longer than was necessary.

"Sea nymphs shouldn't cover their hair, no matter how pretty the bonnet. A very Happy Christmas, Marietta."

"And to you, Stephen." My pulses were hammering in a most alarming manner. Would this happen every time that we met?

"I think I've hit on a plan for this afternoon," he said in a low voice. "But it may take a little time, so don't be surprised if—" He stopped abruptly. I turned and saw that Philip Coulter had come down the steps and was well within earshot, watching us, a quizzical look on his face.

I presented him with a good view of my shoulder.

"I think someone is intruding," I murmured.

"Yes, unfortunately. Until later." He bowed and moved off down the path.

As we gathered for Christmas Day dinner, Hazard served the traditional drink made from sorrel, red as the poinsettia blossoms in the courtyard. But in spite of the pretty drink, the holiday spirit was beginning to wear thin. There was no candlelight to soften our faces; even the gold and silver table decorations looked dull and tarnished in the daylight. Tension was more apparent with every course; and attempts at conversation during turtle soup dwindled by the goose. The time for the celebrated passing out of yearly checks was drawing close.

"Uncle James does it after the plum pudding," Molly had told me earlier. "He tries to make a little ceremony out of it. So useless! All anyone wants to do is rip open the envelope and see what's inside."

The pudding, flaming in its silver dish, was carried in and picked at with token appreciation. Finally, James Thaw stood up and cleared his throat for attention—a needless gesture, as complete silence had descended upon the company.

"Elizabeth, my dear." He bowed in a courtly manner to his sister. "We thank you for your efforts to give us as happy a Christmas as possible, under the circumstances. You are the pivot around which our family life revolves, and we are all, I know, deeply grateful." Clapping and fond looks for Mrs. Coulter.

"Also, I am happy to welcome Marietta Jackson to this occasion, and perhaps I should explain the Thaw tradition to her." I gave him a pleading look; I would far rather have been excused from the room than singled out in this way, and murmured something about not wishing to intrude.

"My father's great desire," he continued solemnly, "was to ensure the family's interest in Repose, for which he himself worked so long and hard. To do this, to bring the family back to Repose, he began the custom of dividing the year's profits equally among those who are seated at this table for Christmas Day dinner. Some have not observed this custom for reasons best known to themselves"—he glanced pointedly at Philip—"but in general, I think we have all come to appreciate the wisdom of the patriarchal decree. This year, we are deeply saddened by the loss of my nephew Gerald, who would have stood here in my place one day. A grievous blow to the family. And it would not be right to omit a tribute to Nanny, our faithful friend for so many years. But enough in this vein. I will now call on Nicholas to distribute the envelopes around the table. I hope the contents will prove useful, and that 1880 will be a happier year for all of us. Will you do the honors, Nicholas?" With another bow, he seated himself, with the air of one congratulating himself on a job well done.

Nicholas, restless from church and the long dinner, performed his duty with great zest, running from place to place, handing out the large white envelopes. Mrs. Coulter was the first to receive hers. She pulled out the check rather gingerly, and her eyebrows lifted slightly. Pamela's expression did not change. Serena gave a gasp, her hand flew to her throat—the first indication that all was not well. Last of all, Nicholas handed an envelope to Philip. He opened it slowly; all at the table watched the rugged face attentively. For what seemed an endless moment he studied the enclosed bit of paper; then he laid it carefully beside his plate, and turned to his uncle.

"Uncle James," came the measured voice. "I realize that my coming here was a surprise and that it means less profit for everyone else at the table. Still, I think I must ask you for an accounting. On behalf of us all." His eyes narrowed, and he pushed away the check with a deliberate gesture.

James Thaw stiffened. "Accounting, Philip? What precisely do you mean?"

"What I say. A year's earnings at Repose, even divided seven ways, and taking today's sugar market into consideration—no, this, *this* calls for an explanation." There was complete silence in the room. We looked at James Thaw.

"I see no need to give you any explanations, Philip," said his uncle quietly. "I have followed the same procedures at Repose this past year, and if the results are unsatisfactory, I regret it very much, but I am not accountable for what is beyond my control." In spite of his low voice, a mottled red color showed in his face. The conversation was beginning to take on an ugly aspect. Mrs. Coulter laid a hand on Philip's arm, but he ignored it.

"Well, then, I suppose I should rephrase my remarks. If you are not responsible then who, may I ask, is? The money from Repose can hardly have been reduced to this pitiful amount without some unusual reason."

James interrupted him angrily. "Are you accusing me, sir, are you accusing me of taking the money. If so, I warn you—"

"No, Uncle James. But I do question your management, let us say. You know the old saying—'The best fertilizer is dirt from the master's boots.' No owner can spend a few weeks out of the year at Repose and expect it to run itself the rest of the time."

"Repose does not run itself. Morris is here."

"Ah, yes. Morris. We all saw how effective Morris was this morning. He does not stir out of his house, he knows none of the Negroes by name. There's the problem, clearly. I suggest that you pension Morris off and hire a competent overseer."

"*No!*" The force of James's reply made us all jump. "No," he continued, with slightly less vehemence, "that is impossible. Your grandfather left instructions that Morris should always have a place here. I would be failing a trust if I were to send him away. He has nowhere else to go."

"I did not mean to send him away. He could be pensioned off, given a place to live. Let's be blunt about this, Uncle James. We all know, even Miss Jackson knows, that Morris is your father's illegitimate son. And as that son he has certain rights. But does he have the right to virtually control the Thaw family fortune, year after year? Particularly in the light of this inexcusable failure. Let's not delude ourselves. We are caught in the trap of absentee ownership that has destroyed so many fine plantations." His voice softened slightly. "If you like, I'll take it up with Morris myself. Surely you can see that he must be replaced."

The servants had been standing motionless against the wall, enthralled, no doubt, with this conversation. Suddenly, Mrs. Coulter became aware of them and motioned them to leave the room.

After a few seconds' pause, James Thaw resumed. "Philip, I insist that you allow me to make the decision. In spite of what you may wish, I am master here. You yourself have shown no interest in Repose. Now you suddenly appear and begin to give orders. For this and other reasons, I absolutely forbid you to contradict me in this manner."

Philip was silent, drumming his fingers on the cloth. I felt sorry for James Thaw, pitted against this younger and stronger man. I hoped that Philip would have the kindness, for his mother's sake, to drop the argument, at least for the moment.

When he spoke, it was with a deceptive gentleness. "Forbid is a strong word, Uncle. When losses on an estate reach this point, I'm not sure that even the master has the right to forbid." An amusing thought seemed to strike him. "You are a student of local customs, Uncle James. Do you remember what happened, in the old days, to the head of a family accused of a breach of trust? It was such an unforgivable offense that hanging wasn't punishment enough. No, they went out and burned him alive!"

A collective gasp came from the listeners. "Philip!" Elizabeth Coulter was ashen, as though she might faint. I wanted to run from the table, sickened by this degrading family quarrel. Indeed, Molly had been right to dread Christmas Day dinner.

Philip Coulter now had the grace to subside. "I beg your pardon, Uncle James. That was an inappropriate remark even as a joke, and I apologize. I should have discussed these matters with you privately, not at this time."

I let out my breath. Mrs. Coulter pushed back her chair, feeling, as I'm sure we all did, that the sooner we left the room the better. Throughout the exchange, Serena had been gazing into the distance, her attention fixed on something beyond our sight. Now she looked at us.

"What does it matter where you talk?" she said in a high, clear voice. "There is nothing left. Nothing. We all know it now. This place killed Gerald. It soon will kill us all. The family is cursed, God help us! I've known it for some time. This family is cursed!"

There was a dreadful silence. Then Nicholas began to cry, a harsh, gulping noise, breaking the paralysis that held us in our seats. Molly, her face so white that every small freckle stood out, went to her mother. Together, she and Pamela led her away. Philip walked quickly to the verandah, his heels making a sharp sound on the wood.

"We'll go to your room now, Nicholas," I said, trembling, not knowing what else to do. "We can play the game that Molly gave you. You'd like that, I know. Nicholas, did you hear me? Would you like to do that?" I took his arm and pulled him toward the door. He seemed dazed, a small boy who had been cruelly exposed to the raw anger of grown-ups; a child who had heard his mother rave and curse his family. Though he might not have understood, the terrible sound of her voice must have shaken him deeply. The tears had stopped by the time we reached his room, but his face was set in a despairing way that made me want to take them all and rattle them to their senses. You are going to destroy this child, I addressed them silently. How can he grow up properly in the midst of this—this turmoil?

I too had been shaken, more than I realized. Perhaps my family life had been unusual, but I could scarcely remember a harsh word spoken under our roof. I could understand anger on a large scale—anger against war, or slavery—but at Christmas dinner, and over a check! My childhood might have been dull and confining, but I would not have exchanged it for this uncertainty.

Jilly got up from her basket, stretched, and limped across the floor to meet us. Her leg was healing fast; only a few large scars showed through her coat, and she was losing the hungry look of a dog that had lived by its wits; her ribs were covered with a layer of fat, and the little belly was rounding out from the scraps

that Nicholas filched for her. Her eyes never left him, she knew
very well to whom she owed her pleasant existence.

I put the toy soldiers out on the floor, and we marched them
up and down until I saw his lids begin to droop.

"Why don't you take off your shoes and tuck up on the bed?" I
suggested. "Not a nap, of course. Nothing like that, but just to
be comfortable. Shall I go on reading about Henry Morgan?"

In the wall of bookshelves along the passageway in our wing, I
had found a few children's books among the mixed assortment of
old volumes. None of them had been touched for years, it
seemed, and it distressed me to see the leather bindings falling
apart. I promised myself that after Christmas I would spend a
few hours pulling out what was worth saving. But for now, the
battered book of Henry Morgan's life was exactly to Nicholas'
taste, and he climbed onto the bed without protest. As I resumed
the tale, Sir Harry, the buccaneer turned statesman, had just
boarded the French sloop *Trompeuse*, and was transporting the
rich cargo of gold into the swaggering town of Port Royal, head-
quarters of the pirate world, the "interlopers" as the irate town
fathers called them. We were about to start the next chapter,
"The Great Earthquake of 1692," when I glanced up and saw
that Nicholas was fast asleep.

As I tiptoed back down the hall past the bookshelves, an anti-
dote to the Christmas dinner came to mind: sorting the books
would put the Thaws out of my thoughts for a while. I was
heartily sick of them. Poor Mrs. Coulter, I thought, gathering up
a large armful of volumes to take to my room, what a dreadful
position for her, caught in the battle between her brother and
her son. I could sympathize with James Thaw, for why should
Captain Coulter suddenly arrive and expect to run the estate? At
least he had the decency to apologize, I thought, yawning, as I
arranged the books on the floor. I would have a short siesta in
the long chair before beginning to clean them.

I must have dozed off, for I was wakened by a loud banging
on the door. "Marietta, are you there? Guess what," shouted
Molly. "There's going to be polo at the Shepheards' this afternoon and Philip is going to play. Granny says we may go in the
buggy. Hurry, or we'll miss the first chukker!"

I scrambled to my feet. Hastily, I thrust the books into a corner; they would have to wait, and anyhow they looked like a worthless lot of stuff. My hands moved with maddening slowness as I washed them free of dust. My gloves were in the wrong drawer; I ran to find my parasol and tripped like an awkward child.

"Hurry, Marietta, we're all waiting for you!"

"Yes, one second!" As I tied on my bonnet, I could see in the mirror that my eyes had deepened in color as they did in moments of excitement. Stephen had found a way to meet me on Christmas Day afternoon! This had seemed an impossibility, but somehow he had succeeded.

CHAPTER 9

Who climbeth highest, most dreadful is his fall.
JOHN LYDGATE: *Miscellaneous Poems, c. 1440*

The game was already in progress when we arrived. We waited until the play went to the other end before making our way around the goal to join the thirty or so spectators in the small, awninged tent. As we slid into empty seats in the front row, the players thundered back, hoofs thudding on the hard, rough ground. It was my first sight of polo and I gasped as two ponies nearly collided; then one broke free and the rider set him wildly at the goal, the long mallet arched through the air, and the ball sailed through the posts in a great curve.

"Well done, Coulter," came murmurs from the group. "We'll have a shot at winning the tournament this year, I believe," someone remarked.

The players were trotting back, horses blowing white foam from their bits. "Uncle Philip made the goal," breathed Nicholas worshipfully, hanging over the rail. "Someday I'll be as good as he is, Marietta."

"Of course"—but I was looking at a slighter figure sitting easily in the saddle, face half covered with a white helmet. It should be an armored visor, I decided, and he should have a sword instead of a mallet and heraldic emblems on the shield—or perhaps on a banner?

The play was on again; the ponies wheeled and plunged, someone shouted in the melee. But this is dangerous, I thought in alarm. A horse could fall, a rider could be struck with a mallet. I sat very still, twisting my fingers and discovering to my astonishment the heady excitement of watching men engaged in battle. Wars were made for women, went the saying—and this was a mock war, on Christmas afternoon, before an audience of smiling, prettily dressed women and girls. Two combatants raced for the ball, one tall with broad shoulders, the other slim and wiry. My heart jumped as the bigger man cut in roughly, and the ball went back to the center.

"Hard riding, that," said a voice behind me. "Coulter's not going to let up on Thaw today. He's pressing hard."

"Another family feud? Oh please, no." A woman's voice, followed by laughter. Major Shepheard came to join us. "I wasn't planning to have a game this afternoon, but young Stephen Thaw said he could get up two scratch teams if I'd lend Philip a pony. Must have been a good idea—look at the number who've showed up, I'm glad to have the stand used, seats are here anyhow. M'wife is in the tea tent so go on over, because we'll have a break after this chukker. Hot work out there, even for the young fellers."

"Aren't you going to play, Major Shepheard?" asked Molly. "You're the best of them all."

The heavy-set man laughed, obviously pleased. "Getting out of shape as you can see, my dear girl. Pace is too fast for me now, even if I did teach most of them everything they know. Hallo, young Nicholas! Won't be long before you're out there, and those fellers will be the old-timers like me. Are you learning the strokes, boy? Got a pony?"

"Oh yes! I know two strokes already. My father showed me. But the pony won't turn. I kick him, and whack him, but he won't turn properly."

"Good player, your father. One of the best, and I can see that you take after him. You come down one of these days, and we'll see what you can do on a real pony. See what you can do!" He got up and went in the direction of the tea tent, a separate awninged enclosure nearby. Nicholas looked after him sadly.

"He doesn't know how well I can ride," he said in a woebegone voice. "I don't think he believed me when I said that I know two strokes, even if they are forehand ones. Do you think he really will ask me to come down, Marietta?"

"I should think so. He seems a very nice man."

"He is, but people always say they're going to do things, and then they forget. I *have* to show him how well I ride!"

"Well, we'll hope he remembers," I murmured, no longer paying attention. The players were dismounting, handing the reins to grooms who had been standing with other horses under a clump of trees. I watched Stephen take off his helmet and wipe the sweat from his face. The shirt clung to his body, outlining every muscle. He was coming toward us, and my heart jerked wildly against my ribs.

"Good afternoon, ladies, Nicholas. Ready for tea? I know I am." He stood there gracefully, flicking his crop against his boots. Pamela was smiling at him, and I felt a stir of misgiving. Is he asking us all into the tent? I wondered. Will we have any chance to be alone together? I looked away, afraid that the disappointment would show plainly in my face.

Two other players joined us, young men who appeared to be acquainted with the Coulter girls. "Miss Pamela," said one, bowing low, "may I have the pleasure of escorting you to tea?"

"Come on, Molly," said the other. "Hurry up before the bun fight begins." The girls were being hustled out of their seats with no chance to refuse and Stephen smiled at me.

"I'll bring Miss Jackson in a minute, after I speak to my groom." Pamela gave him a cool look; it was so neatly done that I almost laughed.

Nicholas, however, lingered. "Don't you want some cake and buns?" I asked hopefully.

"Well of course I do, but first I have to talk to Uncle Philip about something important. He's over there, with the horses." I looked and saw him standing with one of the grooms, running a hand over his pony's leg.

"All right, but don't be in the way." He ran off, and I turned to Stephen eagerly.

"Well done all round," he said in a low voice. "What luck, but we'd better make the most of the moment. Shall we walk to that little spot of shade under the trees?"

I recall the white stones in the grass that cut into my slippers, the smell of sweat and horses that was so strangely agitating, the rising voices in the tent beyond. I was Stephen Thaw's girl, I thought exultantly. Out of all the others, I was the one he had chosen. I don't care what Pamela thinks of me, I told myself, looking at Stephen's well-shaped hands, the long fingers that could control a headstrong pony—and write books.

"It's not as if you were a Thaw." He spoke intently, with a gaze that so unsteadied me that I had to lean against the nearest tree. "We must meet whenever we can; doesn't Molly help you with Nicholas? You must send a message by one of the servants and I shall do the same. I lay awake until some ungodly hour last night, trying to remember the exact color of your hair. You'll have to forgive me, Marietta, for speaking so openly, but I've never met anyone quite like you. So utterly beautiful, and yet so sweet—so beguilingly sweet."

I could not meet his searching look and stared at the ground, wishing that he would repeat the words: "never met anyone quite like you" . . . "so utterly beautiful" . . . "so beguilingly sweet." Words I would never forget, giving substance to last night's fantasies. I closed my eyes, unable to answer.

Suddenly he swung away from me, turning toward the tea tent, and after a second I realized why. The babble of voices had ceased; an unnatural hush had fallen on the noisy group.

"What is it? What's wrong?"

"I don't know."

Then a woman screamed, breaking the silence, and I saw men running from the tent toward the field in the headlong way that means catastrophe.

"What on earth—"

"Come on." Stephen was running, too, and I followed, tripping on the stones. As I neared the field, I could see that a crowd had formed near the center. Beyond them, several of the grooms were hanging onto the bridle of a plunging, rearing horse, trying to move him off in the direction of the trees. Someone must have been thrown, I thought, and no wonder. That horse looked dangerous, quite out of control.

I stood at the edge of the group and peered in reluctantly, not anxious either to see blood or add to the confusion. But after one look I was pushing frantically through the people.

Nicholas lay on the ground, eyes closed. I saw him clearly, and yet my brain refused to believe that he had been near the horse. It was not possible; he had been walking toward Philip when I left him.

Pamela was kneeling beside him; as I came up she raised her head, and her look was anguished and accusing. She thinks I'm to blame, I thought with horror. She left him with me, but he was going to Philip—what can have happened?

The onlookers parted to make room for Dr. Barrows. I turned to the lady standing beside me.

"Did the horse kick him?" I whispered.

"No, I don't think so," she answered in a hushed tone. "We were having tea, and someone looked out and there he was, out on the field by himself, trying to ride that young horse. He stayed on about half a minute before the animal threw him, the longest half minute I ever hope to spend, and he hasn't moved since."

Dr. Barrows was manipulating the arms and legs gently. "Neck not broken," he said, and a sigh of relief passed through the group. Molly pushed through with a wet towel in her hand which was placed on Nicholas' forehead.

I began to pray. Not another tragedy, God. Not another. Not Nicholas. I had tried to believe that no shadow hung over his head, that the fears of his great-uncle and mother were morbid imaginings. But here he lay, not dead, his chest moving slightly with his breathing, but there could be internal injuries, the frightful list went through my mind. Tears were running down Molly's cheeks as we stood, waiting. I closed my eyes, unable to bear the sight of the small motionless body.

"Coming round," said Dr. Barrows. When I looked, Nicholas was staring up at the doctor, bewildered.

"All right, young man. You had a fall, but not too much harm done." He got to his feet briskly. "Two of you gentlemen lift him up carefully and bring him over to the tent. I want to get a better look at him in the shade."

I caught Molly's arm as they moved off. "I shall never forgive myself! I thought he was with Philip! He was going over to him when I—when we—"

"It was my fault as much as yours. We were all in charge of him, after all. But how could he have done it? It was so frightful to suddenly look up and see him on that animal and there was nothing anyone could do! Look, Marietta! There's Philip. Now we'll find out what happened."

The other horses had been infected with the excitement, and tossed their heads and struck the ground with their forefeet; some of the ponies were being walked at a safe distance. As we came up, Philip was directing several unsmiling grooms to take the frantic young horse away while he talked to the man in charge.

"Now then," he said at last, sternly. "Why was my nephew on the back of that horse?"

The man did not—or could not—speak. His chest was heaving, the sweat poured from his face.

Philip waited a moment. "Who put him up? He certainly didn't get on by himself. I want an answer."

"—not know," the man muttered.

"Tell me the truth, man! Plenty of people here saw what happened. How did he get on that horse? Speak up, now!"

This was implacable authority; at last the man broke.

"Him want to ride so bad, Mast'! Him say, 'Put me up, put me up right now!' What to do, Mast'? What to do!"

I could see that Philip Coulter was furious under the outward control. But his voice was even as he began another line of questioning.

"What's this horse doing here? He is obviously not fit for the game. He seems quite unbroken. Why is he here?"

"Him too young, Mast'."

"I can see that for myself. I'm asking you, why is he here?"

"Him come to be with other horses. Him combolo to other horse."

"You brought him to get used to being with the others. Well that I can understand. But to let the boy ride him—couldn't you see that he might be killed?"

The man shook his head, mumbling. He's not bright, I

thought, or else he's pretending to be stupid, to save himself. Finally, Philip turned to the others in exasperation.

"Whose man is this? Who owns that horse?"

"Missus Anna Thaw's man, suh. Missus Anna Thaw own dat horse."

There was a heavy silence. The black faces watched us impassively. Philip let out a deep breath and swung away in the direction of the tent while Molly and I followed. It was unfortunate that Stephen should be hurrying toward us.

"The stupid fool!" he said worriedly. "I'll see that he's well punished. Luckily, the boy doesn't seem to be hurt." Philip walked by him without a glance, the most humiliating answer he could have given. Stephen looked after him, frowning.

"Oh, Stephen," I said, almost in tears.

"Yes, poor little chap. And it isn't going to help matters for us. I know what the Thaws are going to say—that my grandmother is responsible, which is ridiculous, but all the same—"

I could not speak. Serena's words came back to me: "This family is cursed!"

"Try not to worry, Marietta. And let me know how he is, as soon as you can." He touched my hand and went on.

The buggy was brought around, and Nicholas was lifted in. His color was better, but he lay back on the seat, saying nothing. Molly, Pamela, and I squeezed together opposite. I hoped that Molly would explain to Pamela that Nicholas had been on his way to Philip when I left him. I would always have a feeling of guilt for what had happened that afternoon. As Molly said, no one was strictly responsible, but I would not have urged him to go off alone had it not been for Stephen.

Nicholas was beginning to revive. "Why do I have to lie down?" he complained. "I can't see down here."

Molly leaned forward. "You complete clod," she said angrily. "What were you thinking of, to get up on that horse? Look at all the trouble you've caused, just like the cliffs. Why, you can't be trusted for two minutes."

"No, Molly." Pamela interrupted calmly. "He's had enough for now."

Molly flushed. "I know. I'm sorry, Nicky. It's just that I—" We understood, and so did he, that the outburst was her expression of affection.

"Nicholas," Pamela said softly, taking his hand, "why did you ride that horse? You could have asked Philip or Stephen or any of the others to lead you around on a pony."

"Because I didn't *want* to be led around, that's why! I'm not a baby! I wanted to show Major Shepheard what a good rider I am, so that he will let me play. I told the groom what a good rider I am, and he put me up. I didn't *mean* to fall off, you know. I didn't *know* that the horse would do that!" He was close to tears, and Pamela did not press him.

So that's it, I said to myself. He was showing off to Major Shepheard. A foolhardy, childish impulse that might have killed him. And we would never know if the man deliberately led him on, aided and abetted him. That groom was not nearly as stupid as he pretended to be, in my opinion.

The carriage was starting up the hill when Pamela spoke again. "Perhaps we'd better not say anything to Mother. I'll tell Granny, quietly."

"But she's bound to hear about it. Someone will tell her. Isn't it better to prepare her a little?"

"Yes, but not tonight, Molly. Not after such a particularly bad day. Let one night go by, and the accident may not seem so—so inevitable."

Pamela is right, I thought. Serena will see this as a carrying out of all her doomsday prophecies.

"And," she continued, "Marietta will be just as pleased if nothing is said, I'm sure."

The unexpectedness of this remark so enraged me that I almost leaned forward and slapped that disdainful face. Molly, sensing my anger, looked at us wide-eyed, waiting for my retort. I swallowed hard; there must be no more unpleasantness just now, though I vowed to myself that I would settle accounts with this girl.

"It makes no difference to me what you say," I replied with all the coolness I could muster. "Why on earth should it?" We entered the courtyard in silence. She is jealous, I told myself, as we stepped down from the buggy. She must be first in everything.

Well, she will not spoil my happiness with Stephen. This she cannot do.

Nicholas was soon undressed and in bed; I let Jilly curl up beside him on the sheet, but when we heard Mrs. Coulter's footsteps in the hall, I picked her up quickly and put her in the basket.

"Pamela told me about your fall, darling," she said gently, stroking his forehead. "How are you feeling now? I don't think you have any fever, but it would be best if you stay in bed, just for tonight. I'll have Louisa bring you a tray. Is there anything special you'd like?"

"Granny, you know!"

"I can't quite remember. Is it guavas and coconut cream, or 'spotted-dog' pudding?"

"Guavas, please."

"And lemonade right now, perhaps?" Whatever she might be feeling, however she might have longed to scold him, her emotions were well concealed. How extraordinary, I thought. How much wiser to give him affection rather than a scolding, in his state of mind. I looked at her with admiration as she left.

Jilly had been quiet. Now she showed herself again and stood on her hind legs, paws against the bed. "Look at that," Nicholas exclaimed. "She doesn't forget a thing; she's such a clever dog. I wonder where she lived before she came here. Chitty says she just came to the back door one day and wouldn't leave."

"Poor little thing," I said jokingly. "Maybe she was an abandoned little orphan, with no parents and no home." Seconds later, I could have bitten my tongue. Nicholas' eyes filled with tears. "But *you're* not an orphan," I added quickly. "You have your mother and your granny, sisters." It was no use; his hand plucked at the sheet, and tears ran down his cheeks.

"I want my father, I want my *father!* None of these things would happen to me if my father was here. He wouldn't have let me get up on that horse; he was teaching me the strokes so that I could play polo, too. Everything bad has happened since he died!"

I stroked his hand silently, letting him cry. He doesn't mention any of the other troubles, I noticed, feeling close to tears myself. Oh dear Lord, I wonder how old one has to be to value the rare moments of happiness? To recognize them, draw them out as long as possible?

Finally, I went to the drawer for a handkerchief and wiped the wet face, putting an arm around his shoulder.

"You know," I said gently, pulling him closer, "I was thinking about my own father just now." The ruse was successful. He stopped crying and gulped once or twice, his attention diverted.

"You were?"

"Yes, I miss him very much. My life has changed, too, you know, since he died. But I don't think he wants me to cry about it. I think that would make him sad, to see me unhappy."

"Well, how would he know? Do you think he sees you?"

"I can't tell, Nicholas. But I think he cares about me. And I think your father cares about you. I don't think he would like to know that you were doing foolish things. He loved you, and he wouldn't want you to be hurt, would he?"

"No, he wouldn't." There was silence for some time. From the frowning expression on his face, I could see that Nicholas was considering my words and I waited, longing to put an end to these self-destructive impulses.

"For instance," I began tentatively, "I don't suppose he would want you to go to the cliffs, would he?"

To my great surprise, Nicholas pushed away from me. He turned and looked up with an accusing stare.

"Yes," he said indignantly. "Yes, he does want me to go to the cliffs. I know that he does."

"Now why do you say that?" I asked, stifling the automatic objection, and watching him with concern. He appeared to be in the grip of a fierce inner conflict. His hands held mine tightly, his face was flushed, and he looked about the room, from door to window and back again, as if he might be overheard.

"What is it, Nicholas?" I was beginning to feel alarmed.

"Nobody else knows, Marietta."

"Knows *what?*"

"Knows about the hidden gold treasure in the cliffs."

I bit down on my lip, to keep back the exclamation of surprise.

"What did you say?"

"The gold treasure in the cliffs. You think I'm making up a story, don't you? I'm not. Please listen to me, Marietta! The night before he went away, my father came into my room. It was very late. I think I had been asleep, but the squeaky door woke me. I was going to sit up, but I was so sleepy that I just lay there with my eyes closed. He thought I was still asleep. He began to talk to me, as if he was talking to himself. He was talking out loud, you know the way?"

"Yes, I know."

"He said he was going to Repose to bring the gold out of the cliffs. He said, 'Someday it will belong to you, Nicholas. That's why I'm going.' I remember those words, plain as day, I swear it. And then he was dead—trying to find it for me. *Now* do you understand why I have to go to the cliffs?"

I nodded. I could not trust my voice. So the treasure—the gold chalices—had never been recovered. They had remained hidden all these years. In spite of myself, I felt a surge of childish excitement.

"Nicholas, I believe you. For reasons that you couldn't possibly understand, I believe you. But don't you think that someone else might know about the gold? Uncle Philip?" I thought of him that morning by the rocks. "Or your Uncle James?"

"It was a secret," he said stubbornly. "I think it was a secret and my father was going to surprise everyone. If it wasn't a secret, everyone would be talking about it. Molly blurts out everything she knows."

"Yes. But Nicholas, do you think it's wise to keep this a secret now? Don't you think it would be better to tell someone—your Uncle James, for instance? He could help you find the gold and that would be so much better than trying to do it alone. The cliffs are so big—it might take a lot of people to search."

"Yes, I know that. But he won't believe me, Marietta. He'll say I was dreaming, or maybe that I'd read about buried treasure in a book and was making up a story. Suppose everyone worked and worked and nothing turned up? They would be so angry! No, he won't believe me. I have to keep looking myself, until I find it."

So many choices, so many uncertainties! I tried to think clearly. I must do what was best for Nicholas at this critical moment.

"Nicholas, I see exactly what you mean. I do, truly. But you mustn't try to do this by yourself. It's impossible, surely you can see that? Would it help if I spoke to your Uncle James? If I tell him the story, and say that I think you are telling the truth?"

He sat straight up, and I could see the growing hope in his eyes.

"Oh, would you, Marietta? He might listen to you; he probably will, because you're old. Then we could have a treasure hunt! Will you ask him right away, tonight?"

"We'll see. I can't promise. It's been a long day, and I don't want to disturb him. *But—*" And I paused dramatically.

"But what?"

"You, Nicholas Coulter, must make me a very solemn promise. Sworn on the blood of your ancestors, the faith of your fathers, on the Bible."

"What is it? *Tell* me, Marietta!"

"You must promise that if I speak to your Uncle James, that you will never, never go alone to the cliffs again. Do you understand? An oath, on your sacred word. Now say it."

"I promise that if you speak to Uncle James I will never, never go alone to the cliffs again. I swear it to infinity. Amen!"

I caught him by the shoulders as he bounced up and down on his knees.

"Well, that's settled, then. I expect you to keep your word, and I'll do my best to persuade your uncle to make a search. Look out! You're going to squash Jilly! She's under the sheet."

"Why can't I get up, Marietta? There's nothing wrong now, only a few bumps on my head."

"Certainly not. Do be quiet for a while; it's the least you can do after giving us such a scare, Master Nicholas."

My first opportunity to speak to James Thaw came as we went in to dinner. I asked if I might see him on a matter of importance; he invited me to his sitting room after coffee. We were a small gathering around the table; Phillip and Serena did not appear and I was able to mull over Nicholas' story, feeling—so I imagined—like an archaeologist who has made an exciting discovery: two similar bones, two matching pieces of pottery. Gerald Coulter's words to his son confirmed my grandmother's letter: there *was* a hidden fortune in gold! But how to find it in the cliffs?

Although James Thaw was expecting me, I hesitated before knocking on the sitting-room door. It had been a trying day for him; perhaps I should have waited. On the other hand, he had been affable at the table, as though nothing untoward had happened earlier.

"Come in," he said, opening the door. "Come in and tell me your interesting news."

But after seating myself, I could not begin. The phrases I had so carefully planned seemed weak and implausible. It would be all too easy to assume that Nicholas had been dreaming.

"It's this," I stammered. "The thing is, Nicholas swears he heard his father talking to him the night before he left for Repose, last October. He stood by his bed, talking to him; he said that he was coming here to look for gold treasure in the cliffs." I paused, hoping that James Thaw would make some comment but he did not; the expression on his face was gently skeptical. "But you see," I hurried on, "you see, this is why Nicholas runs to the cliffs. He is trying to find the gold! He swears that his father talked to him, that it was not a dream, and he is so certain of this that I thought I had better come to you." I stopped, breathless.

I had not anticipated James Thaw's reaction to this news. I had not supposed that he would leap to his feet and organize a search party, but I did expect that he would give it serious consideration. Instead, he crossed his legs, encased in the smooth white linen, and pressed the palms of his hands together, blue eyes twinkling at me.

"Now, Marietta," he said in a teasing voice. "Let me understand you. Nicholas has just revealed, after all these months, that he woke up late one night and heard his father talking about treasure hidden in the cliffs. This in itself is odd. Why hasn't he spoken of this before?"

It was a sensible question. "I'm not sure," I answered softly. "But I think he was badly frightened this afternoon, and perhaps for the first time he sees that what he is doing is wrong and dangerous. But now he's afraid that no one will believe him. He's afraid that people will think he's making this up. He doesn't want to appear silly, and that is why I told him that I would come and talk to you."

"I see, yes, I do see. A pity. I'm devoted to the boy, as you know, and the last thing I would want to do is hurt his feelings. He has enough to contend with, poor little fellow. And a fortune in gold would be delightful, a delightful windfall for Repose. But I really think, my dear Marietta, that I would have heard something about this treasure, over the years. I don't believe this would have escaped my ears. And unless I'm very much mistaken, Gerald would never have set out on such an adventure without consulting me. No, I cannot conceive of his doing such a thing. I'm afraid, my dear, that this story is a product of Nicholas' lively imagination. There's a great tradition of pirate treasure on the island—and haven't I heard him talking about Captain Morgan lately? It's easy to see that he's indulging in some wishful thinking."

I was silent; there was nothing more I could say. Wishful thinking, indeed! I had presented Nicholas' case, one which I knew to be true, and failed.

All at once, anger rose in me, sweeping away caution. Nicholas and I would not be dismissed so lightly; James Thaw might be the head of the family, but he was also a pompous, fussy man who seemed to consider himself omniscient. When I was certain that my voice would not betray me, I began again.

"Mr. Thaw, do you remember that when we went over my grandmother's things, I asked you about an amethyst set?"

"I believe I do."

"When Nicholas told me about the hidden gold this evening, I remembered something else that might interest you. There were several letters with the inventory, and in one of them she said that the valuables at Repose were being hidden because of a

slave uprising. Do you suppose that the amethysts and the gold
that Nicholas talks about could both have been hidden in the
cliffs? Could still be there?" I watched sharply for a change of
expression, a glint of suspicion. There was none. Instead, his
smile widened, and he began to laugh.

"Marietta, Marietta! You're as bad as Nicholas! Between the
two of you we'll have Spanish gold bullion buried under the barbecue! If my father *had* hidden any family treasure away, he
was not the kind of man who would leave it for long. No, I cannot become excited about your gold, much as I wish to."

He rose, trimmed a smoking wick, and returned to his chair.
"I am a little perturbed, though, that you bring up the matter of
the amethysts again. I wonder if you think that I am holding
them back from you. If so, I wish you would speak out plainly.
Do you believe you have not received all you are entitled to?"
His voice was dry, and I fought back the same sense of humiliation I had experienced when Serena accused me of stealing.

"No," I replied as steadily as I could. "No, I have no reason to
think that, Mr. Thaw. But I'm disappointed for Nicholas' sake;
he wanted so much to have a treasure hunt, and find the gold."

"Ah, but he shall. We'll have a fine treasure hunt, though not
on the cliffs. I'll speak to my sister first thing tomorrow. And
Marietta, forgive me if I spoke sharply to you about the amethysts. It's been a most trying day. And now this business of the
horse. We must be thankful that Nicholas was not badly hurt, or
worse, and it bears out exactly what I told you. Anna is a diabol-
ically clever woman. If Nicholas had been killed, we might have
suspected her hand in it, but nothing could have been proved. I
fear her, I fear her very much. We are not dealing with an ordinary sort of hate, and now that her grandson is back, it may have
flamed up with added incentive. If she has taken it into her head
that she wants Repose for him, she will stop at nothing!"

I heard him out—the subject of the gold forgotten in his anxiety over Anna Thaw; finally I was able to bid him a good night,
and slip away.

Tonight, thousands of tiny phosphorescent lights silvered the
water. I stood for a moment on the verandah, rubbing my aching
head and listening to the tree toads, noting how the jacaranda

tree cast long shadows on the hillside. It was getting late; the servants had gone to their quarters long ago, and the drums sounded softly from the village. No one was about, and yet I had the feeling of being observed, that odd sensation that makes one turn quickly to see who is watching.

Foolishness, I told myself. The warm evenings seemed to affect me in a restless, disquieting manner. And I was tired, as much from the strain of the past hour as from the long day. On an impulse, I went into Nicholas' room. Jilly's eyes gleamed and I heard her tail thump against the side of the basket as she recognized me in the dim night light. Nicholas was sleeping soundly, his breathing even and soft. For the moment, he was safe.

I'm sorry, I told him, silently. Even though I did my best to persuade your uncle, there will be no expedition to the cliffs. But —you must not forget your promise to me; you must live up to your part of the bargain. For your own good, Nicholas.

I leaned over and pulled the sheet up over his shoulders. I could not forget the sight of Nicholas lying unconscious on the ground, and my own feelings of guilt. Never again, I vowed, would my desire to be with Stephen interfere with my duty toward this boy.

CHAPTER 10

When I left the gentlemen, I took tea in my own room, surrounded by the black, brown, and yellow ladies of the house, and heard a great deal of its private history.

LADY NUGENT: *Jamaica Journal, March 1802*

I went to bed, but in spite of my fatigue, or because of it, I could not sleep. Questions flitted about in my head, up and down and round about: Could Anna's groom have been acting on instructions to kill Nicholas? Did Gerald Coulter actually speak to Nicholas about the gold? Could Philip have been looking for it that morning at the cliffs? Why had they kept this secret from James? I relit my lamp and climbed down from the bed.

The room was stifling. Earlier, I had been too tired to open the sash window—a victory for Cubba in our battle over night air— but now I thrust it open with a crash. The house remained quiet; no one came to investigate, and the only noise outside was that of the drums, beating with a monotonous, dreary sound.

The books lay piled in the corner where I had left them. To go on with the sorting might be soothing, and I carried an armful close to the lamp. It was sad to see the fine leather bindings fallen away; my father had spent much time dusting and oiling his books and often I had helped him. Some of these titles were as dry as the leather: *Sketch of the Lives of Lords Stowell and Eldon; Comprising, with Additional Matter, Some Correction of Mr. Twiss's Work on the Chancellor,* by Surtees. Then came a

set of illustrated periodicals of 1827, stained, mildewed, the value
gone. A book on bovine disease, household account books which
I studied with some interest: "July 17: 3 lbs. molasses sugar, 4
lbs. lard, 12 candles, 5 bottles sweet wine." More account books,
and then—jammed in among them—a small book with a scrolled
leather binding and a tarnished gold lock. It had a slightly more
interesting look, and I held it up to the light. "Journal of Martha
Thaw." The elegant script embellished the front page. Martha
Thaw—the mulatto housekeeper my grandmother had so greatly
disliked. I laid the little book carefully on the table, and began
to read.

The first entries were filled with elaborate descriptions of
clothes and preparations for a journey; there was nothing of interest here, and I was about to toss the book aside when a name
caught my eye.

December 10

So I end my first day at Repose. Mr. Thaw sent the carriage
for me this morning, a mark of respect for which I am grateful.
The journey lasted over two hours, during which time I could
fear this step, and yet be thankful that Mr. Thaw would buy me.
The child will be known as his, and I will see that he or she is
sent away to school, as I was. Mrs. Thaw is gone to England and
I am to be housekeeper. I must think of the child and keep my
temper with the servants, who will surely attempt to disobey me.
I know both sides of the fence, which may be of advantage in this
unsettled time, and I must quickly discover the loyalties of the
Repose slaves. My room is comfortable enough, though situated
in the rear of the house.

December 15

Little of interest. Mr. Thaw continues kind, though I weary of
hearing him rant and rave about lawyers, trustees, and the indo-
lence of the planters who, he says, treat the land like a gold
mine, taking all and putting nothing back. Mrs. Jackson is civil
enough, though she is at a sad loss to understand my position. To
her, "concubine" is a word in her precious Bible, not a woman
under the same roof. It is clear to her that I am more than the
housekeeper, but I must confess that I am uncertain about her

position. Mr. Thaw tells me that she and her husband are guests, but it is a peculiar guest that rides out with the owner every day to inspect and helps manage the estate. The Jacksons are American, and Non-Conformist in their religion. They are sadly confused about our ways, though I assure her that Mr. Thaw is a good master who uses only the cat-o'-nine-tails, never the cart whip. Five more months of waiting for my small one. In the meantime, I sew and walk in the garden and write in my journal.

I paused from the task of deciphering Martha's ornate flourishes, and let my mind dwell on the incongruous picture of the strait-laced New England couple struggling to adapt to this vastly different life. And the baby—could the baby have been Morris? I drew the light closer and turned the page.

The Grignon trouble at Salt Spring has caused more furor than is customary over a flogging, however unjust. I suspect that the rumor of the free law is at the bottom of it. I will try harder to discover the temper at Repose, which is perhaps why Mr. Thaw has brought me here. I will surely advise him, to save myself and my child; he is a hard man, and I can scarcely like him, but it is to my advantage that neither he nor Repose suffer. I do not doubt that a few young troublemakers are at work, as the older slaves know that violence will cost them more than they gain. "Who gib fish and cloth?" they ask. And I cannot see that trouble will benefit people of color. We will be caught in the middle of black and white, as always.

December 22

The mosquitoes are frightful. Yesterday Mrs. Jackson and I went for a long drive in the sociable, roads steep and rocky, and woods very thick. She very much feared the precipice on one side, with the river running below, but enjoyed the ferns and bamboo which grew along the way. Most of the time we meet only in the garden or in the hospital. She cannot, I know, reconcile my color with my educated ways. It is more usual in America for mulattoes to work in the fields than to be sent abroad to a school like Chelsea. I could tell her stories about the

loneliness of the sea voyages over and back and about my
mother, the mistress of a planter who sent me to school in England.

More news about the Salt Spring affair. The driver and his
wife and several others have escaped into the hills, fortunately,
as they would have fared badly at the hands of the militia, one
of whom was almost flung into a vat of boiling sugar by the
slaves.

I have made friends with the midwife, and am learning far
more than birthing from the old gossip. The missionaries are creating bad feeling by telling their congregations that they are not
freed men, while at the same time the peddlers are selling
papers saying that freedom has been granted by Parliament and
that the planters are endeavoring to keep the news from them.
She says that we have two or three Korymantyns here who are
part of a group ready to rise against the planters. I informed Mr.
Thaw, expecting him to dismiss this as nonsense, but he did not.
Evidently there is concern among his friends, although I think
they are more incensed with the missionaries than with the
slaves! This is what comes, they say, of allowing them to make
converts and start schools. They would like to forget the warriors
who lay shackled below deck in their kennels, arriving more
dead than alive for the seasoning period. No, I see both sides
and fear them both. The days of breeding lists, cart whips, and
treadmills is gone, but what is to come?

December 25

Christmas again, and not a happy time; the unrest has destroyed our meagre holiday spirit. Yesterday Mr. Thaw asked
me to bring to him the household silver and other valuables so
that he might hide them. It was all I could do not to laugh as he
took the silver, being careful that I should not see his collection
of Spanish gold chalices. Did he think that I, after being in the
house these days, would not have found them? He is quite right
not to trust anyone with these valuable cups, but I laugh at his
gullibility in thinking that he could hide anything from me. My
eyes were dazzled by this collection; I wonder how he came by
it? He is no thief, so it must have been purchased, perhaps from

a merchant or seaman down on his luck, for a fraction of its worth.

Mrs. Jackson gave up her amethysts with great lamentations and cries of "What is best to do?" She wishes that she could know where they have been hid. I could tell her, if I had a mind to. Last night Mr. Thaw returned late, his legs and arms a sorry mess from small sharp cuts. He had been on the cliffs, there could be no doubt about it. If only I knew the exact place!

Yesterday he debated whether to give the slaves the holiday to go to ground and collect their food, and I persuaded him to follow the custom, as though nothing untoward was in the air, and today Mrs. Jackson and I distributed the annual gifts. She has been helpful in sorting the piles of clothing, and is glad, I think, of something to occupy her time, as she is missing her little boy and is most anxious to leave Repose. I cannot see what in the world detains them and if I were in their places I would go as speedily as possible. However, there is no use in alarming her. There is an odd quiet about the blacks, a sullenness that I cannot like. Still, it may come right, as Mr. Thaw is known to his slaves. More than anything in the world, they fear a master they do not know. But nothing will save us if they break into the rum. Mr. Canning, at Dorset, is working his slaves into the ground, hoping to break their spirit, but I would rather rely on Mr. Thaw's reputation as a hard but fair master, though I may be proved wrong in the end.

Reluctantly, I put the journal down again, closing my eyes to ease the strain. I tried to picture the two women at Repose; my grandmother's consternation at finding herself in close company with a mulatto mistress, walking with her in the garden, conversing across the table at dinner, though there had been no mention that she dined with the Jacksons and Mr. Thaw. My ignorance was as great as my grandmother's in these matters. Little love was lost between the two, I felt. Martha had a rather self-satisfied manner and my grandmother had probably been quite right in labeling her an opportunist of the first degree. Although the hour was late, I could not leave this fascinating tale.

December 26

Boxing Day, and very quiet. I wish more of the tradesmen would come for their yearly presents as they do in England. It would make a diversion in our dullness. The Baptists are to dedicate a new chapel. If only we can keep control through the holidays—always an unsettling time. Then cropping will begin and no one will have time to think of freedom.

December 29

It has happened, what we dreaded, and I count myself lucky to have survived. The day of December 27th was spent as usual. The two men were much occupied in seeing that all was being made ready for cane cutting. They had dined at five, and I was in my room, working on my endless embroidery to pass the hours. It was long past sunset, and I was puzzled to see a glow in the sky, in the direction of Dorset. Suddenly I knew that it was fire, but there had been no shell blow to summon help—an ominous sign. Mr. Thaw came and bade me join the others in the living room. Mr. Fenwick the overseer and the two bookkeepers had also come to the Great House.

We waited, scarcely speaking, not knowing what we should fear. Then all on the sudden we heard the shell blow, not the usual long blow, but wild, uneven blasts.

"That will be the signal for our slaves to rise," said Mr. Thaw, and we extinguished all the candles in order that we should see better, and not be seen ourselves. The men went to the loop holes and Mrs. Jackson and I placed ourselves at opposite windows to watch the village. It was like the breathless moment before the hurricane strikes. I strained my eyes, but could see nothing out of the ordinary; a few lights, but no sounds of drumming or shouting. Perhaps they will stay quiet, I prayed. Perhaps the trouble is only at Dorset. But then Mrs. Jackson screamed out "Another fire!" There was a great light in the sky in the direction of Hamilton Hill, and we knew then for a certainty that the uprising had begun. The house servants had disappeared—a sign that Repose would not be spared.

I cannot describe my terror, waiting in the dark for the slaves to strike. The whole sky was aflame, as though every plantation within hundreds of miles had been fired. The conch shells could be heard in every direction. Mr. Thaw was cursing and swearing that he would save Repose or die in the attempt. The Jacksons, on the other hand, were far more anxious to save themselves, as I was. Mr. Fenwick, I believe, was not unhappy at the thought of shooting, while the bookkeepers said nothing, as usual.

To our surprise, though, the hour passed and there was no sign of trouble from the village. Even I, the least hopeful, began to think that we might be spared. Suddenly, Mr. Thaw groaned. Peering out, we could see the faint glow around the trash house. In seconds it was blazing up, the dry cane stalks making a perfect fuel.

"The fools!" he cried. "Their own houses will go next, and then the mill!" I could see that he could hardly restrain himself from running down the drive. The mill meant more to him than wife or child. But we were unprepared for the horror when the fire reached the animals. Some of the cattle broke loose, and we could hear the pounding of their hoofs as they ran down the hill to the road. Others were caught in the flames, and I can never forget their screams. No one who has heard animals burned alive can forget that sound. The night was so clear that we could see the slaves running about witlessly, shouting. I think they had finally realized their predicament—that they were in danger of losing their own houses and all their possessions.

It was just at that time, as I recall, that the argument started between Mr. Thaw and Mr. Jackson. Mr. Thaw was all for seizing on the slaves' confusion, and going down to organize the fire fighting, in hopes of saving the mill, and the year's cane crop. Mr. Jackson flatly refused to go, and with Mrs. Jackson in near hysterics, crying for her little boy, I could not blame him. But unfortunately the other men took his side. Mr. Thaw was out of his head with anger, calling him a Yankee coward. Mr. Jackson called Mr. Thaw a thief and a swindler, swearing that he would be off at the first opportunity and that he would sell his share of Repose—and not to Mr. Thaw's advantage. I began to understand why the Jacksons were at Repose, and I cannot guess what might have happened if the danger to us all had not been so great, the sky on fire, as though the end of the world had come.

Finally Mr. Thaw returned to his loop hole, and Mr. Jackson to his, and things were quiet between them for the rest of the night. Mrs. Jackson and I laid ourselves down on the long chairs, though once I slipped into the dining room for a sip of brandy. We could hardly credit it when the first light appeared and we could be sure that we would not be attacked. The Great House was untouched, though many of the other buildings had been burned to the ground. This sight set Mr. Thaw off again, but when he saw that the mill had been spared he began to talk of getting in the cane. He said that they would go out and find the oxen and build a new trash house and a new boiling house. As though no words had passed between them, he began to figure out the costs, and to tell Mr. Jackson how they would rebuild.

Mr. Jackson would not listen. He announced that he had no further interest in Repose, and that he expected to be repaid in full or else he would sell his share of land. He said that he and his wife would be leaving immediately, on foot if necessary. Poor man, he would have done better to hold his tongue.

I left them and went to rest in my room, afraid that after the terrible night I might give birth to a half-baby, and I must have slept soundly for a few hours. I was wakened by Mrs. Jackson beating on my door. "You must help me," she was crying. "My husband is very ill!" I went to their room, which overlooked the ocean. What a dreadful sight! Truly, I could not have imagined such agony. The spasms of pain were so terrible that I thought he must break his back, trying to escape them. Then for a few seconds he would lie still before it would begin again. The sweat poured from him, his voice came in a croak—it was spent with crying out.

I asked Mrs. Jackson when the pain had started. Three hours ago, she said. After I had gone, the men had finished the brandy and the remains of the dinner left on the sideboard when the servants ran away. Mr. Thaw had gone out with the other men, and her husband had been helping her pack when he was seized with pain and vomiting. She had given him paregoric, but it had not relieved him. "We must have the doctor," she kept saying, clutching my arm. "Someone must fetch the doctor. What do you think can be the matter?"

"Food spoils very quickly here," I told her, "if it has been left out," but another thought had crossed my mind. As for the doctor, who knew where he would be, after such a night? I was tempted to go to my room and stay out of this horrid affair, but out of pity I went in search of Mr. Thaw. He was in the cattle pens, and the stench almost turned my stomach. To my amazement, the head driver, most of the trade workers, and even some of the field hands were at work, setting things to rights as though nothing in the world had happened. I watched Mr. Thaw's face closely as I told him the news.

"Tell Cudjoe to ride for the doctor," he said. "God alone knows where he can be found, or if there's a place standing in the whole parish." And you would not ride out to see, I added silently. The whole parish could burn and you'd not care, as long as Repose was saved.

I returned to the house. In that short time Mr. Jackson had weakened terribly. He no longer had the strength to fight the pain and seemed to be losing consciousness, which was a mercy, in my opinion. Mrs. Jackson sat by his side; I think she realized that he was beyond hope. I went to the abandoned kitchen and made coffee. She looked at it and shuddered. I knew then that poison was on her mind. Suddenly she turned to me. "Martha," she said, "what shall I do? Tell me what I should do. Nothing matters to me now except getting back to my child. You'll soon have a child and then you will understand. You must help me."

I hardly knew what to answer. If my life had not depended on Mr. Thaw, I might have told her to go to the magistrate. But if Mr. Thaw should be convicted of poisoning, what of me? I had to think for both of us, and quickly.

"Mrs. Jackson," I said, "you must go home as soon as possible. You must convince Mr. Thaw that you have no interest in Repose. None whatsoever! For your own safety. Do you understand me?"

She recognized her own danger; she was not a stupid woman and her child was now her main concern. When her husband died, I pulled the sheet over his head and led her from the room. The burial took place early this morning and by noon she was gone; the young minister who read the service took her into town. There was no way to retrieve the amethysts and she didn't seem to care—in fact, she left most of her things behind. I did not attend the service, as Mr. Thaw ordered me to take this opportunity to go through her things and find any papers pertaining to Repose. I found nothing, and he was angry with me. But I am used to his tempers and pay no heed.

A man from Dorset came yesterday to tell us that nearly half the estates on our side of the island were put to the torch, but miraculously no whites were killed and our slaves were quick to blame the fire here on an outsider.

I laid down the journal. I had read enough. My grandfather had died with the sunlight pouring into the room—"the spasms of pain were so terrible that I thought he must break his back, trying to escape them."

My fingers were numb from gripping the pages. I had been angry, in James Thaw's sitting room, but now the fury was so strong that I clenched my teeth painfully to keep from crying.

"I know what I have to do," I whispered, staring at the journal. "I know what I have to do. I shall take this book back to the lawyer. The claim—and the journal—will be used as evidence. This matter is going to be settled, whatever the cost. The Jacksons are going to have what belongs to them, at last."

After a time I was able to calm myself. I gathered up the pile of books and thrust them back on the hall shelf. The journal I wrapped carefully in a handkerchief. No one must know that I had found this piece of damning evidence that had lain so long with the household accounts; neglect had played into my hands; I must not lose the advantage. But as I studied the room, there seemed to be no safe hiding place. Cubba was forever handling my things, Charmian was constantly polishing the floor with orange skins and coconut husks; it could not be kept under a piece of furniture. Finally I placed it behind the triple mirror of the dressing table that stood by the window. The chance of a general housecleaning was small, judging by the heavy dust that had accumulated in the corners.

The moonlight was so intense that I turned down my lamp and could see every object in the room, strangely distorted in the pale light. It was very late but still the drums went on, louder than before, drowning out the pleasant night sounds. I could not sleep and turned restlessly on the pillows, unable to put Martha's story out of my mind: the man's cries, the woman's despair— "What shall I do?"—Martha's search for the claim in the midst of the funeral service.

At last I fell into uneasy slumber, and I remember that I dreamed of figures in the room, moving silently, outlined against the open window.

CHAPTER 11

He that fleeth from the fear shall fall into the pit; and he that getteth out of the pit shall be taken in the snare.

JEREMIAH: *XLVIII, 44c.*

The caves where Nicholas and Molly had begged to picnic were not, in my opinion, proper caves, but sprawling formations of honeycombed limestone. The huge upended rocks and deep sink holes looked like a giant's plaything—toys that he had picked up and smashed in a fit of rage. But it was a fine place for a treasure hunt provided one did not lose oneself in the myriad hiding places.

Our little cavalcade had left Repose on horseback, preceded by the pack donkey with the luncheon. James and Serena were resting and Philip had declined to join us, so we were a party of ladies escorted by Nicholas, Hazard, and three boys who had gone ahead with the food.

I was delighted to leave Repose and go up into the mysterious hills—a very different aspect, I discovered, as we climbed above the tropical vegetation of the shoreline. The fields reminded me of my New England pastures; Mrs. Coulter named the trees and bushes. "Logwood, you know, and guava, but over there is star apple; do you see the gold on one side of the leaf? Sweetsop, genip—and look, a 'wait-a-bit' bush. Look at the thorns! If you should happen to fall in, you would have to 'wait-a-bit' until someone came along and pulled you out. And many of the grasses, Marietta, are used for bush tea. Scorn-the-earth, tree of life, cow tongue, snake leaf—I only know a few, I'm sorry to say."

I gazed about, enchanted with this small patch of field and with the flashing birds I was beginning to know by sight and name: the emerald tody, so much like my robin; the banana quit of the oriole family with yellow underparts. If there were only crows and maples here, I reflected, this bit of land would seem familiar.

The path became narrow as we climbed, single file, into the higher hills. The horses picked their way with care; there would have been no room for the buggy wheels as we wound around the side of the mountain, the overhanging rocks on one side, the river below on the other. Then thick green enclosed us again— trees intertwined with vines, as well as a profusion of ferns with great moist fronds, wedged tightly together into the rocky slope.

I had not imagined that we would go such a distance into these uninhabited hills. There had been only one cluster of houses far back—a few shacks huddled under the spreading trees, fenced in with "quick stick." The women and children sitting on the steps had been cleanly dressed, with an air of well-being that surprised me.

"It's the climate, of course," explained Mrs. Coulter, who was riding beside me. "It's impossible to starve here, as my father would say to anyone who brought up the subject of slavery. 'I'd rather be a slave at Repose,' he would tell him, 'than a free coal miner in England.' I realize, of course, that slavery had to end, no matter what the cost to their owners. But all the same, I agree with him. I would have preferred to be here, clothed and fed, than to see my children starving and dying of overwork in the mines or the mills. Very few ever died of overwork at Repose, even in the old days."

I laughed, thinking of the endless sociability under my window. "'I'll pick up the basket when I'm minded to'" seemed to be the motto.

"But up here—does anyone at all live up here?" I asked. "It's so wild, so very isolated."

"Oh no, I wouldn't think so. The maroons are not in this vicinity. Maroons, you know, were the slaves left behind by the

Spanish after the English occupation in the 1610s. They went up into the hills, and were joined over the years by numbers of runaway slaves, causing a great deal of trouble until they were made independent of the rest of the island. No, we never go farther than the caves and I always bring several of the men; one could get hopelessly lost in the hills, but it's become a tradition to come at least once over the holidays. It's a nice change from the water—and I rather like the feeling of being cut off from the rest of the world, don't you?"

The men had arrived at the caves ahead of us; the food had been unloaded from the panniers and Hazard had spread a cloth in a shady place. As always, Chitty had outdone herself. There were cool drinks in stone bottles, salads, fruits, sticky buns, cheeses, cakes, sandwiches—the same overabundance of food as at the Great House. Folding stools were produced, rugs, extra sunshades—and our horses were taken away to a distant pool.

We ate without ceremony, helping ourselves to whatever we fancied. Mrs. Coulter's eyes were bright with pleasure, like a child enjoying a special treat. How seldom she escaped from all her responsibilities, I reflected: the buffer for James's demands, Serena's hysterics, a mainstay for her grandchildren, and mistress of the shifting household. Most of all, I wondered at the quiet acceptance of Gerald's death, and Nanny's. Where had she found the strength to put the needs of others before her own? I wished that I might ask, as one might ask for a treasured recipe.

My feelings about the Thaws had undergone a profound change in the early hours of the morning. I no longer felt like an intrusive guest, paying my way by helping with Nicholas. No, I was now on an equal footing, a person to be reckoned with. The intense anger was gone, and my affection for Mrs. Coulter, Molly, and Nicholas remained. But it was just as well that I had not seen James Thaw that morning. He was "sporting the oak," Mrs. Coulter had said, explaining that he was not to be disturbed except in dire emergency. Pretentious little man, I thought. If I had appeared in his sitting room, waving my claim to Repose, he would not "sport the oak"! But this was no longer a matter that we could settle between us, thanks to his father.

As I finished a last bit of cake, I glanced at Pamela, observing that she had chosen a place where she would not have to face me across the rug, the interloper to whom Stephen was paying court. Like James, she had the annoying facility of never appearing untidy; her light habit fitted perfectly. Molly and I, on the other hand, were rigged out in two old skirts that bunched up around our makeshift side saddles. Fine feathers, but your great-grandfather was a murderer, I said to her silently. How would that impress your crowd of eligible suitors?

Even Cubba had felt the change in me, the anger that needed some form of expression. I had waked heavy-eyed from lack of sleep when she came in with my tea and I had not greeted her in my slightly self-conscious manner; instead, she was told bluntly to go away and come back later. The eyes had rolled, and the lips had pouted, to no avail. No longer was I in awe of the family or their servants.

Molly had busied herself with the treasure hunt, first sending Nicholas down to the horses, and then putting the treasure, a bag of leftover Christmas candy, under Mrs. Coulter's skirts.

"Don't send him too far into the woods, Molly," she advised. "We don't want him running off in the excitement and losing himself."

"No, but the clues can't be too close, either, or it won't be any fun for him. Marietta and Pamela will have to scream and pretend they're on his heels."

"Can he read the messages, dear?"

"I've drawn them, Granny. The hollow log and so forth. I'm ready. Come on, Nicholas!" she shouted. He came quickly, eyes round with excitement. I needn't have been so concerned with James Thaw's verdict, I realized. He had accepted it quite easily when told about our trip to the caves. At his age, one treasure hunt was almost as rewarding as another. But I made a point to remind him of his promise. "You'll not go to the cliffs alone, Nicholas, will you? You'll remember your promise to me?"

"*Yes,* Marietta! Why do you keep asking me? I *promised!*"

"Now listen to me, Nicholas," said Molly. "These are the rules —when I say 'go,' everyone runs to find the first clue, which is in a cave. From then on, no help, not even for you, Nicholas. This is a really hard treasure hunt. Now on your marks, set, go!"

Bless you, Molly, I thought as Nicholas sprang off like a hare toward the nearest rocks; we could hear him scrabbling around, talking loudly to himself. Pamela grimaced, lifting the hem of her riding skirt; I shall let her go well ahead of me, I decided. I had been strangely tired all day, and started slowly to the distant caves; underground tunnels, Nicholas had said, with bat droppings everywhere, and I was thankful that we were not allowed to hunt there. I watched a pair of banana quits argue for a place on a nearby branch until a shout from Molly sent me reluctantly on my way again. It was cooler near the rocks and I pushed the sun hat back from my eyes and peered gingerly under a narrow overhang. No paper clues there, nor in the sink holes beside it. The other two were off to my right somewhere; I could hear Nicholas' shrieks as Pamela closed in on him; she was an affectionate sister, I had to admit. The Coulter family sense of obligation was strong.

Yawning, I sat down with my head against a rock. I'll close my eyes for a second, I decided, and pretend that I've found a clue. But I must have dozed, for when I raised my head, Pamela was standing above me, an expression of disdain on her face.

"We're done," she murmured, "and Granny wants to leave. You *are* getting into a habit of going off." I scrambled to my feet and we stood eye to eye for a second.

"It's nothing," I said lightly. "I waited to give you a head start; I thought perhaps you needed one." Her gaze did not waver, and we returned to the others in silence.

"I won, Marietta!" shouted Nicholas. "You're the biggest slow poke. We thought you were lost!"

"Lost! I'm not quite such a ninny as that. What lovely candy, enough to last you all week."

"It's half gone already," said his grandmother, smiling. "Now I think we had better be on our way, before the sun starts to go down. Oh dear, I hate to think our picnic is over for another year. Nicholas, run and tell Hazard and the boys to bring the horses, will you, darling?"

We mounted and turned the horses' heads toward the path,

the donkey and his panniers going ahead. Quite a procession we were—Mrs. Coulter and Pamela on the riding horses, Nicholas on his pony, Molly on a work animal that belonged between the shafts. I followed her on an equally dispirited beast and Hazard brought up the rear on a mule. The going was slow, as we picked our way down the rocky path, and I dozed again, moving loosely with the swaying motion, letting the reins hang slack.

The disaster, when it struck, took me utterly by surprise. My stodgy horse let out a scream of pain and began to dance about, as if to rid himself of an unbearable aggravation. I grasped the pommel of the saddle, trying to gather up the reins as we continued in a whirling jig. Then to my horror, he plunged sideways onto a small path that branched off from the road at this juncture, the only avenue of escape from his torment. I could hear the others shouting, but I was helpless as we careened along; I could do nothing but try to apply the fragments of horsemanship that flashed through my mind: to keep my head down so that I would not be struck by a branch, to turn the horse, to saw on the bit, to loosen my foot—all quite useless. There was no place to turn; the bit might have been a piece of straw for all the good it did me as we plunged farther and farther into the wood. I think I was screaming, though I have no recollection of it as I clung for my life to the pommel.

We fled on. I sensed that he was tiring; lather spattered my face as I hung low on his neck and his breath came in heaving snorts. In the end, he stumbled and lost his footing. Mercifully, my simple saddle lacked the strap that would have held my foot tightly in place, and I rolled over onto the ground, the breath jarred out of me by the fall. When I raised my head, he was trotting back down the path, reins dangling from his neck. I called wildly, but he kept going and soon was lost from sight.

My first feeling was one of simple relief at finding myself alive. I stood up cautiously, amazed that nothing was broken or even sprained. Then, tying my hat firmly on my head, I started back along the path. The others would have rushed after me, I knew that we would soon come face to face; and I hoped that they would not be alarmed by the sight of the riderless horse. "Coming," I called. "I'm all right, I'm coming!"

It must have been a quarter of an hour later when the nagging suspicion that I might be going in the wrong direction crept into my mind. There had been no time to notice landmarks on my headlong journey; it seemed to me that the horse had gone in a straight line, but as several small paths converged, I was not sure. He might have veered off to left or to right, and I would not have known. Praying that my sense of orientation had not failed me, I chose the path that showed the most signs of use. It went raggedly along and I followed the turns, calling out and listening for an answering cry. The birds taunted me from the trees; there was no other sound.

Still, I would not admit to myself that I had missed the way. "Here I am!" I yelled at the top of my voice. "Here I am!" and I ran on, assuring myself that I would soon meet the others.

The trees along the path were thick, but not unlike those that separated Repose from Anna Thaw's land. I had become accustomed to the heavy foliage, so I thought. Suddenly, without warning, I stood in a narrow passage; the branches joined over my head in an impenetrable tangle; my feet sank into foul-smelling mud, and moisture dripped from above. This was what I had feared: the heart of the woods; the hidden evil I had dreaded in my first hour on the island. Holding my breath to keep from screaming, I turned back. Several slimy cords had fallen as I passed, almost cutting off my escape. I pushed at one, expecting my hand to blister, and another took its place. Panic overcame me then, and I ran in blind, unreasoning flight. I ran until I thought my heart would burst; each breath was a torment, and the trees became a solid, blurred line. I must flee this place, and I would run until I collapsed.

When the path dropped sharply I was too blinded to see and I pitched forward, catching at the roots to break my fall. For some time I lay stunned, wondering when I would feel the crippling pain. It was the warmth of the sun on my neck that roused me, at last. There had been no sun in the woods.

I pulled myself up quickly and stared. My flight had ended abruptly in a small meadow, a tiny round circlet in the hills; the contours of the land had changed, as though the tunnel formed a distinct boundary. This was new country. Although the hills overlapped one another around the narrow valleys, the earth had been compressed and the hills pushed upward.

I dusted myself off and tried to collect my wits; the extreme fright I had experienced could not have been sustained for long, no matter how grave the situation. As calmly as possible, I tried to assess my situation. Look for another path, I told myself. Where there are paths, there are people who use them. Moving away from the spot where I had fallen, I skirted the meadow and was delighted to see faint tracks leading into the woods—ordinary woods—but in any case, I had no choice. What sort of people would live here, I wondered, as I trudged along. You must not show fear, I told myself. Speak quietly, don't stammer, and above all, don't run.

But there was no sign of the living. Like a thread winding on a spool, I went around one little hill, then the path dipped down to another meadow exactly like the first. Then on again to another path, another hill. Many of the trees were familiar friends —flame of the forest, casuarina, mountain apple, mango, and I heard the comforting soft voice of a dove. Strangely, I did not feel either lost or lonely. My feet touched the ground lightly and without effort. I could have gone on endlessly, surrounded by such beauty. Even the color in the sky, forerunner of sunset, did not really alarm me; I ignored the thought of the approaching night.

It was the bird calls that first warned me of the footsteps. Listening, I became aware of the steady, muffled tread behind me. I stopped, and there was no sound. I repeated this procedure— walk and stop, walk and stop. Someone was following me. With huge relief I opened my mouth to shout—and stayed silent. Who was this person with the furtive step? Why did he not call out my name?

I lost the floating, even pace, and hurried forward, stumbling in my haste. The sky was deepening into a pale gray, and the potoo, the fading-light bird, was barking his gruff "he-whoo" as an unpleasant expression came to mind: "the hour between the dog and the wolf." Should I keep ahead of the stranger, or wait? Should I look for a place to hide? My feet were dragging with weariness as the trees thinned, showing that another meadow lay before me.

Another meadow, another hill—on and on into the night I would go. Why hadn't I waited, miles away, where the horse had thrown me? It had been stupid to think that I could have found my way back to the road; much better to have stayed where I was, until a search party could be organized. What an unfortunate end to the treasure hunt, I thought, and all the time we worried about Nicholas losing himself.

The path was widening with unmistakable signs of use. I drew a deep breath and listened. There were voices ahead, many voices. A village with women and children where I would be protected by the sheer number of people. They would stare at me, no doubt, and point to my hair, but they would surely lead me back to the road. Here was deliverance from the footsteps and from the night. With an enormous sense of triumph, I gathered up my skirts and sped toward safety.

CHAPTER 12

The offense of sorcery is so vast and so comprehensive that it includes in itself almost every other crime.

PAUL LAYMAN:
Processus juridicus contra sagus et veneficos,
1629

A huge cottonwood tree marked the center of the large, open clearing; there was no village, no women and children. In my elation, I had run forward from the sheltering trees and now stood at the edge of the field, staring at the extraordinary sight before me. Men, hundreds of men, were dancing and making a sound that was something between a choke and a dog's bark—the sound I had heard from the path. As my vision cleared, I began to distinguish different patterns: all were black, naked to the waist, and wearing handkerchiefs tied about their heads in precisely the same way. Like large beetles they bobbed about, reaching up as though trying to pull unseen objects from the air. Another larger group was engaged in races. Each man carried a small box which he waved frantically as he ran and barked with desperate urgency. As I watched in stunned astonishment, I became aware of the focus of this wild activity. Directly under the wide branches of the cottonwood stood a masked figure, taller than the others. His hands grasped the ankles of another man whom he was whirling about in dizzying circles—faster and faster. Then slowly, he lowered the body until it lay unmoving on the ground, senseless or dead. Now the tall man began to dance—bending down to place something in the victim's mouth, jumping away and returning again as his cohorts continued their own racing and leaping.

I stood near the trees, not knowing what I should do, nor how to interrupt this frenzied ritual. I supposed that it must be a ritual, and tried to remember if Stephen had mentioned an obeah dance. It could go on all night, I thought weakly, it could go on endlessly, like the drums, and I'm tired, so tired.

Then as if by unseen signal, the dancing stopped abruptly. The men joined hands to form a large circle around the tree; the barking ceased. Now the head man began to wail loudly, stamping his feet, and as his chant rose in pitch and tempo the human circle began to move in a rhythmic rotation. Arms and legs flailing the air, the leader was working himself up to a crescendo; I expected to see him fall to the ground in a fit. But then he slowed, like a top running down, and went back to the prostrate figure, which had not moved throughout the performance. With a great cry, he seized the body in his arms, raised it, gestured triumphantly, and stepped away. Miraculously the man did not fall but remained on his feet, grinning and shaking his head in a stunned, sheepish way. A great sigh rose from the onlookers. They dropped hands, and, one by one, flung themselves down on the ground as if exhausted.

The ritual was over, and with it my momentary respite. Unless I crept back into the woods, I would soon be noticed. It was a dreadful choice: to remain at the edge of the field or to hide; to brave these primitive men, or the blackness of the night. I could not make the choice, and stood motionless, waiting.

A few seconds passed, not more, although they seemed like hours. Then one man pivoted in my direction and pointed; the others, lying on the ground, grew rigid. There was no sound whatsoever, far more ominous than shouts. Slowly they rose and faced me—a mass of bodies in silent confrontation. The faces under the bandannas were expressionless, but I was conscious of anger. I had spied upon these men, I had watched their secret meeting. It would have been far better, I now realized, if I had come running from the woods in obvious fright and startled them. To stand and observe had been a horrible mistake.

Commonplace phrases came flooding into my mind: "I am lost and I need help. Someone is following me. Take me back and you will be well paid." I walked forward a few steps, toward the leader. Still no one moved. It occurred to me that they might never before have seen a white woman; perhaps I appeared as an evil spirit, with my pale hair and skin. I stretched out my arms in a pleading gesture, trying to convey my helplessness. The leader's face was hidden behind the mask; I knew that he was the one I must reach.

"Help me, please. Help me," I said, forcing myself to move forward, willing him to understand. Another long moment passed; the hostility surrounded me, invisible yet solid as a wall. Now I pointed in the direction of the path, and ran several steps, beckoning him to join me. It was no use. The men began to fan out around the field, forming a human net, hemming me in.

The leader began to speak softly in guttural tones accompanied with gestures—slowly, then gradually increasing in tempo. I knew without the faintest doubt that something terrible was being planned for me; when he brought his followers to a certain pitch they would obey him. The only question was: how would I be punished?

Until the past August I had thought little about death, and seldom about my own. If pressed, I would probably have pictured a very old, white-haired lady drifting peacefully into a coma. "She's going," whispers the nurse, and a sound of suppressed sobs rises from the children and grandchildren gathered around the bed. Or after giving birth to the beautiful little boy or girl, the anguished young husband clutches my hand. "I won't let you go, Marietta—you cannot leave me, beloved." Never, never in a faraway field, at the hands of a savage tribe.

The blood was going from my head, but though I felt faint, my mind continued to function clearly. I was stricken with a sense of frightful waste. I would not see Stephen again; there would be no Venice or Paris for us. My poor mother—the Jacksons would never receive their share of Thaw land. My heart began to beat erratically. The leader's voice was rising wildly. He shouted a question and the answer came back with a shriek. The dialogue was repeated, over and over, and the men began to stamp. Soon they would break loose and come toward me, a wave of running bodies. Any thought of meeting them with head held high vanished as my knees collapsed. I crouched on the ground like a wild animal, hands over my eyes, trying to make myself invisible. Oh God, I prayed, let it be over quickly. That's all I ask—let it be over quickly.

Pounding feet behind me—I cried out, anticipating the deadly blow; it did not come. After a few seconds, I became aware that the shrieking and shouting had suddenly ceased; the field of men was silent. Slowly, I raised my head, and then pulled myself up onto my knees. The man who had run past me stood by the leader; they were facing one another in a challenging stance. I brushed at my eyes, scarcely able to believe what I saw: the man was Hazard; he must have followed me through the hills. But why in God's name hadn't he called out and prevented me from going so far? Would he now become a victim of these men?

As I watched in anguish he began to speak, pointing to me and telling a story with an authority that seemed to impress the men, for they listened attentively. I could not understand a word, but as surely as rain sinks into parched earth, the anger began to evaporate from the field. After what seemed an endless time, Hazard stopped and bowed ceremoniously to the leader, who bowed to him and signaled with his hand. In seconds the field was deserted; the fan of men had slipped away into the woods.

I had been kneeling motionless, and now I stood up, trembling from head to foot. "Hazard," I whispered, as he ran toward me. "Hazard. They were going to kill me. How could you—how did you—"

"Later, Missie, not now." He pulled at my arm. "Hurry, it be dark soon. Hurry!" The fading light, and the urgency in his voice brought forth my last reserve of strength. I followed him to the path and we began the journey back through the twisting hills, the narrow valleys, the tiny rounds of meadows. On and on.

Once or twice he halted to let me catch my breath and also, I felt, to listen.

"Why didn't you call?" I asked him, weakly. "If only you had called out, I would have stopped. I never would have seen those men."

"Later, Missie." And he hurried me forward again. When we came to the entrance to the tunnel, I pulled back, shaking my head.

"I won't go in there. No, I will not!"

"Yes, Missie. Only way to road. Only way." The smell was strong in the rising vapor of the night, a choking, putrid stench. I clung to Hazard's shirt as he groped his way forward through the vines, unnatural ropes that swung down as though to prevent our return, but in a surprisingly short time we had made our way through them and were embarking on the last long stretch of level path. He had been wise to hurry me; we were going blindly, guided by the dark masses of trees on either side. In a few minutes the vague shapes would have been lost in blackness.

The reserve of strength that had brought me back through the hills was gone; my legs would not go where I wished, and without Hazard's supporting hand I would have fallen.

"Look, Missie!" he said suddenly. "Look, lights on the road. They are waiting." Ahead, a short distance ahead, the glow rose up out of the night. With a final effort I set my feet to moving on the path like mechanical toys, jerking along, closer and closer, until finally we emerged from the trees into lights and voices and a stir of excitement. "There they are! He found her, he found her. . . . Look oh, look! Missie and Hazard!" Molly flung herself at me.

"Marietta, what *happened?* The horse came back hours ago! Then Hazard went after you and we went back to get Philip and the others; we've been waiting until it was dark to go into the woods, so that you could see the flares. Oh, Marietta, we've been so *frightened.*"

"All right then, Molly. Let her sit down, over here." I recognized Philip's voice, and his looming height. "Are you all right, Marietta? Not hurt? Hold the torch, Molly. Let me look at her."

In the flaring light I could see the concern in his eyes as he looked down into my face.

"I'm all right," I whispered. "It's my legs—I walked so far, and then—and then—" I put my head in my hands.

"But you're not injured?"

"No."

"Good. Drink this." He held a flask to my lips, raising my head, and I swallowed, choked, and pushed it away.

"Never mind that. We must go, quickly! There were men and they were going to kill me and then Hazard came—they may have followed us. You don't understand—not just a few men— *hundreds* of them." I heard my voice rising shrilly.

"Yes, we are going, don't worry." Phillip turned to the others. "Well done, Hazard. Sam, you and Quaco lift Miss Jackson; I'll take her up in front of me. Hazard can ride Sam's donkey." His commands were hastily carried out and I found myself handed up into Philip's arms as another man held the horse's head.

It was an odd feeling, to be in a man's arms, a man whom I had taken great pains to avoid. It would have suited me better to ride alone, and I tried not to lean back against him. But to my dismay, I began to shiver with a violence that could not be concealed.

"Relax, Marietta," he said quietly over my head, as the horse began to lurch down the steep path, picking his way in the dark with care. "Try to relax. Imagine that you're back at Repose now, in your bed. Don't think about what happened; you can tell us later. You're back in your bed, asleep. You have walked a long way, and you are very tired, very tired and sleepy." As he talked, my head nodded and before long it was resting on his shoulder. The hours of running and walking, the wrenching falls, the shock of facing death overcame my resistance. I wished that the arms around me were Stephen's arms, but I was glad, as a child is glad, to be held securely, safe from the night and its unknown dangers.

Lights were shining out at Repose as we entered the courtyard. Cubba took charge of me with a fine air of importance, removing my torn clothes and helping me up into bed. She would have an attentive audience later, I knew, as she described the legs covered with bruises, the ruined shoes. Mrs. Coulter had given strict orders that no one was to visit until I had eaten and rested; it was several hours later when she came to the room.

"How are you feeling, Marietta? Better? We are all on tenterhooks to hear your story—where you went and how Hazard found you. Oh, my dear, the thought of you lost in the hills! The horse took off so suddenly, and we were so helpless. Then the hours of waiting after the search party left. Well, I have never been so thankful, the joy of seeing you coming into the courtyard on Philip's horse." The tears in her eyes surprised me; I could not imagine Mrs. Coulter in tears.

"I've given you so much worry. I'm sorry."

"It doesn't matter, not in the least, now that you're back safe and sound. Do you feel like talking? My brother is waiting in the hall. He has been very anxious and concerned."

James Thaw. I had vowed that I would treat him with coldness, but when he appeared, carrying a bottle of his best port, I could not summon back last night's hatred. The narrow escape had damped down all other emotions.

"She's very pale, Elizabeth," he said, handing me a glass. "Drink this up, Marietta; it will do you good. And now tell us exactly what happened to you. We have been in almost unbearable suspense."

The story was a simple one: a bolting horse, the flight along the paths and the hills—I could not bring myself to describe the tunnel—and finally the dreadful ritual. I noticed James Thaw's shocked expression as I described the men with the boxes, the whirling victim, the grunting noises.

"Boxes, you say? Did they wear handkerchiefs tied round their heads?"

"Yes, they did. In exactly the same way."

"And the man stood up, though he seemed to be dead?"

"I thought he *was* dead, until the leader with the mask put him on his feet. Why, do you know who they were, Mr. Thaw? What they were doing?"

James Thaw did not answer. Rising from the chair, he went to the window, rocked back and forth on his heels, and then turned.

"What you saw, Marietta, was the Myal death and resurrection ritual." There was silence in the room. I had never heard of the Myal, but there was no mistaking the awe in his expression and voice.

"Myal," said Mrs. Coulter, slowly. "Isn't that—aren't they something to do with obeah?"

"It was an African cult that became very popular after the Emancipation. I didn't know it still existed, frankly. But I've read about the barking noise, and the racing and the little boxes made to represent coffins."

"*Coffins?*"

"Part of the ritual. The witch doctor, or chief, was displaying his supernatural powers, you see. The man was dead, and he brought him back to life by a trick, no doubt, using a powerful drug. I have never heard of anyone actually seeing the Myal rites. Or, if anyone saw them, he did not live to tell the tale."

I gasped, and saw Mrs. Coulter's hand go to her throat.

"James, what are you saying? That Marietta would have been killed simply because she came upon them accidentally?"

"I most certainly am. You don't grasp the situation, Elizabeth. These are primitive people, living far back in the hills. They undoubtedly prize their isolation, which allows them to practice the old customs, and the last thing they want is to draw attention to themselves. Suddenly a white woman appears and observes them. Do they want her to go free, to return and possibly tell the authorities what is taking place? Certainly not, and what could be easier than to kill her on the spot, make an end to it then and there. Is that your feeling, Marietta? That they would have killed you?"

I felt a coldness on my spine, remembering the seconds of waiting before Hazard appeared. Killed me? There had not been the slightest doubt in my mind.

"I'm sure they were going to kill me. They were just reaching fever pitch—and then Hazard ran by."

"Ah, Hazard. I find this strange, very strange. Hazard arrives miraculously, having let you go on ahead, talks to them in their own language and persuades them to let you go free. You say that he was just behind you when the horse bolted? At the one entrance to the woods? Something very peculiar must have put that horse into a frenzy; cart horses do not run, as a rule."

"He was behind me, yes. But I thought the horse had been stung, the way he acted." James turned to his sister.

"How did Hazard seem, Elizabeth, after the horse disappeared?"

"Calm, but very much perturbed, I thought. He went after Marietta on the mule, and then in a few minutes he was back; the mule could not catch up and he didn't know which path she had taken. We waited, and then the horse came back. We were all dreadfully alarmed—Nicholas was crying. We decided that I should bring Nicholas back and get help, and Hazard volunteered to go into the woods again, alone. He knew the countryside better than anyone else, he said; if people went in all directions there would be even more confusion. So I let him go. It seemed best, at the time."

"Yes, of course. But why did he follow at a distance, letting her walk so far? I will have to talk to Hazard. You were spared, Marietta, and that is a great mercy. But I am greatly concerned. I'm sorry to say this, but I very much fear that you are still in danger from the Myals."

I lay quietly, aware of the creeping chill.

"Still in danger? What do you mean?" Mrs. Coulter's voice trembled. He turned to me, running his hand over his face in an uncharacteristic gesture.

"A pity to alarm you, after what you've been through. But shall I be blunt? Because of Hazard, you were not killed this afternoon. But you are, nonetheless, a continuing danger to them. I am sure of this. As long as you are alive and able to talk, you are a threat to these people."

"But—what should I do? Surely they wouldn't come here."

"We shall see to it that they don't. I will talk to Hazard at once. Then I shall alert the village and everyone on the place to be on the lookout for strangers, for the odd circumstance, for anything out of the ordinary. Marietta, you must be cautious; you must not leave Repose without protection. As they say, 'forewarned is forearmed.' I wish you could put this unpleasantness behind you, my dear, but I know what I'm talking about. These are strange, primitive men."

He left the room, and I watched him go with confused feelings. There was logic in his fears; I was grateful for his concern, and yet I could not imagine being threatened at Repose, so full of people and activity, so far removed from a lonely meadow in the hills. Mrs. Coulter seemed to share my bewilderment; she walked about absent-mindedly, touching my brushes on the dressing table, straightening a cushion.

"My brother is right," she said finally, "and you must be extremely careful, Marietta. On the other hand, he has had such worries—first Gerald, then Nicholas, and now you, this afternoon."

I raised myself on the pillows; an idea had occurred to me. "I know. I can understand that he must be very upset. Especially after the business of Miss Anna and the groom. He has often warned me, you know, that she wants to destroy this branch of the family, that she would harm Nicholas if she could. I wondered if perhaps he was, well, overanxious, and I wanted to ask Molly, but somehow that didn't seem right." I paused, hoping that Mrs. Coulter would speak out on this matter which had greatly puzzled me. There might never be a better opportunity. She was pulling at the jalousie cord; I could see her fine profile, the eyes considering the situation.

"I'm glad you didn't ask Molly. She's too young to be involved in these complications; and even at your age—well, I wonder if you would be able to understand, Marietta. Your life has been so far removed from ours, such different standards and customs."

"I could try."

"Yes, and I believe we owe you an explanation, after the past few days. You must be very much confused, as well as frightened. Now, I know nothing about the Myals, my dear, but I can tell you something of the Thaw family history." She crossed the room and settled herself in the long chair. I raised myself on the pillows. Mrs. Coulter rarely spoke at length. Her story would warrant my closest attention.

"I was the younger sister," she began, folding her hands in her lap. "I wasn't told much about family matters, no more than was thought fit for my ears, but you know what children are; they have a special awareness and there's very little that you can keep from them." She paused, looking up into the shadows of the high ceiling.

"My mother left the island when I was ten, and I spent most of the year with her in London, with long holidays here at Repose. After I married, we came with the children for Christmas. My father died in 1844, still with a great sense of a family dynasty, hoping that his children and grandchildren would come to appreciate Repose and his life's work. The Christmas check custom was his way of ensuring a bond between the Thaws and the estate." She sighed, and then began to speak in a different tone.

"Marietta, I wish I could paint a picture, describe Repose in the old days, when I was a girl—the great wealth, the parties, the visiting back and forth among the big families—such gaiety, compared to today. But under the lavishness there was enormous strain—sickness, for example. So many people died, and died so suddenly. Friends would come to dine, and a few days later we would hear that they were dead of the fever. A slight headache, nothing at all, was often the first symptom of a fatal attack. And I suppose that because life was so precarious, there was much overindulgence. Some of the men drank heavily, starting with a planter's punch when they came in to second breakfast, and on into the night. We children used to laugh, to see them hoisted into their carriages and taken home. The ladies did not drink openly, but their vice was almost worse. My mother told me long afterward that she and a number of her friends could not have existed here without their laudanum—tincture of opium—which they carried everywhere with lumps of sugar. I think it was why she left the island; she became dependent on the drug and feared she would never rid herself of the habit. Yet without it, she could not endure the trials of running the household and dealing with the slaves; there was no time for painting or music, pastimes she could enjoy in London. And always the uncertainty —one year, falling prices, the next a storm to ruin the crop; once it was a plague of rats—" She stopped speaking and looked up at the ceiling again. I lay silent, hardly breathing for fear of interrupting her train of thought. Gaiety, tragedy, unexpected death.

After a long moment, she continued, hesitantly:

"There was another problem, Marietta, far more demoralizing than liquor or drugs. The men, some of them, kept one or more mistresses. 'Custom of the country' it was called—acceptable, and even encouraged by a few white wives. For the black and colored women it was their only chance to rise in the world, and oh, their children! Many were beautiful, though frail and highstrung, but all, all of them were at the mercy of the father's whims. Some would be domestics while others were sent abroad to be educated. Some had their freedom bought for them, others starved. Now you may wonder why I'm telling you this, but I'm coming to the point in a roundabout way. There were certain rules among the planters, unwritten but carefully observed: one was that a man did not marry his mistress.

"Now my father was a self-made man, determined to see his children do well for themselves. He adhered to the unwritten rules and expected his sons to do the same. I don't know when my brother met Anna; probably at her family's house on one of his long holidays."

"Her family's house? But weren't they colored?"

"On the mother's side. She was a fey old lady, not married to Anna's father. He had come to the island as a trustee for one of the absentee landlords and he was a substantial person in his way. Charles might easily have gone into town for an evening of cards or dancing at their house, though she would never have been asked to Repose. Charles was a rebellious and sensitive boy. He resented my father's heavy-handedness, and something about Anna appealed to him."

"Did you meet her? What was she like?"

"Thin, with a strange sternness. I was surprised at the attraction, I must admit, for he generally liked pretty girls, but perhaps he had need of her strength. I have only seen her two or three times because, you see, my father would have nothing more to do with Charles when he married her. It was an unforgivable blot on the Thaw image."

"But he gave them the land next to Repose."

"He had already divided the land as an inducement to keep Charles on the island; he couldn't take it back. I was here, in fact, when my father heard about Anna. He tried to reason with Charles, to force him to set up housekeeping with her, but Charles was insulted, and Anna's hold on him was too strong. It was dreadful, when Father finally understood that they were to be married. He swore that Anna had bewitched Charles and cut him off from the Thaw family. Charles and Anna withdrew to their own place and seldom left it. They had one son, Stephen Thaw's father, who was sent away as a child to escape the stigma of being disowned by the Thaws. Even in England, he was too proud to call on us and he never came back to the island. James was particularly hard hit by all this as he was only two years older than Charles, and they had been fond of each other. He has always blamed Anna for the loss of his brother."

I had followed Mrs. Coulter's story with attention, but my question was still unanswered.

"I can see that," I said thoughtfully. "It must have been very difficult. But what I don't understand—Miss Anna did nothing to hurt the family in all those years, did she? Why is there such fear of her now?"

"Ah." Mrs. Coulter unclasped her hands and spread them in a gesture of uncertainty. "How can I answer? Anna has an odd reputation. The black people have always gone to her for help, and there is a feeling in some quarters that she practices obeah, though it may only be that she cures them with medicinal herbs. After Charles died she lived alone quietly, and I would have said she meant no harm to us. Then two years ago the grandson, whom she had never seen, began to visit her."

"You don't think *he* is involved, do you?" I was almost afraid of the answer; Mrs. Coulter's judgment weighed strongly with me.

"No, I think quite certainly not. He's a talented and presentable young man; the children meet him in London, and I see no reason why they should not; there is no need for this quarrel to be kept alive in their generation. He has made his own place in the world and I don't think he would have any reason at all to hurt us. But for Anna—it's quite a different matter. Who knows what hatred, what grudges she has held over the years? And now she is reunited with a grandson who is not received at Repose. She may want revenge for his sake, she may even want to see him established as master of Repose—who knows? No, I can't forget that we have had a strange series of tragedies, and if Anna is responsible, there will certainly be more, for she would be a most relentless enemy. I truly pray that James is mistaken about her, but nothing can be proved, one way or the other."

There was a long silence; then Mrs. Coulter rose. "How late it is! You should have been asleep long ago. I can't think why I talked so much, except that I hope it has helped to put the afternoon out of your mind. Don't dwell on it, my dear. It was a freakish accident—one that could never happen again, a story to tell your grandchildren. Now sleep well, and don't get up tomorrow until you are quite rested." She came to the bed and adjusted the coverlet, touched me gently on the cheek, and departed, closing the door quietly behind her. Dear Mrs. Coulter—she was right. Such a freakish accident could never happen again.

The door creaked open and Molly peered in. "What on earth have you been talking about all this time? I thought that Granny would never leave. Oh, Marietta, you'll die, positively die, when you hear what's happened!"

I sighed, too tired for Molly's ebullience. "Well, what *has* happened? Tell me, quickly; I can't keep my eyes open any longer."

"You'll open them wide enough when you see this!" And she waved a large white envelope at me. "It's from Stephen. One of his men brought it over. The idiot was supposed to give it to Cubba, I think, but instead he came right to the front steps and asked for you."

"Oh no! Who was there?"

"Not Uncle James, luckily. He's giving Hazard the third degree in his sitting room; I heard him having at it. But Philip was there, and Pamela. You should have seen their faces! I snatched it out of the man's hand and said I'd take it to you. Marietta, he really must be madly in love to do such a thing—there's never been any going back and forth between the servants."

I took the envelope from her and opened it, trying to ignore the conspiratorial gleam in her eye.

My dear Marietta,

My man told me that you were lost in the hills and now the news has come that you are safely back. I cannot describe my feelings, first of horror, then relief. You must realize that mermaids should exert the utmost caution when venturing out of their element!

We must meet tomorrow without fail. Surely with Molly's help you can slip away for a few moments. I shall be waiting in the woods opposite the bridge from five o'clock on. Do you know Browning's "Song"?

> Because you spend your lives in praising;
> To praise, you search the wide world over;
> Then, why not witness, calmly gazing,
>   If earth holds aught—speak truth—above her?
> Above this tress, and this I touch
> But cannot praise, I love so much!

Yours always,
Stephen

I read the letter over quickly, trying to absorb the delicate meanings. I would meet him tomorrow. Nothing on earth could stop me.

"Well, what does he say? Or shouldn't I ask?"

"He wants me to meet him tomorrow afternoon at five, beyond the bridge and you're to help me." Molly's eyes grew round.

"Lawks! A secret rendezvous? Marietta, didn't I tell you I felt something would happen between you? I knew it! Of course I'll help. Nicholas—I'll keep him out of the way; no, I've a better idea. We should all start down to the stream together, in case anyone is watching; then Nicholas and I can go to the barns. That will put Pamela and Philip or anyone else off the scent!"

I stirred uncomfortably. "Really, Molly, I'm not going to act like a criminal. No, don't misunderstand, but to be too dramatic would spoil everything. I won't flaunt my meeting Stephen, but I won't hide it, either."

"A meeting in the woods. Oh, this *will* be fun!" She paced about, humming the wedding march, holding up an imaginary train. Somehow, I must restrain her.

"Oh, Molly, you're rushing ahead! We hardly know each other."

"Well, he's going to change that as quickly as possible. Don't deny that you're all in a state, Marietta, you should see the expression on your face. Love's young dream, my dear. And you can count on me to help you." With soulful upcast eyes, she departed through the door, shutting it heavily behind her.

Once again I read the letter, and in spite of a wish to be sensible, my breath caught in my throat. It was almost a declaration. Did I know my Browning? Yes, and—even better—my Elizabeth Barrett. My friends and I had cried over the sonnets and wondered about love; she was our heroine. Perhaps Stephen would take me to the Casa Guidi; we would stand on the terrace looking out over Florence. Mrs. Stephen Thaw—wife of the British novelist. The young couple will make their home in London, after extensive traveling abroad. I thrust the letter under my pillow and lay quietly in the dark, contemplating the bits and pieces of the eventful day, the contrasts between desperate fear and present exhilaration. Like Nicholas, I had swung easily from one emotion to the other. Nicholas. As I arrived back at Repose he had come running down the steps, face alight with excitement.

"Marietta! What's *happening?* Yesterday I was almost killed and today it was you!" His words returned with an odd impact. My whole concern had been Nicholas' safety; now I must think of myself. The picture had reversed itself: I was no longer the protectress, but the victim. No, James Thaw is exaggerating the danger, I said to myself firmly. Meeting the Myals *was* a freakish accident, as Mrs. Coulter said; something to tell my grandchildren about. I can dwell on the afternoon, filling my mind with obeah, suspicion, and fear. Or I can fill the remaining days with sunlight, flowers, and my growing love for Stephen.

CHAPTER 13

To labor is the lot of man below;
And when Jove gave us life, he gave us woe.
ALEXANDER POPE: *Trans. of Homer, Iliad*

Cropping, the life's blood of Repose, began at daylight. I woke
to the sound of clanking machinery, and a strange, sweet smell
in the air. My window framed a busy, distant scene, like a
Flemish painting come alive: in a far corner of the fields tiny
figures moved slowly along the lines of green fronds, toppling
them with a slashing machete while others bundled the brown
stalks and carried them to the large carts. The drivers, hidden
under huge-brimmed straw hats, touched the cattle with long
whips and the thin cream-colored animals moved forward; they
too must relinquish the easy pace in a great effort to bring in the
crop—an effort that would continue for four months. Already a
straight black column of smoke rose obtrusively into the pure
blue of the sky.

I was struck with a sense of unbroken tradition. A young Elizabeth Thaw, leaning on the sill many years ago, would have observed the same orderly, time-honored work. The sun would
have shone as brilliantly on the hibiscus and red ginger spikes, a
fork-tailed doctor bird might have appeared on the nearby jacaranda. How quickly one was captivated by this warmth and
beauty, forgetful of bitter winter, lulled on a bright morning into
delightful apathy.

I had reread Stephen's letter many times; I knew the phrases by heart—and at each reading I found myself more convinced that I was truly in love. I had looked forward to falling in love, of course, but expectations were pale forerunners of the reality. A preference for brown eyes was now translated into a particular face, an expression, a smile. Did Stephen feel the same? I knew so little of men. Philip, for example, had shown a gentle side I would not have guessed at in that towering figure. Could Stephen on occasion be angry and demanding? If only I had a brother—even a cousin.

My thoughts were interrupted by an outburst from under the verandah. I was accustomed to the low murmurs and laughter but this was a loud and quarrelsome noise. Cubba's voice rose above the others.

"Me no give a damnee, I tell you."

"Oh now Cubba, what for Hazard do?"

"Put you mout' on it, neger," and a shrill argument ensued in which Hazard's name was repeated. Hazard. I should have thanked him last night, I realized with dismay. It was the least I should have done, and I would waste no time in seeking him out. When Cubba appeared with the tea tray, I questioned her.

"What was all the noise about? Where is Hazard?" She pushed out the lower lip and tossed her head. She had never liked the man, I knew.

"Him gone. Mist' James, he tol' him to get out and go, quick!"

"He *what?*" I was astounded. I had been certain that Hazard would have a reasonable explanation for his actions. This was news, indeed!

"Him gone, Missie. I tell you afore, him bad neger. Better him go to the hills where he belong."

To the hills? Which hills? I had a vivid picture of myself, crouched on the ground, waiting to die; Hazard had come and spoken to the chief in his own language, and the powerful man had obeyed him.

"Cubba, do you think—could he be one of the Myals?" Until now, the idea had never entered my mind. Hazard had seemed particularly intelligent, most unlike the savage Myals. I had assumed that he had, by virtue of this intelligence, persuaded the man to spare a harmless, lost girl.

Nodding vigorously, Cubba answered me. "Dat is so, Missie. Dat is so. Him no busha servant, to be sure. Him a scuffler."

"A scuffler?"

"Tiefer, thief. We say, 'Where cow tie, deh him eat grass.' Hazard come to trouble us. Lawd a mercy, please to take him back far away, far away from here!"

I took a sip of the strong tea, trying not to show my misgivings. For Cubba's denunciation was far more threatening than James's rather fussy warnings. Had Hazard left in anger, planning future mischief?

As I sat down to a late breakfast, I noticed that the ocean was not in its usual state of tranquility. The white edge of breakers came far closer to the cliffs, and the blue beyond was rough and dark. No one was about except for Mrs. Coulter, who sat in her favorite wicker rocker giving the orders of the day to Charmian. Yesterday Hazard would have received them.

"For luncheon, you can dress the table for ten. Major and Mrs. Shepheard will be here. Now, Charmian, you and Louisa must manage until we can find another butler. If you need help, come directly to me before giving orders to the others. I don't want Mr. James upset by your quarreling. Do you understand?"

"Yes, missus."

"Good. And fetch more coffee for Miss Marietta—the pot is almost empty." There was an unusual undertone of irritation in the firm manner. As Charmian left, Mrs. Coulter turned to me with a sigh.

"Such a morning. We are once again without a butler. Hazard has gone."

"I know. Cubba told me when she brought my tea. She said that Mr. Thaw had—let him go."

"My brother talked with him last night, as you know, and was not at all satisfied with his story. He is still afraid that he may be in league with the Myals."

"Cubba certainly thinks so. She thinks he *is* a Myal."

"Does she? Oh dear! I don't like that at all! But aside from that, another problem is that he came from Mrs. Shepheard as a special favor to us, if you remember. He was her yard boy's brother. James should have talked to me first before sending him off. I would have paid him, smoothed things over. Now he has every right to feel that he has been badly treated and can bear a grudge. A disgruntled servant causes no end of trouble."

I swallowed hard. "What—what could he do?"

"Well, hopefully nothing. With any luck he's gone back to wherever he came from and we won't hear of him again. I wouldn't speak of it to Mr. Thaw, Marietta. He looks ill today; his heart is not what it should be, you know."

"I'm so sorry; can you manage without Hazard?"

"Oh, one can always manage. You will learn that, my dear. And when I think of what might have happened to you in the hills, this is the merest annoyance. I shall never forget the waiting, wondering if we should ever see you again and what I could possibly tell your mother. Dreadful. Are you feeling rested? No ill effects? I shouldn't push yourself today, what with the Shepheards' party tomorrow night. It is our great annual event, you know, done in Mrs. Shepheard's grandest manner, which is very grand indeed. I think you'll enjoy it; now, where on earth is my list? I had it right here—I don't ever remember my mother having a list and I can't move without one."

"It's by your chair." And I quickly retrieved it for her.

"Ah, thank you. I think we can put off going to town until tomorrow. And really, don't run about, Marietta. A quiet morning will do you no harm at all."

So I lingered over the fresh, hot coffee grown on the hillside, idly taking pleasure in Charmian's soft voice singing hymns, the hanging baskets spilling over with delicate flowers; the sun that unfailingly appeared day after day, made bearable by the mild breeze. Could that changed look of the ocean be the harbinger of bad weather? The peaceful spell was broken by running feet, and Nicholas came dashing around the corner.

"There you are! That silly Molly wouldn't let me into your room. Marietta, Uncle Philip and I are going to the mill and you must see the sugar all boiling up. Nanny used to say it was like the gates of hell—wouldn't you want to see *that*?" He was flushed and breathless, his voice warning of heartbreak if I refused this opportunity.

"All right," I said, smiling at him. "But I must fetch my hat. If you go slowly, I'll catch you on the path."

The noise was quite deafening as we approached the mill; I was relieved when Philip met us at the entrance and took Nicholas by the hand.

"Be careful," he shouted. "The floor is slippery with juice." I stared with awe at the great vertical rollers, rumbling and clashing as they squeezed the cane and the empty stalks fell away to be gathered up for fuel. Juice foamed down the long runnels into the boiling house and I could see that Nanny had spoken truly. The fire under the great copper vats was intense; steam rose in thick clouds, as the sweating men skimmed the mixture with copper ladles, their faces gleaming in the light.

"That fellow over there is adding lime wash, to make it granulate," Philip said, in my ear, pointing. "The pure fluid will go into more coppers and then into the cooling pans. The rest will be drawn off for rum and molasses."

"Rum and molasses, not sugar?"

"Yes, and it's no joking matter; scorched sugar is wasted money. The trick is not to let it burn; our best men will be pulling it, testing for the right color." I almost tripped over a boy who was curled up, fast asleep, and wondered if he would be punished for slackness. The heat and the cloying smell were making me feel queasy; I turned toward the door that led out into the yard where mules plodded patiently in a circle, providing power for the grinders. Philip and Nicholas followed.

"Most of the big places have steam now," said Philip with a grimace; he proceeded to stop a man who was running in our direction, carrying tools. From their conversation I gathered that one section of the runnels had sprung a leak. Other men paused in their work of rolling hogsheads toward the cooling shed to listen; half-chewed bits of cane dangled from their lips and Philip sent them smartly on their way. I wondered where Morris was keeping himself on this important day. For an overseer, he was strangely out of sight; I had not seen his face except on Christmas Day, and I wondered if he drank heavily, which would explain his sickly look.

As Philip returned, it occurred to me that I owed him a very real debt for his kindness the previous night. "You seem to know a lot about sugar," I remarked conversationally.

"Well, I used to spend a lot of time down here, just as Nicholas does, and you can't help but pick it up. It's the Thaw inheritance, after all. Damn, that leak in the runnel should have been fixed before grinding begins, not after." He rubbed his chin, looking remote and angry.

"Does it look like a good crop?" I persevered. We were standing against the paddock rail and the horses came slowly over to investigate, flicking their tails. Privately, I thought them dusty and ill-kempt.

"No way of knowing yet. The fields should have been fertilized last spring and some of the plants replaced. The old-timers say that there's a norther on the way. That's why we started early, to get in as much cane as we can, before the storm hits."

"A norther? How long does it last?"

"It may blow over in a day, or last nearly a week."

"I thought the sea looked odd this morning. A different color, darker."

"Yes, that's one of the signs."

Nicholas had been skipping about, kicking at stones. "June too soon," he began to sing. "July stand by, August come it must, September remember, October, all over." Philip cuffed him lightly on the ear.

"We're talking about northers, not hurricanes. Don't get your hopes up, young Nicholas. Fetch your pony a banana, why don't you? Look at him, begging for it."

I could see why Nicholas admired his uncle. He was a man's man; it was hard to imagine him courting a girl in his abrupt manner. Whereas Stephen—I imagined myself walking down to the bridge and into the woods. Would he meet me just beyond the bridge or nearer the fields? In any case he would be smiling, his eyes humorous and conspiratorial; Philip Coulter was speaking.

"—meant to apologize for my rudeness to you that morning, but there never seemed to be the right moment; and once one gets off the track with a person, it's hard to get back. I realize that what I was doing must have looked strange to you. But you have to understand that it was a bad time for me, looking at the place where my brother was killed, trying to figure out how it might have happened. It made no sense; it still makes no sense; that journey in October, and why the devil he was trying to climb the rocks; he was not a foolhardy sort of person. I wanted to study the place, think about it, before going up to the house. When I saw you standing there, watching me, I'm afraid I lashed out. I didn't know who you were, of course, or why you were there. So—will you forgive me?" He smiled down at me in a friendly way, as if wanting to make amends, and I returned the smile hesitantly. There was no reason to rebuff Philip Coulter, particularly after this apology. It would be easier to be on pleasant terms with him.

"Of course. It seems a long time ago, and to be truthful, I should have spoken when I saw you, or come forward. I don't know why I didn't."

"Thank you. I wanted to clear the air because—" He stopped and cleared his throat. I glanced at him inquiringly.

"Because—well, forgive my bluntness, but you're young and alone in this part of the world, you know. I've no right to advise you, of course, but I think you should be very careful what you do, where you go."

"You mean because of the Myals? That they may still want to do away with me?"

"There are the Myals, yes. But they're only part of it. My advice is not to leave Repose by yourself. For any reason." I felt the incriminating blush rise to my face. He had seen the man arrive with the note from Stephen; I was being warned off. The family feud again. Not trusting my voice, I turned away.

"Look out, Marietta!" came a cry from Nicholas. "Look out! You're going to fall over the hogshead. Uncle Philip, I thought you were going to the toolhouse. What are you fetching? Can I come in? It's always locked." A welcome interruption; Philip Coulter was already halfway across the yard.

"I'm going to the toolhouse," he said in a clipped voice, "because there's a particular tool for that job, though Lord knows if it's about. All right, come on in, Nicholas. But don't mess around." Tools did not interest me; I remained outside until a sharp exclamation from Philip made me jump. Oh no! I thought, Nicholas has broken something, and I hurried to the door. The two were standing against the far wall, looking down. Philip prodded what appeared to be a coil of heavy rope almost hidden behind several barrels.

"What happened, Captain Coulter?" I asked, seeing the bewilderment in Nicholas' face.

"Happened? Nothing happened. This rope doesn't belong in here. It'll rot in no time, and rope is damned expensive."

"Well, perhaps you should move it," I said reasonably.

"Thank you, I've reached the same conclusion. One more stupid mistake, rope in the toolhouse. Come on, Nicholas. Help me pull it out into the sun."

Together they began to haul the heavy coils from the corner and across the floor. It was a very long rope; it took Philip Coulter's considerable strength to move it. Suddenly there was a sharp jerk and the rope held fast. With a muttered oath, he went behind the barrels. His face, when he came back, was angry. He really is a bad-tempered man, I thought; Nicholas continued to tug.

"Aren't you going to help me, Uncle Philip? This would make a capital climbing rope, you know. We could hang it on the poinciana tree. I should practice every day, because I think I might change my mind and become a sailor. Yes, I think I'll be a sailor."

"Never mind that now." Philip's tone was so sharp that we both jumped and stared at him. "Leave it be. I'm going to lock up." With his thumb, he indicated the door. I was only too glad to go, but Nicholas was of a different opinion.

"But Uncle Philip, you said yourself that it would rot. So let's pull it out now before it gets any worse."

"Nicholas!" It occurred to me that Philip Coulter strongly wanted us out of the toolhouse for some reason connected with the rope. Something out of sight, hidden. I marched back, took Nicholas by the shoulders and headed him toward the door.

"Don't tease, Nicholas. Maybe he'll hang the rope later, but not if you tease." My head was aching; I was far more tired than when I had left the house. Philip followed, locking the door behind him.

"Uncle Philip," said Nicholas irritatingly. "You forgot the tool you came for."

"Yes, well, nip along. Go on back." There was no doubt that Philip Coulter was anxious to be rid of us. With dragging feet, we started up the hill toward the graveyard. When I looked around, he had disappeared.

Agnes Shepheard, neighbor and good friend to the Thaw family, had the delightful gift of creating fun; the Repose dining room was filled with the unusual sound of laughter and animated talk. Seizing a verbal needle, she drove it straight into a selected target, which happened to be James Thaw, on her left. Even Serena was laughing, an impossibility, I would have thought.

"How dare you appear on Christmas Day in that dreadfully old hat! Don't you know that the provincials depend on you for the new styles? Why, some poor man might actually copy that stovepipe, thinking it the latest rig." In vain did James protest that he saw no need to bring clothes from London when these served him well enough.

"Insult to injury! We aren't fine enough for your better wardrobe, it seems. Well, Pamela, I expect you to redeem the family at my party tomorrow night, and shine in the latest fashion. And you too, Miss Jackson." I replied that I hoped she would not be disappointed, but I had nothing elegant in the way of ball gowns.

"Ah, but that's of no importance," said James, giving me a courtly nod. "Miss Jackson is an adornment to society wherever she may be, and in whatever apparel." I smiled at him gratefully, for I was becoming apprehensive about the party, which would be far more elaborate, I suspected, than our simple affairs at home. But Stephen would look after me. Strange, I thought, how happiness pushes out the horrid feelings of anger and resentment; my rage at James Thaw had quite evaporated and I fell into a reverie of patterns and color: the yellow muslin with the embroidered yoke for this afternoon and the pale blue silk tomorrow night; I could do my hair in a dressy fashion, with long curls down the back and a few on the sides, pulled back with a blue satin ribbon.

Major Shepheard, the genial polo player, had been occupied with Serena; now he turned to me. "By the by, Miss Jackson, I hear you had a most unpleasant experience in the hills yesterday. Most unpleasant, and I congratulate you on your pluck. Most girls would be in bed with the vapors after such a day, and here you are, pretty as a picture." I smiled and murmured that it now seemed like a bad dream—I had almost forgotten my fright.

"Excellent. I'm glad to hear that. And I'd let sleeping dogs lie, you know, except that this falls into my line of duty—I'm a local magistrate. I had no idea the Myals still existed; rum bunch; thought they'd been wiped out years ago. D'you mind telling me about them? The number of men, for instance? It might come in handy, one day, to have the information."

I twisted my hands, hesitating, wishing that I need not answer. Didn't the major understand that in talking I might be contributing to my own peril? If it became known that I had been describing the Myals to the local magistrate—I glanced at Louisa and Charmian across the room. How far and wide would this conversation be reported?

In a low voice, I gave him an outline of the events, aware that Philip Coulter was observing us from the other side of the table. As I paused, he broke in; ordinarily I would consider this rude, but now I was profoundly thankful.

"Sir," he said, "I've been meaning to ask you when the matches at Lintowel begin. I have a feeling H.E. took me on with them in mind. I put out some feelers for the job because I wanted to be on the island for a while, and luckily he needed a chap to fill out the team."

"Nonsense, Philip. You're too modest, by far. From what I've heard, and I do get a bit of the gossip, you've done well, extremely well. Heard about Anstruther's—tricky business, too. I wish your father was here; proud, he'd be."

"Thank you, Major. I had a good legacy there, even though I can hardly remember him."

"Great feller, great man with a mallet, too. I remember one time in Egypt—" I picked up my fork, and breathed again. Had

Philip Coulter seen my predicament or had his intervention been accidental? Perhaps there was more subtlety behind the bluntness than I had realized, and I studied his face as he talked shop with the major. If he had not offended me at our first meeting, if I had not fallen in love with Stephen, would I have liked Philip Coulter? He was undeniably handsome, in a rugged, powerful way, and apparently outstanding in his chosen career. His mother doted on him; her eyes followed him lovingly whenever they were together, and he was gentle with her, and affectionate toward Nicholas. But then there had been the callous attack on James. One could depend on the man, I decided. But my heart would never leave my body when he looked at me.

At long last we were moving to the living room for coffee; I wished that I could excuse myself and go to my room. The heavy food, the heat, and—though I was reluctant to admit it—a headache was pressing against my forehead and making me feel ill. I longed to lie on my bed with the jalousies drawn.

"Bless you, Elizabeth, for inviting us up here today," said Mrs. Shepheard, fanning herself vigorously, red-faced from overeating. "Each year I vow it will be my last party, but I have a feeling that when we get back the lanterns will be up, the furniture moved, and we will probably survive. By the way, where's the butler? Tilford came straight up the other day, but they told him in the kitchen that someone was already hired."

There was a sudden halt in the conversation. Mr. Thaw carefully set down his cup.

"I don't quite understand, Agnes. We thought that Hazard, the butler that came, was sent by you. At least, we assumed it. This was not so?"

Mrs. Coulter, who was never awkward, had spilled coffee on the tray; she was staring at Mrs. Shepheard in consternation.

"Tilford, was that the name? I didn't take it in at the time, I'm afraid, and when Hazard appeared he told me what he could do and seemed pleasant and well trained. I simply took it for granted that he had come from you. Do you mean that Hazard was not the man you sent?"

"Nothing to do with me, my dear. Tilford is my yard boy's

brother. What has happened to Hazard, then?" Mr. Thaw and Mrs. Coulter exchanged looks.

"In one way," Mrs. Coulter began, "this makes it easier. We— that is—I felt unhappy about it—"

"What Elizabeth is trying to say," her brother cut in, "is that I dismissed him, too summarily, she felt. He was one of the best butlers we've ever had, but the truth is, I did not trust his story of following Marietta into the hills and persuading the Myals to let her go, and in their own language, mind you. Not that it wasn't praiseworthy, but when I asked him some rather searching questions he was most evasive. There was something wrong there and I don't want him around the place. Now, after hearing this, I'm even happier to be rid of him. What do you think, George?"

"Hard to say," the major said slowly. "You know nothing about him, where he came from? Didn't he give you references, Elizabeth?"

"I didn't ask for any; I thought he had come from you. Ordinarily, I would have been more particular. Oh dear, this *is* strange!"

"What I *don't* understand," said Mrs. Shepheard, "is how he knew about the job so soon after the other fellow left. Someone here on the place must have told him. I'll never understand the speed and efficiency of the grapevine, and why can't it be applied in a few other directions! I ask you! Well, would you like Tilford after tomorrow night? He has a gimpy leg and will probably drop a tray of glasses, but he'll do in a pinch, as I told you before. Better than nothing."

"Agnes, I am truly mortified. It seems that you are always saving us from household disasters, and there's no way I can thank you or repay the kindness."

"Nonsense. Glad to be of help now and then. Will we see you and James tomorrow night?"

"No, my dear. It's too soon, we think, after Gerald. The young will enjoy themselves and tell us all about it."

"Quite right," said Mrs. Shepheard. "Much better to stay peacefully at home. It'll be a frightful crush, and I almost pray for the norther to strike in the afternoon."

"Hah!" said her husband. "What a pack of balderdash! You'd be out shaking your fist at the sky, telling the rain it's not allowed to fall. Now, my dear, are you finished gabbing? The carriage is waiting."

"Never kept the carriage waiting in my life, George!" He winked at us behind her back, and Molly put a hand to her mouth. Mrs. Shepheard looked at her sharply. "What's the matter with you, gel? Oh, I see. Well, hardly ever!"

There was a general laugh, and the Shepheards descended the stairs. As the carriage moved out of the courtyard the peacock followed, shrieking angrily. He seemed unusually cross and I wondered if he was announcing the norther. If only it will hold off until I meet Stephen, I prayed, as I hurried to my room.

When I awoke from heavy sleep my headache was gone, but the reflection in the mirror showed unbecoming circles under my eyes, pallor in my cheeks. I pinched them to bring back the color. Surely I was not falling ill, not at this crucial moment! With growing nervousness, I gathered up my parasol and my bonnet, tied and retied my sash several times, and put cologne on my handkerchief. Down the hall I could hear Molly arguing with Nicholas; a serious difference of opinion, voices raised. Oh no, I thought, he can't, he simply can't put on one of his difficult moods just now. So much depended on his willingness to go with Molly.

We made a peaceful procession going across the field toward the stream, swinging a pacified Nicholas between us. But when we reached the water, there was another altercation; he wanted to play in the water.

"It's *hot*," he yattered. "I don't want to go to the mill, it's too hot there. And I don't want to see the horses, I want to be in the *water!*" Molly and I looked at each other over his head.

"Oh!" I exclaimed, with inspiration wrung from desperation. "Here's a new game you've never played! Now Molly ties her sash around your eyes and I hide. You must count to fifty ten times. When you open your eyes you have to see me without moving from the stream. If you see me, I lose. If you don't see me, you win. And the winner gets a candy prize!"

"What a fine game," said Molly, instantly. "That's an American game, isn't it? Well, come on, Nicholas, quick, let me tie up your eyes. No peeking!"

Poor Nicholas. He was given no chance to reason with us, and I slipped across the bridge and into the woods. The air was cool, after the sultry meadow, and I walked slowly along the narrow path, enjoying the constricted feeling in my throat, conscious of my hammering pulse. Around this bend—or perhaps the next? The sound of footsteps lent speed to my own feet.

"Hurrah! Well done!" Stephen said, taking my hands in his. "Did you have any trouble?"

"No, none. Molly helped me. She has poor Nicholas blindfolded by the stream."

"Good girl. I knew she'd help. So at last we have time to ourselves, with none of these annoying interruptions." He smiled, and his eyes were exactly as I had pictured them, searching and humorous. "How lovely you look," he said, under his breath. "I don't believe you have the slightest idea of how lovely you are."

He had brought a rug and a tea basket and we established ourselves in a small open spot just off the path. "My poor girl," he said, passing me the biscuits, "what a narrow escape! My groom came running to tell me about the white-haired missie from Repose, lost in the hills. I had a wild notion to saddle my horse and go looking for you, but it wouldn't have done any good. It's a miracle, you know, that you're here. Those bloody hills—that butler fellow was lucky not to lose himself as well."

Hazard, I thought, with a sharp pang of fear. Hazard, are you angry? Are you coming back? I told Stephen the story as we drank our tea. "You must be careful," he said, with a look of deep concern. "I only wish I could be on hand, to look after you." After our refreshment, he packed up the basket, refusing to let me help. "No, you're not to lift a finger," he said, as though I were a fragile bit of glass. He had brought a book, but there was too much to say; we had no need of Mr. Browning.

"Will you save me most of the dances tomorrow night?" he asked. "We needn't dance them all, you know. Mrs. Shepheard has a garden where we can sit. There's something—something I want to say to you, but not here. Not now." My breath caught in my throat.

I listened, watching each expression on his thin, sensitive face, a writer's face. We talked about his travels, and I admitted that I longed to see distant places, the out-of-the-way cities. He spoke about the ones he would show me someday, his favorites. "Don't you believe me?" he asked. "There is so much I have to learn about you; I never know if you are quite serious or laughing. Do you remember when Molly and I teased you about the fortune-teller and you pretended to be angry, or when—" He stopped suddenly, and dropped my hand. I listened, also. There was the unmistakable sound of footsteps on the path.

"Who—"

"I don't know." Footsteps coming closer, and now voices, one deep and one shrill and chattering. Philip Coulter and Nicholas. We rose hastily. I have a perfect right to be here, I found myself saying silently. They came into sight, Philip holding Nicholas by the hand, pointing out a particular kind of tree. Oh no, I thought; you didn't just happen along. You watched me go. You planned this.

Nicholas saw me and pulled away. "I won the game," he shouted. "I didn't see you anywhere. Then Uncle Philip came and he said he would play. Now we've found you, Marietta! Hallo, Stephen. Do you want to play, too?"

Nobody spoke. I was far too angry to trust my voice, and I sensed that Philip was trying to put us on the defensive. Finally Stephen broke the impasse.

"Well, Philip? What brings you this way?"

"I've come to fetch Miss Jackson," he said curtly. Stephen took a step forward; the muscles in his neck stood out. My mouth opened to tell Philip Coulter what I thought of his effrontery, but I held back the angry words. Nothing would be more un-dignified than a fight—and in front of Nicholas. With a great effort, I turned to Stephen.

"Thank you, Mr. Thaw," I said with a pleading look. "Thank you for the tea party. I enjoyed it, and I'll look forward to seeing you at Mrs. Shepheard's tomorrow night." Seizing Nicholas' hand,

I started back toward the stream, yanking him along in my agitation. I must maintain my self-control because of Nicholas, I told myself; I must not look at Philip Coulter, but keep straight on to the house. I saw, as if in an illustration, Marietta in her yellow dress, Stephen in tan linen, sitting together in the glade. He is holding her hand—perhaps she should have withdrawn it—but he is so tender, gentle with her. Now the picture was blotted out, ruined; the enchanting thread brutally severed. Philip Coulter had no right to interfere!

As we passed the graveyard, I could hear his steps coming up beside me. He was wearing riding clothes, and must have gone out after the heat of the day.

"You're angry," he said, matching his pace to mine. "I would be, too, in your shoes. But I haven't changed my mind since this morning. You must take care, Marietta. Don't go into water that may be too deep for you."

I stopped and faced him, not meeting his eyes. "I d-don't care for your w-warnings," I stammered. "It's obvious to me what you're doing—carrying on the family feud. I saw you riding Stephen down at the polo, cutting him dead when he tried to apologize for his groom. But doesn't it occur to you that it's absolutely no—concern of yours where and when I meet him? I'm not a Thaw or a Coulter, thank God, and I do as I please." I kept my eyes on his belt buckle. If I had looked up and seen amusement in his face, I would have hit him.

"As you say. But I still feel an obligation to warn you, no matter how much you may dislike it."

"Oh really!" I was almost strangling with rage. "Just go your way, Captain Coulter, and in the future have the goodness to leave me alone." Once again I set my face squarely toward the house; he did not follow.

In a moment, a small voice spoke up tentatively.

"Why are you and Uncle Philip fighting, Marietta?" He was looking up at me from under his lashes, but not in fun.

"I'm sorry, Nicholas," I answered as calmly as I could. "Grown-ups do that, sometimes. But don't worry about it. It's nothing to do with you, pet."

Molly was waiting in my room, as I suspected she might be. "Oh my stars," she said miserably. "Marietta, it was so dreadful—and there was nothing I could do."

"What was so dreadful, Molly? What's happening?" There was a touch of panic in Nicholas' voice.

"Oh, nothing to worry your head about," said Molly quickly, almost in my words. "Go feed Jilly right away, Nicholas. She's been whining for you ever since she came back, and next thing you know, she'll be barking." He left, and I sat down on the dressing-table bench, fighting back the tears.

"It was—bad?" she asked.

"I have never been so humiliated, never! 'I've come to fetch Miss Jackson,' he said. Imagine!"

"We played that silly game for a while, until you were out of sight. Then I let him paddle in the stream. Suddenly there was Philip, asking where you had gone. I tried to look vacant, you know—'my goodness, she was just here,' and then Nicholas began to talk about the game. 'Shall we go find her?' he says, and that was it. I couldn't bear to face you; I came up here to wait. Oh, what did Stephen *do?*"

"I thought they were going to hit each other; then I dragged Nicholas away. A fight would have been even worse. I gave Philip my opinion, on the way home; I shan't speak to him for the rest of my visit."

"Oh heavens," Molly groaned. "Well"—and she brightened—"what did Stephen say before he came?"

I felt the color in my face. "He brought tea," I said, "and we talked about traveling, cities; he wants to show me—" I bit my lip, but it was too late. Molly's eyes had grown round.

"Mercy on us, did he *propose?*"

"No, no! But—oh Molly! He asked me for most of my dances tomorrow night. We will sit in the garden, he said."

"Well then he certainly plans to propose. Only fiancés have more than three dances, I think. Oh, Marietta, you will be my cousin! You'll come to see us in London, and maybe here, though I can't quite imagine you staying with Miss Anna. What joy, not to lose you after all!"

"Nothing is settled, you know. Nothing at all." But I jumped

from the bench and whirled about the room, skirts flying. Endless hours, minutes, seconds until tomorrow night. Molly gazed
after me, grinning.

"What if Philip should follow you into the garden? What
would you do?"

I halted in mid-turn. "He wouldn't dare! At a party? Without
the excuse of saving me from Hazard or the Myals? I should tell
him—oh, what I told him this afternoon would be mild as milk-
weed! He spoiled my afternoon, but he will not spoil tomorrow
evening, I can promise you that."

"But if you aren't going to speak to him—"

"That wouldn't count. If your Uncle Philip interferes with me
again, he'll find himself in a battle he'll never forget."

CHAPTER 14

*Do not make me kiss, and you will not make
me sin.*

H. G. BOHN: *Handbook of Proverbs*

The following day was unpleasantly hot, for the breeze which
swept away the heat dropped long before its task was done. The
sunset was fiery, marked with long, livid streaks. I found myself
watching the sky fearfully as the cutters stepped up their pace in
the fields; the wide swaths grew larger, and women joined the
men in their haste to gather up the stalks.

The house had been unusually quiet during the day. Philip
Coulter was not to be seen; James Thaw kept to his room, feeling the heat, according to Mrs. Coulter, and Pamela departed for
town late in the morning. I overheard her grandmother gently
remonstrating with her for not taking a companion and instructing her to be back early. "It's quite an innovation," she told us at
luncheon, "to arrive just before the dancing. We used to be
taken ahead to rest for the entire afternoon. Marietta, let me
warn you, the night air here is treacherous, particularly in this
weather. Be careful about sitting outside after twirling about." I
tried not to blush, and Molly gave me a knowing look across the
table.

Washing my hair had occupied most of the afternoon, and
required the help of Cubba, Molly, and even Nicholas. The zinc
tub had been carried to my room and Cubba fetched rain water
from the cistern. Finally I was pronounced ready for curling.

"Rapunzel, Rapunzel, let down your hair," said Nicholas, untangling a strand. "*When* is this silly business ever going to be done?" Molly gave him the curling rags to hold and he was promised a walk and a chapter about Henry Morgan.

"It's beautiful, worth all the trouble," Molly exclaimed later, as she untied her handiwork. Instead of a low, rolled chignon, long curls fell on either side of my face and down my back. "You look so romantic, like a lady in a portrait; you should have a little dog, and a fan. Mother has a lovely shawl with silver threads running through it; it would be perfect with your hair and the dress. Blast, blast, and blast. It's so maddening to be fifteen, too young for all the fun."

"I thought you didn't care for parties and that nonsense."

"No, I don't. But I want to see you and Stephen together—and think of the delicious food! Shall I run and fetch the shawl?"

I hesitated. "I don't know—I have the feeling that she still suspects me of stealing."

"Oh, no. She's very generous when it comes to her own things. It's only bad when Nicholas and Repose are involved."

"If you're really sure—but Molly, shouldn't you be helping Pamela? The buggy came back ages ago; I don't want to monopolize you." Molly, looking oddly guilty, shook her head. Her face was too open to conceal her thoughts, and I wondered what had occurred between the sisters. The dress, perhaps. Molly had confided that Pamela would wear only her chemise and one petticoat. "Granny would faint if she knew, but I'm no tattletale!"

Promptly at eight o'clock, Quaco brought the large carriage around to the verandah steps. The entire household assembled to see us off; we might have been departing on a long, hazardous voyage.

"O ki, the hair," came the familiar murmur as I stepped from the living room. Then a sigh of appreciation for Pamela. With a sidelong glance, I noted that her dress was deceptively simple; white folds draped in a classic style, and the hair bound up with a silver fillet—artless yet dramatic. My curls over which we had labored suddenly seemed fussy and old-fashioned. But the real outburst of applause was given to Philip Coulter. As Pamela and

I seated ourselves diagonally in the carriage, protecting our skirts, he appeared at the top of the stairs. The short red mess jacket, faced with green, was decorated with a row of miniature ribbons and fitted tightly over his shoulders. Long blue trousers, strapped over Wellingtons, made him seem even taller. Unwillingly, I was forced to admit that he made a splendid figure as he bowed and then joined Quaco on the driver's seat. He was avoiding me; there was more than enough room behind.

As we passed the village, our lanterns swinging with the horses' cautious steps, fire from the boiling house was reflected in the sky, giving the night a lurid quality. I thought of the men working through the dawn, some curled up for sleep in the corners. Nicholas had told me, with morbid glee, of the man who fell into the mill. "They cut off his arm with the machete that hangs there just in case someone falls asleep!"

Pamela's face was cool and remote in the flickering glow. I wondered if she had ever felt light-headed with anticipation. Or was her mind always on the brilliant match that Molly joked about? Though she could not be interested, romantically, in her own cousin, I wondered what she thought of our growing attachment. She glanced at me, and I quickly shifted my attention to the conversation taking place on the box.

"The Pyle," Quaco was saying, "the white with red belong to Mist' Hamilton. I see him when him just a stag, over to Hamilton Hill. Had to go to the drag pit—very bold. Best bird belong to Mist' Cox's man Jason. Brown and red. Still, I think to put my money on the Pyle."

"Where is the pit this year?"

"By de small horse barn, beyond the cattle pens, Mist' Philip. Dat be farther away from de house den before. All the same, plenty buckra at the pit and not at de party!" he laughed softly, and Philip snorted. Across from me, Pamela stirred.

"You're not—you can't be serious, Philip! A cockfight at the Shepheards' tonight? How disgusting!"

"Not at all. It's a tradition, the Shepheards' annual derby, as much as the ball. Makes the evening, in my opinion, though I haven't been to one in years."

"Does Mrs. Shepheard know about it?"

"Come, Pamela. Mrs. Shepheard not know what goes on at her place? She sends out food and drinks, sets up a tent just as she does for the polo. If too many men leave the party, she goes right out and shoos them back. One has to be a bit judicious—one hour at the pits, one at the party."

"How very nasty." Pamela's face showed her disdain and I was quite in sympathy, though I knew nothing about cockfighting—a mysterious masculine sport like boxing or bull fighting; a sport that Philip Coulter would enjoy.

The horses slowed as we turned off the main road and joined a line of carriages proceeding at a sedate pace. Stone pillars marked the entrance to the Shepheards'; the long, straight avenue was bordered by tall coconut trees. The major had told me that his house, though large, was not old, and had been built to his wife's taste—a very grand taste indeed. As we approached, lights shone out on formal gardens and terraces. Pillared verandahs circled the huge house—the mansion that I had looked for in vain at Repose. A formidable place, and I looked up at the long flight of stone steps with sudden qualms. The shrill sound of voices rose above the fiddles in the background—strangers' voices. Hopefully, Stephen would be waiting.

"I'll be with you in a while," said Philip to Quaco, as he helped us from the carriage.

"What a pity to detain you," murmured Pamela.

"Are you trying to teach me manners?" inquired her uncle equably. "Ladies, we'll be leaving before midnight on strict orders from my mother. Not seemly to dance on the day of the family memorial service."

"But it's not until tomorrow afternoon—"

"Midnight, Pamela. Consider yourself lucky that she let you come at all." I smiled to myself. Pamela's protest did not move her strong-minded uncle.

The band was playing a polka as we reached the top of the stairs and stood in line to greet the Shepheards. Many of the guests were older ladies and gentlemen who had come long distances, I gathered, from the kissing and chattering. And among them were a number of young officers in mess jackets; I recognized one or two from the polo. But no sign of Stephen.

"Ah, the Repose contingent, in its glory!" Mrs. Shepheard was flushed and in high spirits. "Go and have your programs filled, girls. Philip, I depend on you to see that Marietta is introduced and looked after." I smiled, hoping that this would not be necessary.

In the long drawing room, furniture had been cleared away and dozens of small gilt chairs lined the sides. Mahogany columns rose impressively to a ceiling hung with chandeliers, while light from the hundreds of candles was reflected on the glassy floor. "It's like ice!" I heard one girl exclaim as she whirled by. As we stood in the doorway, several young men hurried up to Pamela; her face took on a provocative expression as they argued over her card; she spoke languidly to one, tapped another on the arm with her fan, and moved off with the third, the dress floating behind in soft folds. I, on the other hand, stood anxiously looking about for Stephen. If he did not appear quickly my card would be filled, for Philip Coulter had lost no time in collaring a number of young subalterns and was leading them up to me.

"Will you dance?" he asked tonelessly, congratulating himself on a job well done, I supposed.

"I believe that the next one is already taken—and in any case, I wouldn't think of keeping you from the barn." There was a hint of anger in his look, which pleased me.

"Well, then, twelve o'clock promptly, by the stairs"—and he walked away. The young subaltern led me to the figure that was forming. Poor man, he couldn't know how unhappy I was to be his partner, so I tossed my curls and entered with good grace into the set. Then came a lancers. And a reel. And a polka again. It was desperately hot in the room; I felt an unwelcome trickle of moisture on my neck and, as we turned and pirouetted, I constantly searched the perimeter of the room for Stephen's face. Accidents began to loom in my mind: horse fallen, a buggy overturned, pinning him beneath.

"Would you care for some refreshment?" inquired my partner of the moment.

"Yes, that would be nice—such a warm night." We made our way slowly through the crush, past flowering trees brought in for the occasion, to the immense dining room. The long table was

covered with silver trays of mousses, creams made from ice
brought in on the ships, vols-au-vents, cakes, jellies, meats.
Guests circled slowly with plates, scarcely able to choose among
the lavish array. The heat was quite unbearable. Suddenly I had
a feeling of room and people melting into a hazy jumble—the
noise receded oddly—and I turned quickly toward the door.

"It's the heat," I told the young officer, who, noticing my sudden pallor, shouldered a way back onto the verandah. "I'll be all
right in a moment." He was a most obliging man. After seating
me in a quiet corner, he brought a glass of lemonade and said he
would be back after the next dance. I thanked him, struck by the
profound difference in the American and British military. These
young men were proud, almost arrogant in their regimental fac-
ings and uniforms, the standard bearers of responsibility and tradition; each one, I knew, considered his regiment the pride of
the army. I sipped the cool drink, worrying about Stephen,
watching the dancers bob up and down in a country reel. A
group of men came up the steps, laughing loudly; one was being
clapped on the back by his fellows in congratulation. I supposed
they had come from the cockfight; they had the look of boys returning from an outing and the old ladies seated in front of me
had definite opinions to air:

"—don't understand Agnes and George. Everything of the very
best, everything from Harrod's down to the dance cards, and then
to have a tournament or whatever it's called out in the barnyard.
Look there will you, at John Bresthwing, on the stairs. What
lady would want him for a partner now? Unsteady on his feet—
he can barely walk!"

"Oh," said another, "you'll find that Katrina Hamilton won't
object. And I remember Agnes telling me that this party pro-
duces all manner of interesting alliances. She swears that the
fighting puts men in a daring mood. Katrina may be very
grateful."

"Uncouth, all the same, Mary. How they would laugh at us in
London. Take young Pamela Coulter, for example. They tell me
she is to be one of the belles of the coming Season. What would
she say if she knew her partner had just been holding a nasty
bird?"

"Very little, my dear. She never seems to speak; I really find it difficult to see what these young men see in her, for the looks are nothing out of the ordinary. And that cool manner—I saw her in town this afternoon and she hardly bowed. Her mind on other matters, I should say, than common politeness; Elizabeth Coulter should not let her go about alone."

"Poor dear Elizabeth. She surely can't be charged with lack of duty toward her family; Serena has become quite unbalanced since Gerald's death, you know, and now they've lost that funny old Nanny." There was a pause, while the ladies contemplated the Thaw misfortunes.

"Well," said a third voice, "I shouldn't worry your heads over Miss Pamela. She has her head firmly set on her shoulders, and if all accounts are true, she will make a very good match. James will help to pay for her Season, I imagine, but I suspect the family is hard-pressed. Such a pity about Repose. A charming place it used to be, when old William's wife was there. I can just remember how we loved to go to visit as children—such an easy, delightful atmosphere. Now there is no entertainment whatsoever, and the place is sadly run down, I hear."

"Naturally. You cannot leave a house without a year-round staff and a good overseer; it's false economy to think otherwise. My cousin at Burning Bush did that one winter. She went to Egypt and when she got back the pigs were running through the house; yes, running through the house."

I got up and moved away, unable to bear the prattle. The evening was half gone, the fiddles screamed piercingly. Where was Stephen? Several people looked at me curiously—a young lady standing alone at a dance? Suddenly the gaiety seemed to heighten my sense of despair, made even more acute by the earlier anticipation. The waltz was ending with a flourish, and I saw Pamela leave the floor, attended by admirers. Soon my partner would come in search of me and I would be drawn out of hiding, or I could go upstairs pleading a sick headache. In any case, the evening was ruined. For some reason, Stephen had been prevented from coming to the party.

The dreadful old ladies were observing me, wondering, no doubt, who I was. I turned my back on them and accepted a glass of punch from a limping manservant, Tilford, perhaps. But it tasted strongly of spirits and after one sip I looked about for a place to set it down and thus missed Stephen coming up the stairs. His voice startled me so that the cup fell from my hand with a crash.

"My deepest apologies," he said worriedly. He was breathing hard, as if he had been running, and wiped his face with a handkerchief. "What good luck to find you so quickly. I came as fast as I could but even so I've missed several of our dances."

"I'd quite given you up," I murmured, smiling at him. The light from the candles and torches had suddenly taken on a glowing brilliance, the music was pleasing and sprightly. "I'm afraid my card is filled; I came out for a moment to escape the heat—and here comes my partner looking for me."

"And in vain, poor man. Come! If we dodge behind these old besoms we can make our way to the dining room and out into the garden, and away from these bothersome people." We passed through the crowded rooms and onto the balustraded terrace where other couples were promenading in the cool night air. I remembered Mrs. Coulter's warning, but the shawl had been left long ago on one of the gilt chairs, and this was not the moment to retrieve it.

"What a dreadful racket; worse than a barnyard full of hungry chickens," I said feelingly, glancing back into the dining room.

"Or, as Bacon puts it, 'A crowd is not company, and faces are but a gallery of pictures. . . .'"

"How very elegant! Now you've made me quite ashamed of my barnyard." He laughed, taking my hand.

"Never mind that. Have you forgiven me? I haven't told you how beautiful you look. The hair is dazzling but I prefer it the other way; one sees your eyes better when not distracted by the curls." A man trod on my dress and begged my pardon. "We won't have any peace here," said Stephen under his breath. With a hand on my elbow, he led me carefully down the broad, shallow stone steps and onto the gravel path. In the light from the house, I could see that the garden was extensive, planted in formal squares and semicircles. The colors were blotted out, but the smell of night jasmine was strong and the sound of water came from several fountains. We walked slowly. Stephen's fingers stroked my wrist lightly; no one had ever touched me in such an intimate, caressing way and I shivered, dreading yet longing for the moment when he would draw me close. The most stirring moment of my life was at hand: the bridge from my girlhood to a new life. A golden moment, like a bell, waiting to ring out.

But the garden was not secluded. Other couples walked about on the paths; we heard the murmur of voices, the sound of gravel underfoot. A bench where we tried to sit was occupied. Stephen swore softly, his hand tightened on mine.

"Blast them. Come, Marietta, come this way," and he led me over the grass into the darkened shrubbery. I must have hesitated, but he urged me forward into the deeper shadows. All at once there was a feverish quality in his haste, unlike the gentleness in the woods. The bushes pressed in, almost like the vines in the tunnel, and I pulled back.

"Don't be frightened," he whispered, stroking my hair. "There's no need, when two people want each other as we do. Since that first afternoon I've thought of nothing but this, of having you close to me. Strange, how you appeared from nowhere, like a creature from another planet."

"With my hair hanging down, and my face covered with tears—"

"Ah, your beautiful hair." He touched my face; I was trembling violently. "I have called you a mermaid," he murmured, "but that was wrong. I know better, now. You're on fire with love—I can feel it—as I am. My lovely one, there's a summer house beyond the garden where I can love you, as I must. Beautiful, warm girl." He bent his head and kissed my lips. The smell of rum was strong on his breath. This was not the tenderness I had expected. His hands were hurting my shoulders, and I tried to free myself.

"No," I said, suddenly frightened. "It's too dark here. I can't see. Please, Stephen, take me back to the garden." For a few seconds he did not move. It was almost as though I had struck him a blow.

"Back—to the garden?" he said thickly. "But I thought you—

ah, no! You must let me, you must let me touch you—" And he thrust his hand into my bodice.

I jumped as though he had burned me. If this was love, I wanted no more of it.

"Let me go," I said in a rising voice. "Stop—let me go!" The anguish in my words must have reached him, or the thought that others might hear. He withdrew his hand, tearing my dress, and I twisted away, trying to hold it together. What had gone so dreadfully wrong? Was this how men behaved? I was rigid with shock. I did not know what to do or where to go. Little as I understood what had happened, I sensed that in some way I had been badly used.

He spoke first, harshly. "I thought you wanted me to kiss you. You came very willingly, Marietta." The truth of his words brought stinging tears to my eyes.

"But not like that. And not when you had been drinking." He did not answer; perhaps he had not expected such a blunt reply.

"I waited for you," he said finally, in a different tone, "but you were late. And then someone wanted me to go to the fights for a few minutes. But what does it matter? Marietta, I apologize. I lost my head for a moment—is that to spoil everything? Can we start over and be as we were yesterday? Come, why not?"

"The summer house," I said, still shivering. "Why did you want to take me to the summer house?"

"So we could be alone, you sweet idiot! This garden is like Brighton Promenade. I thought you would want that, and from what Pamela said this afternoon—" He stopped abruptly, but too late.

"*Pamela!* You and Pamela talked about *me* this afternoon?"

"Calm yourself, my dear." He sounded amused. "Pamela and I are old friends, as well as relatives. She merely said you were enjoying our little flirtation. But she also warned me that you might not know how to play by the rules—and it seems that I should have paid more attention to her."

"Play by the *rules?*"

"Well, surely you have these little affairs in America? Mind you, I think permanent liaisons are for married ladies. But the excitement of advances and withdrawals? And milder flirtations for the younger girls? Many of them play with great expertise, you know, and you seemed to be quite willing to join in the game."

Games, advances, withdrawals—and I had been waiting breathlessly for his proposal of marriage.

"And I suppose you would treat Pamela this way, like a drunken beast?" I said bitterly. He did not answer. He was beginning to realize, I think, how much he had upset me.

"Well," he said finally, "I seem to have alarmed you and I'm sorry. Too bad, the whole business. Shall we go back? A pity to spoil the whole evening; you'll still have time for some dances."

Wordlessly, I went with him toward the house, brilliantly *en fête*. But as we reached the steps, I stopped. "I'm not going in," I said. He began to protest, saying that he would find me another partner, if I liked. I was adamant.

"Shall I send Pamela, then?"

"*No!*" I hissed. "Please just go, leave me," and at last he went away. Two couples came down the steps, talking and laughing, and I shrank into the darkness of the wall. No one should see my distress.

For some time I sat on the corner of the step, leaning against the stone as the chill in my body turned to burning heat. I put my hands to my face, trying to blot the past half hour from my mind. If this was how men acted, I would be careful to keep clear of them for the rest of my life. Never again would I be so gullible. And almost as humiliating as my blindness about Stephen was the thought of Pamela's hand in this: her statement that I was "enjoying the flirtation," and that I might not "understand the rules." As I sat there, I began to recognize that I was only reaping the harvest of my naïveté; there had been no one to call a halt to my headlong fancies. And for the first time I was acutely aware of my position—or lack of it—at Repose.

At home I was the daughter of Professor Jackson, a distinguished scholar of solid New England ancestry. Here, I realized with a shock, the Jackson name meant nothing. A pretty girl on a somewhat dubious mission—I was fair game. Stephen Thaw would never have suggested the summer house to one of Pamela or Molly's well-connected friends.

I tried once again to hide the tear in my dress. At midnight I must face Pamela and Philip, and the thought of their cool, curious looks made my cheeks burn. No, it was more than I could bear. I rose from the steps and cautiously made my way along the terraces to the front of the house. Somehow I would get myself back to Repose—alone.

CHAPTER 15

The universe shows us nothing save an im-
mense and unbroken chain of cause and effect.

P. H. D. D'HOLBACH:
Le systeme de la nature, I, 1770

Several carriages were drawn up in the circular turnaround, their drivers standing at the horses' heads; they were laughing as they waited, eyes gleaming in the torchlight. Slipping back into the shadows, I crept by, and only when I had gone what I judged to be a safe distance down the long drive did I begin to run. One thought prevailed: to escape the music, the people, the humiliation, and reach the haven of my room at Repose where no one could see or speak to me. Moonlight shone on the white gravel; I had no difficulty in making my way to the huge iron gates, and paused to catch my breath. To my left lay the coast road and I suddenly began to reckon the length of time it would take to walk it. An hour and a half? Two hours? And if I should hear footsteps, would I dare to hide in the tangle of roadside growth, disturbing what manner of insect or animal? I envisioned myself somewhere between the Shepheards' and Repose, the moon momentarily hidden by a cloud and the vultures, the John Crows, coming toward me—no! It was madness to contemplate walking to Repose. Perhaps I could wait here for the carriage, and thus avoid returning to the house. But Philip would be expecting me at midnight; there would be a hue and cry and searching parties and my foolishness would be known to all.

I stood at the end of the driveway, rigid with indecision, wishing that I could break through the pressing misery and find that it was all a dream, that I was back in my own small room at home. The blow to my self-esteem had been severe; it seemed that beautiful, capable Marietta Jackson was no more equipped to venture forth into the world than a child. Two emotions filled my mind: fear of the long, dark road ahead of me, and a fierce mortification. One thing I swear, I thought, clenching my fists: my life may be very lonely, but never again will I put myself in a position where a man can hurt me.

The sound of approaching wheels brought me back to awareness of my immediate plight. The carriages at the foot of the Shepheards' steps would soon be coming; I should not have waited so long, I realized, shrinking back into the shadows to let the vehicle pass. But it was stopping, and with a sudden tightening of nerves I recognized Quaco on the driver's seat.

"Him go by me sure," he said to the figure beside him. "Dat dress I know. But for why, Mist' Philip? For why run away from de party?"

"That's not the worry," came Philip's voice, sharply. "The point is, where did she go? Which way? Toward Repose, I guess, and she can't have gone far. But it wouldn't matter, if the Myals are about." I had thought of vultures, but not of the Myals, and I ran to the front of the carriage; Philip's hand grasped my shoulder, roughly. "Marietta! Where are you going? What happened?" I clutched his arm, nails digging into his coat.

"Never mind. Just take me back to Repose, will you? Take me back just as quickly as you can—oh please!"

He must have felt the urgency in my voice—and the sharpness of my grip.

"Get in. Quaco, run and get a message to Miss Pamela. She's to spend the night, do you understand? I'm taking Miss Jackson home and Pamela's to stay the night. I'll hold the horses. Now hurry, man."

The leather was cold on the empty seat, and as I shivered in the dampness, I remembered Serena's borrowed shawl left behind in the drawing room. Somehow this was the culmination of the evening's disasters; I twisted my hands in my lap until the knuckles stabbed with pain. Quaco returned; Philip got in beside me. Without speaking, he took off his coat and put it around my shoulders. I sat huddled in the corner, letting the night air fall coolly on my face, listening to the creak of the wheels. If only he would not talk; my throat was tight, as if an iron band enclosed it. If it loosened, I would cry. And I will not cry, I told myself grimly, until I'm in my room, in my bed, and no one can hear.

For a time we traveled in silence; the road was even longer than I remembered; and by now I would have been half dead with exhaustion, let alone fright. My convulsive shudder roused the quiet figure on the seat beside me.

"Can you tell me what sent you running off like that? It must have been something out of the ordinary." His tone was kindly and inquiring and I could say nothing. He had warned me about Stephen; he had every right to be superior, if I were to give him that satisfaction. But I could never explain; he would not understand about fantasies and daydreams—how misleading they could be if allowed too much freedom. His world was forceful and sensible; he would never try to escape from his world as I had from mine.

The rising mist touched my hot cheeks and blurred the swaying lamps. A small animal ran in front of the carriage, causing one of the horses to stumble and snort, and I saw the dark form disappear into the shadows; it had escaped the vultures—the staring eyes, the deadly beaks. Yesterday I had been angry at Philip's interference; now I knew that it had been justified. Was this another lesson to add to the burgeoning list? To learn to accept advice gracefully?

"Well," he continued, not waiting for my answer. "Pamela will be pleased at the change of plans; it means several more hours of dancing for her. Could you manage to have a sick headache, d'you think? Then my mother will forgive me for leaving her, though she's always a forgiving person. Uncle James—that's a different matter. I'm in his bad books forever. Of course I've been hard on him, particularly on Christmas Day, but it was a shock to find the place in such bad condition—Gerald would have handled things better and with a lot more tact. I suppose I should have stayed away and avoided the yearly ritual of the checks, but I knew my mother needed help this year with Serena and the children and Uncle James."

I turned toward him, surprised at the turn of the conversation. "Then the dreadful business of Nanny dying," I said hesitantly. "And the household problems. Your mother is one of the most remarkable people I've ever met. She must be exhausted, yet she never complains and always manages to be kind."

"No, she never complains. And that's another reason why Repose must be set right and produce a decent crop. The land is still good, there's no reason not to have a good income from it. But it takes proper management, and Morris seems to be a sacred tradition, like the checks. Uncle James won't hear of replacing him. I'll try to wield a big stick around the place while I'm here, but it's an impossible situation. Take the business of the rope, for example."

"The rope? The one in the toolshed?"

"Yes. You probably wondered why I ordered you and Nicholas out so quickly."

"I did, rather. I thought perhaps you had found something you didn't want us to see."

"Particularly Nicholas. There was a hook on the end of that rope. A hook that had been caught in a tree. And the other end was cut clean off, as though someone had sliced it with a knife." His face was grim in the flickering light.

"You can't mean—you don't think it was the rope your brother—" I began, and then stopped, horrified. No wonder he had sent us away.

"Yes. I was almost certain when I first saw it. Now I am convinced. You see, I planned to take it to the cliffs. But when I went back to the toolhouse after lunch, the rope was gone. Someone had removed the evidence."

"I don't understand," I said, bewildered. "Are you sure the rope didn't fray against the rocks while your brother was climbing? It was actually cut?"

"Cut—clean and neat."

"But then—someone—why, that—that would be—"

"Murder," he finished for me. "My brother didn't slip. There was no accident. He was murdered. And I intend to find the murderer."

I was shocked into silence. Quaco flicked the whip over the horses' heads, a stone rang out against a wheel. Philip's discovery had opened the door to frightening possibilities, it seemed to me. New possibilities of danger to Nicholas. Had James been right, after all?

"The rope was gone when you went back after lunch," I said slowly. "Was that coincidence, or did someone see us, do you think? I didn't notice anyone watching."

"There's always someone watching, you know that. In a way," he continued, "finding the rope was a piece of good luck. At least I know what I'm dealing with. Before, it was all guesswork. Listen, Marietta, I'm not trying to upset you, but it's Nicholas we have to protect now. You're in charge of him most of the time— and doing a fine job of it." He stopped, and I could see him looking at me reflectively, as if wondering how to go on.

"I understand. This brings the danger, whatever it is, much closer. I know you're worried about Nicholas. Your Uncle James is, too. He thinks Anna Thaw is trying to get rid of the lot of you." I tried to speak lightly, to ward off the anxiety I felt. At least it had driven Stephen from my mind.

"Perhaps Anna. Or somebody else. The point is, my brother's death was no accident. The rope was cut. I want you to promise that if you notice anything odd going on around Nicholas, don't call it a whim or fancy but come to me immediately. Those bloody cliffs." He struck his knee with his fist. "What was Gerald doing there in the first place? That's what I'd like to know."

I sat silently, unconsciously twisting my hands again as I considered. Should I tell him Nicholas' story—the story of the hidden gold? It would be a relief to repeat it to someone with authority, though, like James, he might not believe the boy. And the real evidence, Martha's precious journal, was my secret and would be kept in a remote compartment of my brain lest I unguardedly reveal it. I was thankful for the darkness; it was far easier to converse with Philip Coulter with my face partly hidden. I drew a deep breath.

"Did you ever hear that your brother, Gerald, talked to Nich-

olas the night before he left for Repose? That he went into
Nicholas' room and spoke to him, thinking him asleep?"

"Who told you this? Nicholas?"

"Yes. It sounds far-fetched, I admit, but he swears his father
stood by his bed, talking to him."

"What about?"

"Gold. Family treasure that is hidden somewhere in the cliffs.
He was going to find it, he said."

Philip Coulter moved abruptly; he let out his breath in a long
sigh. "Far-fetched, indeed. Hardly the word for it. Why are you
telling me this? Do you believe it?"

"Yes, I think I do," I answered cautiously. "That was the
reason Nicholas kept running to the cliffs. We thought he was
looking for his father, but he was really trying to carry on the
search alone."

"But—"

"Let me go on, please. It was only after he was so dreadfully
shaken by the fall from the horse that he told me. Otherwise he
might have kept it to himself. His father's words were very real.
I doubt that he could have imagined them."

"I see. Poor little devil. But why did he keep this a secret for
so long?"

"Because he knew he wouldn't be believed. And he was right.
When I went to Mr. Thaw, he laughed and called the story
shades of Henry Morgan. If there had been any hidden gold, he
would have heard of it, he said. That's why we had the treasure
hunt at the caves—to console Nicholas."

"Do you think that will satisfy him?"

"I shouldn't think so, really. But one good thing came of it.
One very important thing."

"Yes?"

"Nicholas made me a solemn promise. He swore that he
would never, never go to the cliffs alone."

"And you believe him?"

"Yes, I do," I replied emphatically. "He's certain about the
gold, but I honestly believe he'll keep his word."

We did not speak again for a time; the silence was calming,
and I was surprised to discover that I had, for a few moments,

forgotten my misery. Philip Coulter had been understanding; he had acted quickly, and he had not pressed me with questions, for which I was grateful. Glancing out, I saw that we were approaching the cottonwood tree where I first met Nicholas. The smooth gray bark was silver in the moonlight, and the roots were covered by the night mist. Home of the duppies—perhaps it was only my imagination, but I thought that the horses stepped up their pace as we passed.

Philip Coulter leaned forward, hands gripped together as if he had come to an important decision. I turned my head inquiringly.

"Yes," he said slowly. "I'm interested in your story. If you'd told me before I had seen the rope, I'll admit I would have shrugged it off—but now—well, there had to be an extraordinary reason to bring Gerald to the island in October, and to the cliffs. And an extraordinary reason to kill him."

"What are you going to do?"

"Look about. Investigate. I'll go down to the cliffs tonight. Better not to have anyone see me poking about in the daylight."

Go down to the cliffs tonight? I thought of the rocks, darkness obliterating the sharp edges, the hiding places from which a man could jump and send Philip hurtling down.

"Oh, that sounds terribly dangerous," I said impulsively. "I really wouldn't go to the cliffs tonight, if I were you."

Unexpectedly, he laughed. "Well, that's calling the kettle black. No more dangerous than walking this road alone, a pretty young girl in a ball dress. No," he added, as I drew back into the corner, "I'm not going to ask questions. I know the answer, I think. Stephen Thaw was at the cockfights. As a matter of fact, I followed him to the house, and when neither of you appeared on the dance floor, and when Quaco sent a message that he'd seen you running down the driveway—well, I'm sorry. Not a pretty ending to the party."

I did not speak. For a few moments I had actually forgotten Stephen, but now the ugly scene came back to me: my eagerness to go into the garden with him, the breathless waiting for his kiss, and then the shock. Philip, it seemed, had known what would happen. And Pamela. I began to shiver. Why had he brought up the painful subject? He must have realized how distasteful it was to me.

"Marietta, have you an older brother?" The voice cut through my distress.

"No," I whispered.

"Well, let me take the place of one, just for a short time. And not to give you a lecture on behavior, so please don't misunderstand. Listen to me, Marietta. You did nothing wrong. The truth of the matter is that a great many young ladies far more sophisticated than you, and older ladies as well, have been deceived by Stephen Thaw."

In spite of myself, I looked around at him.

"Yes, I thought that might be a slight comfort to you, to know that you were in distinguished company. One has to be fair to the fellow," he continued in a thoughtful voice. "Because of the family situation, he's not had an easy life. Lived by his wits, or, I should say, by his charm, and he's been very successful at it; his reputation in London as a ladies' man is well established, not to mention one or two scandals that are not as well known. That's why, when I saw his eye on you, I took it upon myself to warn him off, that afternoon in the woods. I was damned if I was going to stand by, no matter how angry you might be, and let him get away with his little tricks—stolen meetings, secret messages, quotations from Lord Byron washed down with descriptions of Venice, I suppose."

"Not to be taken seriously," I added hotly, "unless one happens to be stupid. Well, Pamela warned him about me this afternoon."

"Pamela?"

"Oh, yes. She went into town particularly to tell him that I was swept off my feet, and I might not understand the rules by which these games are played. Unfortunately she didn't accomplish very much. Quite the opposite. If only he'd gone on with the secret messages and poetry instead of"—I could hear my voice rising—"instead of behaving like a—like a drunken beast!"

There was a long pause, and then Philip said quietly, "I'm sorry. I didn't realize he had been drinking. Generally—well, it's unfortunate. I don't suppose you've had much experience with these things."

"No, I most certainly have not! But I've learned a good lesson tonight, I assure you. No man is ever going to come near me again. Never—"

"Ah, don't be so bitter," he interrupted. "That would be a mistake, to let one bad encounter poison your mind. Stephen Thaw isn't worth a backward look, poor fellow. You should pity him, you know, caught on his treadmill. He's a taker, a parasite. While you—you have so much to look forward to—so much to give." Before I could move, he leaned over and lifted my hand. Lightly, he kissed it and put it back in my lap.

"There, you see?" he said teasingly. "Not all men are savages, carried away by their brutish passions."

I laughed, weakly. He might have been talking to Molly. But his talk had eased my mind enormously; a measure of self-confidence had been restored. After all, if so many older and wiser females had been taken in by Stephen's captivating ways, why not I? Philip Coulter was right. The experience, though still painful, should be relegated to its proper place, like a distasteful book.

The horses were slackening pace for the long climb; the glare from the boiling room grew steadily brighter as we approached Repose.

"Nearly midnight," said Philip. "One good day's work behind us, before the norther arrives."

"It's still coming?"

"Yes. If you'd been through one, you'd notice the difference; the air is so lifeless." Far above us a faint light from Repose shone out. I had not realized we were still in the low-lying fog.

"The Shepheards' house is very grand," I said almost to myself. "But I prefer Repose; it's more of a home."

"That was my grandfather's dream, the dream he worked for all of his life—a home for the Thaw family. The Christmas checks are a form of bribery, of course, and yet, in some ways he succeeded. Nicholas has planter's blood in his veins now; he'll know how to manage Repose when it comes to him." His voice hardened. "And I intend to see that Repose does come to him."

The horses pulled into the courtyard and stopped, breathing gustily. I gathered my skirts and stepped down with Philip's assistance. Tall as I was, my head barely reached his shoulder. I remembered that I had vowed never to speak to him for the rest of my visit; I had avoided dancing with him at the party; I had, in fact, told him that he belonged in the barn. He, on the other hand, had been extremely kind. Oh dear, I thought, as we stood together at the foot of the verandah, I suppose I must thank him, but it will be difficult, embarrassing. He spoke first, relieving me of the necessity.

"No crying into your pillow?" he inquired. "No flight to the nearest convent?"

"No—no, I don't think so."

"Well, good night then. If my mother is up, will you tell her about Pamela? I shouldn't like her to worry. She has the service for Gerald very much on her mind."

A chilling thought came to me: two sons lost on the cliffs—Gerald and Philip. A service for two sons.

"Do you have to go to the cliffs tonight?" I asked. "Can't you at least wait until daylight?"

"No," he answered. "Whatever mischief is afoot must be dealt with—and quickly."

As I went up the stairs I noticed that the tree toads were strangely silent but the moon was still brilliant, occasionally shadowed by a mass of heavy clouds. I studied the sky; it was a habit one acquired here, reading the sky for directions. Below, Quaco was leading the horses away, and a light flared up in Philip's face as he lit a match. I felt most uneasy, but there was nothing I could do to prevent him from going to the cliffs. On the other hand, I was glad that I had told him about Nicholas and the gold. It was a relief to have shifted the burden to his shoulders. Murder, gold, a small boy's safety—no, these matters went far beyond my capabilities.

In the living room, one lamp had been left burning; there was no sign of Mrs. Coulter. I paused, looking about. Without the distraction of people, the room seemed shabbier than ever; I longed to give the Staffordshire figurines a good wash in vinegar and water. So much had happened since I had passed through on my way to the carriage; it would take time to forget Stephen's behavior. In spite of Philip's words, I had been badly hurt, but now I could accept the fact that I had learned the much-needed lesson that my father had prophesied: I had not troubled to search beneath the outward appearances; I had disregarded the hidden subtleties.

In my obsession with Stephen, I had all but forgotten the Jackson claim, but now in the silent house I remembered why I had come. Philip had called Repose his grandfather's dream: how angry William Thaw would be if he could see me here, touching the familiar objects as if they were mine; a Jackson with the power to destroy much of his life's work.

At last, I turned down the lamp and made my way along the dim hall, stepping carefully over a creaking board. The brass knob on the mahogany door was loose, and I turned it cautiously to prevent it from rattling. Only a few hours had passed since I crossed over this threshold, easing my large skirt around the corner, gay and giddy with anticipation. Now I prayed that Molly would not be waiting for me, for I could not face her questions: "How many times did you dance? What did he say about the hair?" And, worst of all, "Did he propose?" My only wish was to tear off the ruined dress, the fancy hair ribbons, and bury myself in the pillows. I knew that sleep would not erase my disillusionment, but it would dull the cutting edge. Molly's questions would not hurt as fiercely in the morning.

CHAPTER 16

*Murder, though it have no tongue, will speak
With most miraculous organ.*

SHAKESPEARE: *Hamlet, Act II*

The lamp in my room had not been lit. Except for a slatted pattern of moonlight the room was dark, and I was alone. My relief was so great that I did not think it odd to find no welcoming glow. In any case, I did not need it; my hair would have to do without its customary brushing.

The hooks at the back of my dress were tiny and hard to reach. I was twisting to loosen them when I became aware of the unpleasant smell that filled the room—so strong and acrid that I stood still, my senses suddenly alert. There had been no sound, no movement in the corners untouched by the moonlight. Yet I knew that someone was in the room.

"Cubba?" I said, backing toward the door. "Cubba, is it you?" I was reaching for the handle, trying not to breathe, when the dark mass by the bed took the form of a moving figure. As it lunged at me I was forewarned, and threw myself sideways away from the door. The knife passed over my shoulder and thudded into the paneling with a sharp, splitting sound.

There was no conscious thought in my mind as I leaped toward the verandah door and seized the handle, tugging at it frantically. It was locked. Whirling about, I saw that the man still lay motionless against the wall; the fall must have stunned him momentarily. I headed for the open window, but I had not counted on the hampering layers of petticoats that would not be maneuvered, clinging to my knees like wet sheets. As I struggled, the man stirred and at that moment I began to scream for Philip. If he had gone to the cliffs—if the man pulled the knife from the door—my shrill, steady scream emerged like a kettle on the boil.

The inhuman noise must have frightened my assailant; it would soon awaken the household, and people would arrive in force. He went past me with a rush . . . over the sill and across the verandah, dropping into the hibiscus bushes. The dampness of the grass absorbed his footsteps almost at once. I stopped shrieking and held onto the curtain, clutching my throat. It was impossible for me to understand that a man had waited in my room, waiting to attack me with a knife; not an accident but a deliberate attempt to kill me.

Hurried footsteps sounded on the verandah and I heard Philip's voice: "What is it? What's wrong?" He tried the verandah door, and, finding it locked, kicked it open. Still in the darkness, I said faintly:

"There was—a man—in here. He's gone—across the grass."

"Are you hurt? Did he touch you?"

"No, but it was—I never—" My knees would no longer support me, and I slid to the floor, feeling faint. The sweat ran down my face.

In seconds, Philip was back. "No sign of him out there. Where's the lamp?" His voice seemed to come from a great distance.

"Table—by the bed." I closed my eyes as the light flared.

"Christ!" he said. My head jerked up and I stared. My big, airy room had been turned into a place of filth. White cock feathers lay in a circle about the bed, and a bloody, headless bird had been carefully placed on the pillows, the gore from his severed neck staining the white linen. Other objects—I could not avert my eyes—were heaped on the coverlet: dirt, bones, bloody clothes. The defilement was complete. I turned my face to the wall and moaned.

In the hall, Jilly's wild barking mingled with shouts. Molly and Nicholas.

"Marietta, let me in. Are you all right? Let us in!"

"Oh no," I whispered. "Keep them out. They mustn't see—" Philip crossed the room and calmly turned the key in the lock.

"It's all right, Molly. I'm here, and Marietta is all right. There was a thief in her room, but he's gone. Take Nicholas away, will you? Take him to his room and keep him there for a bit like a good girl."

"But why was Marietta screaming? Why can't we go in?" I could hear Nicholas' protests as Molly dragged him off. Philip swore again; he was standing in front of the door, staring at the knife which protruded from the dark wood.

"The coverlet," I said shrilly from my position on the floor. "I'm afraid it will be ruined. The blood will never come out. But if you call Cubba and put it in cold water right away—yes, that's what you should do. Call Cubba and Louise and have them take it right away."

Suddenly the room was dark again, and Philip was lifting me up. He held me against his shoulder, stroking my back. "Yes, of course," he answered softly. "They'll take care of it; there's no need to worry. Marietta, try to tell me what happened. He was here when you came in?"

I was breathing hard, as though I had been running, and the words came raggedly. "Yes. I came in and shut the door. He ran at me with the knife and missed—it went into the door and he fell. If he hadn't—and then I began to scream and he went out the window. The knife. If he had pulled it out—I couldn't get through the window. My skirts were in the way. I kept tugging at them—and the door was locked, and I was screaming because you might have gone to the cliffs."

"I know, I know. But did you get a look at him? Did you recognize him?"

I lifted my head, shocked. "How could I! It happened so fast, and it was dark. He was just a dark figure coming at me. If I hadn't jumped, the knife would have gone right through me. He was waiting for me, he came into this house, into this very room —planning to kill me. Somebody wanted to kill me. Why? What have I done? Would the Myals come into this very house and kill me, just because of what I saw? And if they've tried once, they'll try again."

"Hold hard. You're all right. He's gone. Nothing more will happen."

"But the room—the obeah—what does it mean?"

"Obeah won't hurt you. Unpleasant, but it can't hurt you." He pushed the loose hair from my face. "One more question. Do you think the man could have been Hazard?"

"I don't know, I tell you. I don't know!"

"Well, no need to fuss about it now. Can you walk?" And he led me through the door and out to the verandah. Lights were on in the house now, and I could hear calls from the servants' quarters. James Thaw came around the corner, carrying a lantern, followed by a white-faced Elizabeth Coulter.

"The door into the hall was locked; we came around this way," said James. "What happened, Philip? Is she all right?" With my face hidden, I listened to his quick explanation. Mrs. Coulter gasped.

"Oh, no! Not in our house! Not obeah in our house!" James echoed her shock.

"It's unbelievable. Obeah in a white man's house—" He swayed suddenly, and grasped the railing for support.

"James, your pills. Shall I get them?" from Mrs. Coulter.

"No, no. Did Marietta see him? Were you in time to see him, Philip?"

"She saw a man, but it was too dark—"

"Too dark to recognize Hazard? Did he speak at all? I intend to see that boy brought to justice for this."

Hazard, I thought. Yes, he would know the house; he would understand obeah; and there was the link with the Myals. The voices were going on disjointedly:

"—never catch him tonight"—"but the knife is in the door"—"think we should leave the room locked until the magistrate arrives"—"Quaco can ride to Mrs. Shepheard's"—"Pamela could come back with him—"

"Pamela?" Bewilderment in Mrs. Coulter's question. "Didn't she come home with you, Philip?"

"I'll explain later. Can you look after Marietta now? Get her into bed somewhere, but not in this room. She's had a bad fright."

"Of course, of course. What am I thinking of, poor child? Let me think a minute. Take her into the spare room, Philip. And then—Cubba, Louisa! Bring hot bottles to the spare room, and hot tea. The rest of you can go back to your quarters." A murmur of protest arose from the group. "Very well, you may sleep in the house tonight. But there's no need to stand around as though the world had come to an end!"

The shock had been severe. Even the hot bottles on my feet could not warm me, and I gazed around the large room with a growing fear. The sound of the waves reminded me unpleasantly of the cliffs, or perhaps it was because Nanny had died in this four-poster bed. Louisa and Cubba had undressed me; now they returned with more hot water. As they came closer, I could see that their hands were shaking. Cubba put down the basin; it tilted and almost fell. She looked at the ceiling, at the floor, everywhere but the bed. Suddenly I knew the reason: the obeah spell had been laid on me, and who knew how far it would reach? There was no hope for me—I had been touched. I began to shiver convulsively, and when Mrs. Coulter came back, she moved quickly to my side.

"Have you taken a chill? Louisa, how long has she been like this?" The maids shook their heads, wordless. Then she understood. "Now don't tell me—oh, how ridiculous! Go along now, both of you, out of this room!"

"They think I'm going to die," I whispered. "They can't look at me because of the spell. My lovely room, the blood all over the bed. I'm afraid it's ruined."

"Nonsense." She took my hand and began to rub it gently, trying to hide her concern beneath the calm expression. "Tomorrow the room will be as good as new. You should know better, my dear, than to let them upset you with their superstitions. Obeah can only hurt you if you believe in its power. One can't blame Louisa and Cubba for their foolishness, but you and I know better—oh, no!"

A long, reverberating blast filled the room, drowning out her voice. One long echoing blast, and then another. Mrs. Coulter dropped my hand and held onto the bedpost. I found myself sitting up, rigid, with no feeling of having moved. The noise could hardly have come from a human throat and yet it wailed in profound anguish, shattering the night air. As it died away, Mrs. Coulter collected herself.

"The conch—the shell blow. I haven't heard it for years. It did startle me, for a second."

The shell blow, I thought. The shell blow, sounded only at a time of great danger. I began to climb down from the bed, looking about for a place to hide.

"No, no. Get back into bed, Marietta! You'll make yourself worse, my dear. I'm sure it's just to call everyone together. Philip or James will talk to the people, tell them what happened, and they'll spread the word to be on guard against this man."

"But how do you *know* that?" My voice was rising. "If there were more of them hiding, if they came down from the hills—there were so many of them, and they did whatever the tall man made them do, like animals."

"Hush, you are upsetting yourself; I don't believe it's any such thing. But if it will make you feel easier, we'll find out what is happening." She went to the door. "Louisa," she called. "Find Mr. Philip and ask him to come here as soon as he can."

When Philip arrived, his mother met him outside the room. I could hear her hasty explanations. "So please reassure her, Philip, while I collect my night things. I will sleep on the cot; she shouldn't be alone or with one of the maids."

He came to the side of the bed and looked down at me. There was weariness in his face, though he made an attempt to be humorous.

"Well, the village people think it's rather a joke. They say that for once the obeahman made a mistake and went to the wrong house—the white man's house. And they're asking for blue paint; that's a remedy to warn him off when he discovers his slip-up. Seriously, though, they are on the watch—no stranger will set foot on Repose land. You really have nothing to fear."

I moved restlessly on the bed. "I hope you're right," I said, trying to keep my voice steady. He reached out as if to take my hand, and then stopped. An odd look passed over his face, as though he had made an unexpected discovery, and then the weary expression returned.

"I don't wonder that you're frightened," he said slowly. "You've had a rotten time of it, these past few days. I thought that if there was trouble tonight it would be at the cliffs, not here. But try to look at it this way—the danger is out in the open. Now it can be dealt with."

"Dealt with? When we don't know what it is? We were talking about danger to Nicholas in the carriage. Now it's danger to me. Is it the Myals? Hazard?" His eyes narrowed, intent on mine. I looked up at him from the pillows.

"Ah, no. You've been—you've been plucky. Don't give way now, there's a good girl. Marietta, the magistrate came. He asked if you could give me any sort of description, now that you've had time to think. Do you remember anything else?" He spoke quickly, as if anxious to leave. I wondered if he was hiding something from me. The shell blow: had it signified more than a call to assemble? I tried to keep my mind on his question.

"I knew someone was there, just after I shut the door. There was a nasty smell."

"Go on."

"Then he flung himself at me, and missed. That's really all." I rubbed my head, trying to concentrate.

"There is something else, more of a feeling."

"Yes?"

"The man, I don't think it was Hazard," I said slowly. "We've been assuming it was Hazard. But Hazard would never have missed me with the knife. He's much too quick, and he wouldn't have lost his balance and fallen against the door. This man was clumsy."

Philip had moved to the window, and stood looking out. "Yes," he agreed. "Hazard wouldn't have missed. Well, as we get more evidence, we'll track him down, whoever he is. And in the meantime—" He stopped as Mrs. Coulter entered the room.

"I'm ready for the night," she said. "Philip, I know you are busy, my dear, but thank you for coming. Such a commotion. Serena has hidden her jewelry from the thief; I was hoping to keep the trouble from her, but the shell blow wakened her." She shut the door behind Philip and busied herself laying sheets on the cot in the corner. "It's like the old days," she said absently, "the servants sleeping in the halls, curled up everywhere. They always do this in a crisis, except, of course, at the terrible time of the uprising when they set fire to so many of the plantations."

The uprising. The quarrel, followed by the poisoning. She could not have guessed how her words would affect me. Suddenly I understood why I was so frightened: this was the room of my nightmares. Why had I not recognized it before? I lay in the bed where my grandfather had died in agony, murdered by Mrs. Coulter's own father.

My gasp brought Mrs. Coulter on the run. "Marietta, what *is* the matter?"

I turned my head away. There was no way I could explain my terror to her. "The obeah," I finally managed to whisper. "I can't sleep in this bed, Mrs. Coulter. It reminds me of the other, in my room."

If she had lost her temper, I would not have blamed her. Instead, she led me to the cot and, as I huddled under the covers, drew a chair close to my side.

"I'm going to tell you another story," she said softly, "and I want you to listen carefully, as it may make a difference in your life."

I nodded, not trusting myself to speak. For a moment she was silent.

"I was a very pretty little girl," she began at last. She must have been beautiful, I thought, without surprise. "I was also dreadfully selfish, and miserably spoiled." I lifted my head and stared.

"You—selfish?"

"Very selfish. Two parents living apart and two older brothers, all eager to please me. I had a delightful life, I assure you! And I was lucky in my marriage. A fine husband, our two boys, and all the pleasures of army life—the polo, the balls, the well-trained help. When my husband was killed in an Indian frontier skirmish, I refused to accept reality. Nothing unpleasant could happen to me! Instead of behaving like a soldier's wife, I stayed in my compound, sulking and refusing to see anyone, even little Philip, who was only a year old. Gerald was in England by then, at his school. Finally, the commanding officer's wife came around. Not a formal condolence call; she had already made that, and this time she marched right past the servants and into my bedroom. She was tiny and her eyes popped; she herself was a general's daughter. Well, she sat down and proceeded to give me a proper shaking up, one that I shall never forget. She told me the stories of two women whose husbands had been killed. One had gone on as I had begun, and ended up in an insane asylum. The other had rebuilt her life, not expecting anything for herself, but finding happiness in helping others. There was nothing sympathetic about the C.O.'s wife. 'There is an old proverb,' she said. 'If you walk from one end of the country to the other, you must go one step at a time. Now get up off your bed and start.' After she left, I went into the room where Philip was sleeping and looked at him. And then I began to walk, one step at a time. It was desperately hard, but eventually I began to find courage, and strength—more than I dreamed of. That is what you must do, Marietta. You must forget your fright and go on—one step at a time. You're so young and lovely, my dear girl. I couldn't bear to think that your life will be altered by this visit. Do you understand what I'm trying to say?"

Dear Mrs. Coulter. I hoped she would never know why I could not have slept in the four-poster bed. "You've been plucky —don't give way now," Philip had said. My courage had not been destroyed by either the Myals or by the man with the knife. No, it was finding myself in the bed where my grandfather had died that broke me. I had been so sure that I would succeed where my grandmother had failed. Now there was one thought in my mind: to leave Repose as soon as possible.

Mrs. Coulter had risen from the chair and had begun to ready herself for the night; now she was beside me again. "Only two-thirty," she sighed. "An endless night, isn't it? Marietta, I've brought some of Serena's drops; there are times when I think their use is quite justified."

Obediently, I swallowed the laudanum. Presently my head grew heavy, my eyelids began to close as though pressed down

by an enormous hand, and I heard Mrs. Coulter cross the room
and climb into bed. But my last thought before sleep was very
clear: I must leave Repose tomorrow. I must leave tomorrow, at
the earliest opportunity.

CHAPTER 17

There is nobody who is not dangerous for someone.

MADAME DE SEVIGNE: *Letters, c. 1690*

The norther came before dawn, with a dismal chill that, in a short time, crept into every corner of the house as if seeking refuge. It poured out of the walls, one could almost touch it, and neither clothes nor blankets could protect us from its cold presence. At home, an unpleasant day was nothing to be feared; we dressed warmly, sat by the fire, and often enjoyed the challenging weather. But here there were no fires, and no escape from the hostile atmosphere.

After the first drugged sleep, I was wakened by the cold and then dozed fitfully; my head ached and seemed precariously attached to my body. I heard Mrs. Coulter stir and leave the room. I was still firm in my resolve to go from Repose, but practicalities began to present themselves: where would I be welcome until the next steamer could take me home?

The door opened abruptly, and Molly's head appeared. "You're awake," she said, unnecessarily. "Granny says you're to stay in bed; she's sending Cubba with your breakfast. Aren't you frozen? Did you ever feel anything like this cold? Marietta, Granny made me promise that I would not ask you a single question—not one—about the man last night. It's agony for me, of course, but I won't. Do you know that I almost sat up to wait for you? If only I hadn't been so sleepy and gone to bed, he might never have come; I wanted so much to hear about the party, too. Was it gorgeous? Did Stephen kiss you? Did he propose?"

I stared at her, bewildered. The party—Stephen—had blurred in my mind.

"Oh, the party was magnificent," I said quickly. "I've never seen anything like the food, the flowers."

"Yes, but Stephen?"

"He didn't come until quite late. Molly, you might as well know, my feelings about Stephen have completely changed. Please don't ask me why, because I don't want to talk about it. Ever." And in a different voice, "I had lots of partners, though, some of them were at the polo. What about you and Nicholas last night? Was he badly frightened?"

Molly gave me a reproachful glance; the spicy role of go-between had apparently ended. "He's all right," she said, but I knew that she was keeping something from me.

"What is it, Molly?"

"He's sick."

I sat up and the room tilted oddly. "Sick? What do you mean?"

"Well, his stomach is upset. Granny gave him paregoric, and now he's very sleepy, doesn't want to get out of bed. Imagine, Nicholas! Maybe it's just nerves; everyone was in an uproar and now this miserable storm. But all we need is to have Nicholas really ill."

"Molly, he didn't see—he didn't go into my room?"

"Oh, heavens no. Philip wouldn't let us. We heard about it from the maids; they can't stop talking about it, and you were screaming so horribly. They think the obeahman put a spell on you. If only Mother doesn't find out he wasn't a common thief."

"Your mother! Oh, it's too dreadful! I left her shawl at the Shepheards'."

"Crikey! Don't tell her. We'll get it back somehow. But why did Philip bring you home, and not Pamela?"

The inquisition was becoming painful, and I pushed back the covers. "A headache," I said lamely. "A sick headache. Shall I go to see Nicholas? No, tell him I'll come as soon as I've had my breakfast. Here's Cubba with my tray." Her appearance was timely, as I knew Molly would not rest until she had unraveled last night's events from start to finish.

But Cubba's presence proved even more disturbing than Molly's. As she moved about the room, tidying and folding, her words—just loud enough for me to hear—streamed out: "obeahman," "poison lil' master," "him too sick."

Finally I put down my cup. "Whatever are you saying, Cubba? That someone has poisoned Master Nicholas?"

The lip was protruding, and her face was sullen, eyes avoiding mine.

"I say dat Mast' Nicholas poisoned by dat obeahman, dat what I say! And it de truf!" Suddenly the smug assurance irritated me beyond control; I had not forgotten how she had frightened me last night.

"Don't talk nonsense," I snapped. "You're nothing but trouble. How could that man poison Master Nicholas? Through the walls?"

The battle was on, and the bullets came flying; there were oleander leaves, unripe akee, galli galli, arsenic bean, cassava root—"And he could have make a small worm from de juice and cut off a small part and put dat in de food."

I put my hands over my ears. "Stop it, Cubba. Take the tray and go. I don't want to hear any more." With a toss of the head, she left me feeling more wretched than before.

From the window I could see that the cutters in the front field had increased the pace considerably; the cane fell rapidly behind them and the leaves of the trees were beginning to blow outward with a whirring sound, not the usual soft rustle. An unhappy thought occurred to me: could the storm prevent my leaving?

I went out to the main verandah, where Mrs. Coulter and Charmian, assisted by Quaco, were taking down the hanging baskets and moving the wicker furniture against the walls.

"He's had these upsets before," said Mrs. Coulter in answer to my question. "The medicine seems to have taken hold; hopefully he'll sleep it off." She looked wan, but not unduly worried. "Did you rest after I left you? I put another cover—" We jumped as the basket of ferns Charmian was holding crashed to the marble floor. The girl stared down with a horrified expression.

"Charmian," said Mrs. Coulter in an even tone, "that was *not* obeah! You simply dropped the basket. Just sweep it up." And when Charmian was gone: "Pay no attention; a storm always unnerves them."

I continued on to Mr. Thaw's sitting room and found him lying in his long Spanish chair looking gray and ill. It seemed a pity to disturb him with my arrangements, but I had no choice. When I finished talking, he sighed and put his hand to his chest.

"I quite understand, I quite understand. But it distresses me to see you leave under these circumstances. You've been so good to Nicholas and to Molly. We've all become fond of you, my dear."

"I'm sorry, too. You've been very kind, made me feel welcome. I never dreamed anything like this could happen; but Mr. Thaw, the question is—where can I go?"

He was silent for a moment. "That does present a problem, doesn't it? The hotel is unsuitable, we have no close friends in town."

"Perhaps with one of the maids the hotel would be all right?"

"No, no. We can do better than that, I'm sure."

"I did think of the Shepheards'. Mrs. Shepheard is so kind, and the major is a magistrate."

"Yes, that would be far better. I can explain the situation to George Shepheard; he would certainly understand. Yes, that is best, and I will send a message to expect you this afternoon."

I stirred uneasily in my chair. "This afternoon? But I planned to go right away, as soon as possible."

James Thaw looked at me with surprise. "Now? But I think it would be courteous to give them a little notice; they're certain to have a houseful of guests. Why must it be now?"

"Because—because—well, do you think I am safe here, until this afternoon?" He smiled at me, with effort.

"I do believe, Marietta, that you are exactly as safe in the morning as in the afternoon. The whole estate is alerted, and there will be no trouble, certainly not in the daylight. Let me think. The memorial service will be at four o'clock; we should be back by five-thirty at the latest. Then the carriage can take you to the Shepheards' before dark."

I could find no real fault with his reasoning; still, I did not like it.

"Are you sure there is no way I could go earlier? Perhaps in the buggy?"

An expression of annoyance crossed his face; he coughed and said wearily, "Your cases. Are they packed?"

They were not. And I remembered, just in time, another matter that must be attended to: Martha's journal, lying behind the mirror on the dressing table. I could not leave without it.

"No, they're not ready, I'm afraid."

"This afternoon will be best, then. Now, my dear Marietta, I too have a favor to ask. Nicholas is ill, and will not be able to go with us to the service. Perhaps it's just as well, as it would stir up his feelings about his father. In any case, I think it would be unwise to leave him in the care of the maids. Since you will be here, would you look after him for that short time? Otherwise Molly or Pamela will have to stay at home."

I hesitated. "I will be alone with him?"

"No, no. The maids will be told to be in the house, and I will have several men posted about as guards. There is nothing to fear, I assure you."

Again I hesitated—and finally nodded my acceptance. At least I would have the opportunity to slip into my old room. But as I left, I could not rid myself of the feeling that I should have kept to my first resolution: to leave immediately.

It was a subdued group that gathered in the icy dining room for luncheon. The events of the night before, and the approaching memorial service, would have altered the best of spirits, but the weather heightened the gloom; one had total dependence on the sun in this part of the world.

Serena did not appear. She was resting, according to Mrs. Coulter, before the ordeal of the service. Only a few months had passed since Gerald Coulter's death: son, nephew, uncle, father—his absence was particularly evident today. No one ate much, and the conversation went haltingly.

"The gulls are in the back pasture," said Molly.

"Is that a sign of rain?" I asked, trying to be helpful.

"One of the signs." Mrs. Coulter, too, was doing her part. "Another is the cattle herding together; they'll begin to do this even when the sky is clear. But it's always difficult to know exactly when the wind and the rain will start."

"Or how bad it will be." Molly again. "Everyone says it's not the time of year for hurricanes, but how do we know? There's always the first time." There were exasperated looks around the table and she reddened. "All very well, but who could have guessed that an obeahman would come into the house?"

"Molly, please!"

"Sorry, Uncle James. Sorry, Marietta." She subsided with a gusty sigh and I smiled at her. I would miss Molly, and wondered how the next few years would change her; perhaps she and Pamela would become closer as she grew less hoydenish. There must have been a consultation between them after Pamela returned, for they had come—separately—to help me pack the valises that Quaco had brought to the spare room. Pamela had presented me with a velvet choker fastened with a pretty pin.

"I think this color will become you," she had said, holding it out. "Will you accept it as a farewell present? And my mother's shawl is back in her cupboard." Then Molly had arrived.

"I'm afraid I caused you a lot of trouble," she muttered, twisting her skirt in her fingers. "I wanted to be part of the romance, I guess, and to tease Pamela, too. Marietta, I told her that you were madly in love with Stephen, and that you hoped he'd propose at the Shepheards' party."

So! I thought; that explains quite a lot: why Pamela went to town to warn him; why he took such liberties with me.

"Trouble?" I said sharply. "Dear Lord, Molly, you can't imagine how much trouble!"

"I'm dreadfully sorry," said poor Molly, with tears in her eyes. "I've learned my lesson, I really have. I'll never meddle in other people's business again, so please forgive me, Marietta."

"I forgive you, Molly," I replied, after a long moment. "It was my fault, too, but none of it matters now, and the less said the better, believe me." We finished the packing, talking of other things.

Now as the meal progressed through its courses, I carefully avoided Philip Coulter's eye; the easiness I had felt with him last night had vanished, but then, I reflected, our relationship had been all ups and downs from the start. "I will not speak to that man for the rest of my visit," I had stormed. In the carriage, however, there had been plain speaking in a brotherly way; no murmur of sea nymphs, or of waiting on my pleasure—the flattery which had so misled me. As a result, the anguished girl he found at the end of the Shepheards' driveway had arrived back at Repose able to face the world again. Later, as I stood in my room shaking and screaming, he had known how to quiet me with an understanding that one did not expect in a man—but then, he was Elizabeth Coulter's son.

I glanced down, ashamed of the sudden color in my face. What an idiot he must think me! What a provincial, to flirt with Stephen Thaw and then run wildly away into the night! My feelings about Philip Coulter were undergoing another change—but to what point? In a few hours I would be gone; I would thank him politely and say good-bye. Good riddance, he would think; one less problem to deal with. I gazed at the Chinese export plate that Charmian had placed in front of me; it was slightly chipped, as was most of the china, but I loved the green and white pattern.

My attention shifted to the big sideboard where decanters and candelabra crowded together, and at the crystal chandelier, brought over by William's wife. "We used to love to go there as children," the old lady had said. "Such an easy, delightful atmosphere." I'm like the man with a price on his head, I thought sadly, the one who must leave the country and never set foot over its borders again. I could never return to Repose.

As usual, we took coffee in the living room; Mrs. Coulter instructed Charmian to light the lamps. "We really needn't sit here in the dark," she remarked, trying to be cheerful. "Marietta, is there anything I can do for you before we leave? I feel so un-

happy about your going in this way; I shall write to your mother
and try to explain, or do you think it would be better not?"

"I think not. She wouldn't understand. One has to be here to—
to understand the power of obeah."

"Yes, perhaps. But we shall truly miss you, my dear. You've
been so good, so kind to Nicholas, so brave in all the difficulties.
I don't want to lose touch with you; we shall write back and
forth, no doubt. And thank you for staying with Nicholas while
we're gone. He has not been ill again, and I shall give him more
medicine before I leave. That reminds me—James must have his
pills before we go; his color is so bad today, and now let me
think—Philip, the carriage is ordered for three-thirty; you will be
riding? Otherwise, there will not be room for us all. Your uncle
says he plans to ride, too, but I will try to persuade him to sit
with us in the carriage, crowded or not."

As she left, I noticed with dismay that Philip Coulter and I
were alone in the room. He seated himself beside me on the sofa;
I quickly looked down at the worn turkey carpet.

"We won't be gone for long," he said quietly. "I've spoken to
Uncle James about the guards. And if the storm should happen
to break, I'll start back immediately."

His hands were strong, clasped together, the fingers long and
tanned; they had stroked my head, held me. Nervously, I edged
away. "Don't concern yourself," I replied, "I shall be quite all
right until you get back from the service, and the carriage can
take me straight to the Shepheards'."

After a pause, he spoke again. "I was hoping that you would
change your mind about leaving. We've taken every precaution,
I think. A stranger could not set foot on Repose without raising
the alarm."

"No," I said, staring at the carpet. "No, my mind is made up.
The sooner I leave, the better."

He drew a deep breath. "A pity," he said in a low voice.
"You've become very much a part of this place. I can see you
here, in your pretty white dresses, bringing new spirit and happiness—all the things Repose so badly needs."

I could scarcely believe what I had heard and spilled my
coffee. A part of this place. What did he mean? I might have

turned to him and said "Yes, it's true, I love Repose. There's nothing I would rather do than set to work and change it back into what it once was—hospitable, welcoming, gay." But a lingering shame kept me silent. I could not meet him halfway.

"Kind of you," I murmured coldly, moving further away on the sofa, "but I really don't want to stay." He rose abruptly and left the room; I saw that the spilt coffee had stained the frayed damask. It will never come off, I thought, scrubbing at it with my handkerchief. It will never come off, and I can never take back those words.

Half hidden in the shadowed living room, I watched the family depart. The ladies wore somber dark dresses and bonnets, and Mrs. Coulter carried the new altar cloth which she would present to the church in memory of her eldest son. James and Philip were riding, Philip going ahead on the large chestnut, sitting easily in the saddle as the horse sidled and danced, hand light on the bridle—as light as his lips on my fingers.

He did not glance back; he would not be rebuffed twice. I had flounced away from a strong man whose qualities I was beginning to appreciate, now that it was too late. If there had not been that unfortunate first meeting on the cliffs; if Jilly had not run away and led me into the encounter with Stephen; if—I was reaching the heart of the matter—if I had not interpreted his concern as interference, his authority as arrogance.

The horse, followed by the carriage, disappeared down the first steep curve of the hill. I could have loved him, I told myself bleakly. I could have loved him, but I had pushed him away with both hands.

The house was quiet, and I hurried down the hall to my old room. There was no sign of Cubba or Louisa, but I hesitated before the closed door, wishing that I need not open it. I could not forget the sight of the big bed fouled with dirt, blood, and the decapitated bird. Drawing a deep breath, I turned the handle. The room was fresh and clean, as though ready for the next guest. There was no trace of me or my possessions, and I felt an odd sense of regret: my presence had been swept out with the debris; it had been meaningless as the wilting hibiscus on the bureau.

But there was no time to daydream. Quickly I went to the dressing table, and reached behind the looking glass, feeling for the packet, the small bundle, wrapped in a handkerchief.

My fingers swept the narrow space. Nothing. I moved closer and pulled the heavy glass forward, almost tipping it in my haste. The journal must be here, I told myself, as my breath caught in my throat. Of course it is here! No package. Frantically, I seized the corner of the dressing table and pushed it out into the room. I knelt down, running my hands over every surface—floor, walls, table. The journal was not there.

I could not decide what to do and stood still for a moment. Should I make a search of the entire room, of the empty drawers? Perhaps someone had discovered the little book and put it back on the shelves. With mounting alarm, I turned to the task. Still no journal, and after several frantic minutes, I stood once again in the hallway, trying to think clearly in spite of a sharp pain that hammered at the base of my skull.

"Control yourself," I said aloud. "It could have been found and thrown away when the room was cleaned; it could have been lying there for years. In any case it is the document that matters."

With a sudden jolting impulse, I turned and ran to the spare room where my valises stood, strapped and ready to go. My undergarments, in the pretty silk case, were packed in the smaller of the bags.

Quickly, I ripped at the peach silk embroidery. Several times during my visit I had felt for the hidden paper, and it had been there. Now I drew it out. A piece of plain brown cardboard lay in my hand. The document was gone.

CHAPTER 18

Blow wind, swell billow and swim bark!
The storm is up, and all is on the hazard.
SHAKESPEARE: *Julius Caesar*

Inevitable. The word repeated itself as I sat on the floor, the contents of the valise scattered around me. Inevitable that my harebrained scheme should end in disaster; inevitable that a document so clumsily hidden must disappear. Still, I made another attempt to find it, tearing apart the silk bag that my mother had made for my eighteenth birthday, twisting it inside out. I might have returned home none the wiser, I thought, holding back the tears. I might not have noticed the substitution until I was about to meet with the lawyer.

Cubba. It must have been Cubba, always misplacing my things. More than once I had been suspicious but reasoned that she would have no use for such a paper, could not even read it. But if someone else had directed her to search my things—I rose, and flew out of the room.

"Come here, Cubba," I shouted. "I shall get to the bottom of this; your sulks and pouting will do you no good, none at all!" But there was so little time—only an hour. I sped down the hall to the living room with a growing sense of dismay. The big, shuttered room was dark; the furniture loomed up in vague shapes. There was not a sound to be heard, not in the dining room or on the verandah. "Louisa! Charmian! Where are you?" It was impossible to think that they had gone off against all orders and left me alone with Nicholas. Philip had said there would be guards, and now I hurried to the verandah. But what I saw brought me to a sudden halt. The world had undergone a startling change in the past quarter of an hour. The water no longer moved in measured waves; it had erupted into a tormented mass of nature gone awry and out of control. The dark sky pressed down as if in helpless sympathy, while the wind rose in the mounting strength that precedes the onslaught of rain. The storm—a bad one—was coming fast. The household and guards had fled.

Still I was more angry than frightened. I would not—I could not—lose the bit of paper on which so much depended.

It was then, standing rigidly still in the dimness, that I became frightened. There was no time to elaborate, but I instinctively knew that I was being watched. Someone was in the house; someone who did not wish to be known. I could not see beyond the shadows; a footstep, a door opening would be muffled by the rising wind. The safest place for Nicholas and me would be his room, where I could barricade the door and windows until the family returned. The document must wait.

As I ran back down the hall, I planned my course of action. The windows could be locked from the inside, and the tall chest of drawers moved against the door. If Nicholas protested, I would make a game of it: sleepy bears hiding in their caves until the winter was over. Apparently Mrs. Coulter's medicine had put him to sleep, for there was no sound from behind the mosquito netting as I slipped in and turned the key in the lock. It was a few seconds before I realized that the netting had been pulled aside and the bed was empty. I reached under the sheets, and then under the slats.

"Nicholas, come out," I said furiously. "I mean it. And what have you done with Jilly?" No answer.

"I'm in no mood for jokes, Nicholas. And you're not supposed to be out of bed." Silence.

With a groan of exasperation, I started toward the cupboard, a logical hiding place, and for the second time in a quarter of an hour was stunned into immobility. Nicholas was not in the room. His blue and white pajamas were thrown in a heap and, even more significant, Jilly's basket was empty. A hasty search of my old room, and of Molly's produced no trace of him. He was not in any other part in the house, I reasoned, for he would have passed me coming from the nursery wing.

I never thought that I could feel as helpless as I did, standing once again in his room. First the disappearance of the document, and now Nicholas was gone. Why would he run away from the house with the storm coming so fast? Explanations came with dreadful swiftness: the obeah last night, the service for his father this afternoon. "I should never have left him alone," I said aloud. "I should never have left him, not even for a few moments."

The wind blew at my skirts, holding me back as I made my way through the courtyard and around the side of the house to the path. The workers had left the cane fields and the mill was no longer grinding. Raising my hand to shield my eyes, I stared at the line that marked the cliffs. There was no sign of a small figure against the sky.

"Oh, Nicholas!" I said despairingly, and began to run, straining to see ahead in the failing light. This would be the final irony: I, who had tried so hard to keep him from the cliffs, would be responsible for his death. He may still be there, I thought, as I stumbled down the path. Don't lose your head and startle him; don't scream out his name.

The object just ahead of me on the path was almost under my feet as I stopped, swaying backward in surprise. But, as I leaned down, I recognized it immediately: Nicholas' red jersey. He seldom wore it; in fact, had protested violently on the one occasion I had ordered him to put it on.

I can say now that the red jersey saved my life. For a deep-rooted instinct slowed my rush to the cliffs; sick or well, Nicholas would not have bothered to take his much-disliked jersey from the cupboard. And then a picture of his earnest little face came to me, and his solemn oath: "I will never, never go alone to the cliffs. I swear it to infinity, amen." Willful and mischievous he might be, but he had never told me a lie. Motionless, I stood with one hand at my throat, considering. Why had the jersey been dropped on the path? Was I being led to the cliffs? I

looked back at the house; it was too far away to see any movement even on the verandah, but I felt, as I had earlier, that I was
being watched. Turning toward the cliffs, I stared at the line of
horizon, broken by the one large tree. Once beyond that tree, I
would be trapped if someone was waiting for me there. A sharp
push, and then the fall. "Oh"—the story would go—"oh, she must
have run after him, thinking he had gone to the cliffs. It was
dark, perhaps she missed her footing and went over the edge."

Part of my mind told me that my shoes were wet, that the hem
of my dress was torn, and that my hair was loosed by the wind.
But another part pressed for a decision. Was I merely the innocent intruder on the Myal rites, and the accidental victim of a
man with a knife? Or was someone planning my death, step by
step, luring me to the cliffs with Nicholas as the bait? If I
believed in Nicholas' promise—if I trusted him—

I leaned down and took off my shoes, as if to shake out loose
stones. Then, deliberately, I continued down the path for a few
feet before swerving quickly into the field. Then I was running,
running across the grass to the distant drive, faster than I
dreamed I could run and yet it was not fast enough; the narrow
strip of drive seemed hopelessly distant in the wide, green expanse. I dared not look back, and cursed my long skirts; without
them I could have made twice the distance in the same amount
of time. At last I reached the white gravel and sped across,
scarcely feeling the sharp, cutting stones. During the flight, the
drive had fixed itself in my mind as a line of demarcation—once
over, I knew that I could outrace a pursuer to the village. Mercifully, that path, though long, was downhill and my heart lifted
as I reached the first outlying fence. I've escaped, I thought, as I
flung myself past it. No one can catch me now.

Farther along, I stopped and waited to catch my breath, almost strangling with painful gasps. But as they eased, and my
eyes cleared, I began to sense the strange silence. No voices
called out to me in welcome, no children came running. No
lights shone from the tiny rooms, nor was there a clatter from the
barrels that served as stoves, nor the smell of cho cho, callalu,
and pepperpot. Instead of the incessant chatter, a lone chicken
squawked from a slatted coop. Then, as I walked into the vil-

lage, I could see that a few animals had been penned or tied up. The inhabitants must have feared the storm and gone to higher ground. The entire village had departed.

In addition to that surprise, another chilling thought came to me as I walked about in search of one or two braver souls. The stream had grown very high, as if rain had already begun in the hills. It churned furiously down over the rocks, spilling over the banks. If it covered the road, the carriage would not return and I would be cut off from help.

I wandered, too dazed to think of hiding, until the pain from my bare feet became unbearable. Finding shelter under an akee tree, I sat down to rub them, ignoring a goat who cried loudly; the roar of water mingled with sharp gusts of wind that sent branches crashing against the wattled huts. Only numbness kept me from panic, and I remember the words that kept repeating themselves over and over in my mind:

> O Western wind, when wilt thou blow,
> That the small rain down can rain?
> Christ, if my love were in my arms
> And I in my bed again!

The anonymous poet—I felt that he was a man—had been cold and desolate. I saw him wearing a cloak and doublet; he was on the moors and in hiding for his life, with the wind beating on his face. And he longed for his love, as I now longed for Philip Coulter. A breaking branch roused me to my senses; it snapped and fell to the ground, narrowly missing my head. I could not stay here, but a quick sortie toward the stream was enough to show me that it had covered the main road, and that making my way to the Shepheards' would be impossible. There was one other house in the neighborhood—Anna Thaw's. Surely, whatever her feelings about the family, no matter how evil her intentions toward Nicholas, she would not refuse me refuge. As for Stephen, he mattered little except as someone I could enlist in a search party.

I stumbled out of the village and began to climb the slippery bank, crouching low enough to keep out of sight. The bridge was a long way from the village, and there was no path that I could

take and not be seen from the house. The rocks and rough grass
were cruel to my bare feet but I crept on, balancing against the
gusts of wind and peering into the gray overcast of light. Then,
to add to my misery, the rain descended from the hills. Not the
usual tropical rain pouring down as if from an overturned
bucket, but walls of water driven forward in great uneven bil-
lows. Instantly the rocks were whitened by bouncing droplets; I
was drenched, my clothes hung on me like an added layer of
skin. Blindly, I groped forward, and at the risk of losing the way,
I turned into the cane field where tall stalks made a swaying
breaker. The ditches were filling rapidly, forming new patterns
in the soil; I struggled through the mud until I judged that the
bridge could not be far, and turned back toward the stream. It
had become a torrent, furiously seeking outlets above the
confining banks. The bridge, I thought; I must reach the little
bridge that Nicholas and I had crossed on the sunny afternoon
when Jilly ran away, and where I had gone, so gaily, to meet
Stephen. Finally, I could see it. The water pounded close to the
stonework, but it was passable and I limped across and followed
the path beyond. The woods, like the cane, were a protection
against the rain, but the last open stretch across the fields to the
house was almost too much for my strength. My body seemed
detached from my head, totally numbed by the battering rain. I
leaned into the wind and pushed forward, knowing that if I fell I
would not be able to rise.

The gardens were awash and the flowers flattened to the
ground as I struggled down the path to the door and knocked on
it fiercely.

"Open the door," I cried. "Please open the door." Nobody
came and I continued to beat wildly. It had not occurred to me
that the house might be empty; I could not imagine that Anna
would leave the place, even for a storm.

At last the bolt was drawn. With my hair and face streaming
with water, I must have been almost unrecognizable, but I heard
Anna's voice saying "Come in, Miss Jackson." She pulled me forward and put her weight against the door to close it; the wind
had pushed into the house.

I opened my mouth to speak; there was no sound. I stared at

Anna in panic; I had forgotten the piercing eyes that looked through one, with no expression or warmth. But it was too late for withdrawal. I had chosen to come, and she could do with me as she wished. For the moment, though, her intent appeared to be harmless. With a hand under my elbow, she pushed me into the scullery where Nicholas and Jilly had been tended, and helped me out of my sodden clothes. Soon I was wrapped in a blanket, with hot stones at my feet, sipping an astringent drink that burned my throat. But it revived me, and I stared at Anna Thaw warily—the emaciated old woman, with cropped white hair and intense, frightening eyes.

"What has brought you here?" she said at last. I hesitated—wondering if I should inquire for Stephen. Perhaps he could serve as an excuse.

"My grandson is not here," she said sharply. "He left yesterday and I do not expect him back, not in this weather." Then, in a softer tone: "You are in trouble, Marietta Jackson, as I predicted you would be. But why have you come to me?"

I abandoned all idea of subterfuge; only the truth would do for Anna Thaw; it would be impossible to mislead her.

"I know how you feel about the Thaws," I began, as bravely as I could, though my voice quavered sadly. "And there's no reason—to help me. But Nicholas—he's only a little boy; he can't help what happened years ago. And this afternoon, after they left for the service, he disappeared. He's gone! When I went to the cliffs, I had the feeling that someone was trying to kill *me!* And that person was using Nicholas' jersey—" I put my head in my hands.

"Don't waste time," said Anna Thaw coldly. "If you want my help, pull yourself together and tell me exactly what has happened at Repose."

Raising my voice above the wind that rattled the panes of glass, I told her the events of the past few days. She did not interrupt or ask questions, but as I talked, I knew with a frightening certainty that this eerie woman already knew the story. James had called her evil; "eccentric" was her grandson's description; Mrs. Coulter feared her wish for revenge. Might she have spirited Nicholas away, and hidden him in the house where I now sat?

As I ended my tale, she said nothing but bent down, looked at my feet, then went to a cupboard and brought out an armful of dry clothes.

"Put these on," she commanded. "And wait." The time passed, perhaps half an hour. I was almost wild with apprehension when she returned, wearing a hooded cloak and carrying a lantern.

"Come," she said, motioning to the door. "Come. We are going to Repose."

I could not have understood, I decided, and remained seated in the chair. Anna go to Repose? My dumfounded look must have annoyed her.

"Quickly, girl, quickly! There is no time to be lost. And I warn you now, whatever you see or hear, be quiet. Ask no questions. Do you understand?"

I was still aghast at the thought of accompanying Anna to Repose. If the family had by some chance returned, what could I say?

"But no one is there," I faltered. "I don't know when they'll be back, in this storm. The carriage cannot get through."

"Quickly, I say! And give me your word that you will be silent."

There was no choice but to follow her out of the house. We hurried down the path, and I wrapped my cloak about me. To my surprise, the rain had stopped. This norther, though violent, had blown itself away. The wind still gusted fitfully, but the sheets of water had changed to an occasional shower mingled with a rising mist. Even so, the thought of the walk to Repose set my legs to trembling.

At the end of the path, another lantern gleamed in the darkness. I could see the outline of a man, holding the halter of a large animal. As we came closer, the light shone up in his face. I gasped and pulled back. It was Hazard. Anna's hand tightened on my arm. "I warned you, no questions. You will ride the mule and Hazard will lead you."

Once again I was painfully conscious of my helplessness as I jogged along on the mule's back. I could not comprehend that I, Marietta Jackson, was running blindly from one danger to the next; not so long ago, I had firmly believed that terror was to be chased by a bull, or to be accosted by a man on the streets of Boston. Now I held on to the rough halter and prayed to live through the night. Nothing at Repose could be as menacing as these strange companions, Anna and Hazard.

The trees dripped, showering us with moisture; I realized why Anna had ordered me to ride the mule: my cut, bruised feet would not have carried me past the barns. Now, as we came up to the bridge, Anna suddenly stopped and spoke to Hazard in a voice I could not hear. We went on through the blackness and it was not until we were close to the graveyard that the shape of the house became visible through the mist. It was dark, except for one lighted window.

"Which room is that?" Anna asked me, gesturing toward the bright square. I looked at it, trying to orient myself.

"I think, yes, it's James Thaw's sitting room," I whispered. And then before I could stop myself: "But there *is* someone in the house. There was no light when I left, I'm sure." Could the carriage have returned? I wanted to slip from the mule's back and run, hide—anything to escape whatever Anna was planning and in which I must play a part.

Noiselessly, our little group crept up behind the kitchen house and passed the breadfruit tree—familiar places that loomed in sinister shapes, dank and shadowed. Hazard tied the mule to a post and, as I dismounted, Anna spoke to me again.

"The sitting room. Is there a door from the verandah?"

"Yes," I gasped. "And one from the hall."

"Good. Hazard, you know what you must do, and Miss Jackson, I warn you for the last time—whatever you see, do not move or cry out." With her uncanny insight, the strange woman realized how close I was to hysterics—swinging between fright and a feeling of wild amusement. To arrive at Repose in company with Anna and Hazard, to creep with them up the verandah stairs like a scene in a comic opera—she was right to caution me, and I made a strong attempt to take hold of my nerves. After all, the house might be empty and this stealthy arrival a wasted effort. But much as I wished to believe it, my instincts told me that this was not so. Anna and Hazard had hurried me here, through darkness and mist, for a compelling reason.

CHAPTER 19

We should look to the end in all things.

JEAN DE LA FONTAINE: *Fables, III*

The wind muffled the sound of our footsteps as we inched down the verandah, single file, toward the open door of the sitting room. Anna motioned me to stop, and I flattened myself against the wall, unable to see into the room. She and Hazard moved on to a position just outside the bright square of light. There were men in the room, talking; I recognized James Thaw's voice. How had he managed to ride back through the storm? Was Philip with him? But the other voice was strange and slurred.

"I did my best," he was saying. "I did my best. Cannot put no blame on me, no, it not fair to lay blame on me."

"Come, now." James Thaw again. "The fact is, you have bungled abominably. You know that I overlook some discrepancies in the books, but this year, did you take leave of your few wits? Even if the captain had not arrived, I could not have hidden the losses. You will have to leave Repose; I can do nothing to prevent it and I will not. You will have to go."

So the other man was Morris; at last he was being dismissed. I waited for his reply, and it came with a vengeance.

"Bastard. Do you smile that I call you bastard? Oh yes, you thinks, now I be rid of Morris after all these years, but you wrong, dead wrong."

"That will do, Morris. You've told me several times what I

think; in fact, you've said quite enough. Please go. I must rest after riding back through the storm."

My hands loosened their tight grip on my skirt; unpleasantness between James and Morris had nothing to do with me. But as my nerves steadied, a chair in the room overturned with a crash that made me jump. Morris' voice rose in a shout.

"Christ, Mr. James. You think me too stupid. You don't know what hold me here all these years?"

"Morris, I'll see you in the morning. Now will you get out?"

"The gold, man, the gold cups what my mother tell me about. The gold cups in the cliffs!"

"What the devil are you talking about? If you won't leave, sit down, then. You are much too excitable. Try to calm yourself and talk sensibly." There was a short pause, and Morris resumed in a lower tone:

"I knew it something big, very big, to bring Mr. Gerald to Repose that time of year. He come one afternoon, no warning, and say he passing through, that he have business on the other side of the island and he just passing through and be off in the morning. Chitty get him something to eat, and pretty soon the house go dark. But I watch, and about midnight I see a light moving. I follow it down the path to the cliffs and by now I know what it mean. He hook the rope to the tree, go down and come up again, above the first ledge. I hears him swearing and carrying on as he look for the place and try to move the stones and hold the light at the same time. I stay close above him and I follow every step as he drop the stones into the water and begin to bring out the gold. He put it in a sack and pull it up and lay it on the ground. Why, I can near see the shine of the cups through the sack. He make three trips and then he stand for a while, catching breath. He put everything together in one sack and then he go down once more, maybe to close up the hole. One last time he climb down that rope."

"Ah, no! Not even you, Morris—not even you!" James's voice was nearly inaudible; I put my head against the wall, fighting the sickness that rose in me at the thought of the knife cutting through the strands, the recognition of death, and the fall. Nicholas' father. Morris' whine cut through my dizziness: "I take the gold·to a hidy place and when it light I come back and cut off the rope and take it away. Look like he fall whilst clambering around on the ledge. Made me feel bad, it did, to see him like that, twisted up, with the blood run out through the rocks. I always did like Mr. Gerald, you see."

There was a thick silence in the room. I breathed deeply and leaned against the wall, trying not to see Gerald Coulter lying dead, his blood trickling through the rocks. What must Mr. Thaw be feeling? The shock would be severe. As if in answer, he began to cough, a violent spasm that lasted so long I feared he would never catch his breath. Morris laughed.

"Look like you save me the trouble of killing you, Mr. James. Yes, kill you. You know I has to kill you, before I goes away with the gold. Would you like a glass of water before I puts my hands around you neck? Ah, don't look so scared, Mr. James. It come to us all. Just a few seconds more and I be off. Hold still now, Mr. James."

I started for the door, my promises abandoned, for I could not stand in the dark and listen to James Thaw being strangled to death. When Morris saw that there was a witness he would run; if not, Hazard was there to keep him from turning on me.

Then I saw that Anna was leaving the shadows. She stopped me in my tracks with a commanding gesture and walked, slowly, calmly, into the sitting room. Unable to bear my unseeing position any longer, I slipped into the empty place beside Hazard.

"Good evening, Mr. Thaw. Good evening, Morris." The scene before me had the fixed look of an amateur tableau: Anna had seated herself with her back to the verandah; James was stretched out on the long Spanish chair, his trousers filthy with mud. Morris faced me from across the room. I had seen him only on Christmas Day, and was struck once again by the odd color of his hair and his jaundiced look. He turned from Anna to James and then back to Anna, speechless. No duppy, no apparition could have been more startling than the appearance of Anna Thaw at Repose.

It was James who broke the astounded silence. "Something extraordinary must have brought you here, madam," he said in a voice remarkably controlled for one who had been so close to death. "The storm. Have you come for help?"

"No, I have not come for help." Anna folded her hands slowly, as if to draw out the moment. There was a pause.

"Why then, may I ask?"

"You may. I am here because I have recently received information that you will wish to have."

James's eyes closed as if in utter weariness. "Information I will wish to have? From you? Impossible. The storm seems to have driven everyone out of their minds. I don't know what you mean, madam. All I know is that I must have some rest. My heart." Indeed, he looked alarmingly ill, but Anna continued implacably.

"Yes, I will oblige you but only after we have talked of Marietta Jackson."

James's eyes opened. "Miss Jackson? What can you be thinking of? You don't know the girl."

"To the contrary, Mr. Thaw. I met Marietta Jackson the day after she arrived at Repose and was interested to learn that a Jackson was here to visit. Yes, I found it extremely interesting that the only descendant of Daniel Jackson was here at Repose."

James Thaw regarded Anna in a resigned way; he pressed the tips of his fingers together, forming a bridge.

"Frankly, madam, I still have not the least idea what you are talking about. Miss Jackson wrote to me claiming that possessions of her grandmother's were left here years ago. The objects were found, we were able to settle the matter amicably, and she has been a most agreeable guest. If there is anything of importance in this, I do not see it." His voice was calm; he and Anna might have been exchanging views on the weather.

"There is nothing of importance in what you have told me," she allowed. "I would, however, like to meet Miss Jackson again. Is she here in the house?"

It was a presumptuous request. James raised his eyebrows in surprise.

"No, madam, she is not. In point of fact, she was to have stayed in the house with my great-nephew while we were at the service for his—his father." James Thaw's voice broke, and he paused. "Though I cannot see that this concerns you, my great-nephew is here, but there is no sign of Miss Jackson. I am worried about her; Morris is to organize a search party as soon as possible."

Anna sat straighter in her chair. "Well, Mr. Thaw, I believe I can enlighten you. Miss Jackson arrived at my house, not so long ago, fleeing for her life. She was convinced that someone at Repose was trying to kill her; a frightening experience for the girl, especially after her other narrow escapes. Yes, I had quite a time to calm her. What is more significant, she tells a strange story of what has happened at Repose these past few days. Very strange indeed." Anna Thaw stopped briefly and then continued, pronouncing the words slowly and with emphasis: "Marietta Jackson is alive and in my hands."

I closed my eyes and opened them, blinking hard, then shook my head in an attempt to clear it. Nicholas was back, it seemed, but where on earth had he gone? And I did not understand Anna's last words: "Marietta Jackson is alive and in my hands." Carefully, I watched the three people in the sitting room; Anna, motionless; James, unmoved by her remark—and Morris. The man began to twitch as if on the verge of a convulsive fit. Jerking himself forward, he burst into incoherent speech.

"She—this one—she come here and who is to know why? She—what to do?"

Anna's voice was scathing as she turned on him. "Yes, Morris, what will you do that won't end in failure? You are a miserable idiot, a murderous creature. That old trick of placing a dart in a horse to frighten and turn him—oh, your timing was correct and your aim good enough. But why did you wait, after cutting the sheep from the flock? Why did you not kill her? Was it because you discovered that you were being followed?" Morris' lips worked soundlessly.

"Then your next failure, even more foolish. It was clever, yes, to bring obeah into Miss Jackson's room and put suspicion on the Myals. But no obeahman would be as clumsy as you, I assure you. There you were, armed with a knife and unable to kill an unsuspecting young girl. Oh, my poor Morris! And now this afternoon—what a fuss and bother for nothing! The guards and maids sent away, the entire village frightened up into the hills in fear of the storm. The boy and the dog drugged and hidden, the trap laid. There you are, waiting at the cliffs to push the girl over and what happens? She escapes and runs to me. Laughable. Your master is right to send you away, for you are worthless."

By the time Anna finished her castigation, Morris was bent into a crouch, a cornered animal ready to spring. Beside me, Hazard tensed. James rose with effort from the long chair and placed himself behind the big desk.

"Take hold of yourself, for God's sake, Morris!" he said urgently. "Take hold of yourself, man, before you lose your head." He fumbled in a drawer for pills, then seized a half-filled wine glass that stood on the desk and swallowed them.

So it was Morris, I thought disjointedly. It was Morris who followed me through the hills, and waited for me at the cliffs. The man was mad as well as incompetent, and now Mr. Thaw would listen to Philip. He must be shut away, immediately, before he could do more harm.

James Thaw finished the wine and put down the crystal glass with precise care; fine objects seemed to please him; unlike the land, they did not require patience and unpleasant decisions. I supposed that he was asking himself the same question that tore at me: why would Morris want to kill a guest, a stranger at Repose? Fortunately, the pills were beneficial, for when he addressed himself to Anna once more, his voice was stronger.

"You have a great deal of information, madam, a great deal of information," he said evenly. "I'm beginning to understand several things that have puzzled me. I suspected that Hazard was no ordinary butler when I questioned him about the Myals. Did you send him here to spy on us after Thomas left? Was Thomas another of your spies?"

"Thomas is a good boy, but by no means as clever as Hazard. Yes, Mr. Thaw. Until you dismissed Hazard, I knew everything, everything that went on at Repose."

The color of James Thaw's complexion slowly changed from gray to a dark, diffuse red. He trembled as he glared at Anna. "What a low creature you are!" he gasped. "How dare you—how dare you intrude yourself upon us, spying through the servants!"

Another fit of coughing seized him. As he struggled for breath, Anna sat with her hands folded in her lap; the head of white, cropped hair never moved. When at last he regained control of himself, she began to speak in a quiet, conversational voice.

"I have been alone much of my life. I have had time to reflect on greed, and my reflections are borne out by what has happened here tonight. It was greed, James Thaw, that led your father William to poison Daniel Jackson. Oh yes, I know the crime your father committed to keep his land and his gold. Gold chalices so valuable that they must remain hidden from his mistress Martha and her son Morris. A strange inheritance for you, was it not? You alone knew their exact place in the cliffs, and yet you did not have the strength to go after them yourself. Well, they were safe enough, safe until one day in August you received the letter from Miss Marietta Jackson. Ah, the Thaw nightmare had finally come, your father's great fear which he passed on to you. Had the document giving the Jacksons Thaw land been discovered? How much did the girl know? There was only one way to find out—bring her to Repose. And now you were forced to tell one part of the story to your nephew, Gerald Coulter. He was instructed to remove the gold; Nicholas might lose a rich inheritance if it should prove to be on Jackson land.

"Now it was December, the girl was arriving, and you must find out what she knows. Was she bringing papers with her? Who could search her things? There was one person who could help—Morris, who had been robbing Repose all these years. Yes, you could safely blackmail Morris.

"Your plan did not seem difficult, I imagine, in the beginning. Cubba, Morris' mistress, was brought into the house as a maid; her task was to put the sharp-eyed Miss Crowell out of the way while she went through Miss Jackson's belongings. Regrettably, an overdose of poison killed the old lady. But Cubba was free to search and before long she found a hidden paper and brought it to you. How very foolish of Miss Jackson to bring the claim to the land with her. What a triumph for the Thaws! And now came the dilemma—had Miss Jackson left a copy at home? More evidence? There was only one solution—the last of the Jacksons must not leave the island alive. Only when she was dead would Thaw property be secure."

Anna shifted her chair closer to the desk. She leaned forward. "Yes, you look very ill, Mr. Thaw," she said in a softer voice. "It must have been a great strain, to play the part of the kind host and to see all the schemes to do away with your guest come to nothing. One failure after another, and now the girl is alarmed, she is about to leave. A desperate last effort—and she comes to me. Your plan has failed, Mr. Thaw, and Marietta Jackson is in my charge." There was a long pause. Neither James nor Morris stirred. She paused. "Is greed, or should I say family pride, inherited?" she asked reflectively. "However, I did not come here to sermonize; no, hardly that. Shall I get to the point? Your situation, Mr. Thaw, is somewhat precarious. Not only has your victim escaped, but your attempts to murder her are out in the open. They are known. I must ask you—what do you intend to do now?"

I had followed Anna's dramatic unveiling with growing detachment. These astonishing adventures had, oddly enough, begun to seem implausible even to me. And I found it impossible to believe that frail, fussy James Thaw was capable of a driving wish to kill anyone. "He plays a subtle game, your uncle," I had said to Molly after our first game of piquet. But that had been a game. Anna Thaw is obsessed with hatred; she is the deadly opponent, I thought, staring at her. Nothing would please her more than to implicate the Thaws in a scandal.

James had remained in the chair behind the desk; he appeared to be looking straight at me across the verandah, though I was well outside the light. I wished that I could reassure him. "Don't worry, I know that Morris and Cubba are the guilty ones," I would have said. "Anna Thaw is a dangerous woman, as you have always told me. I should order her to go about her business and stop spying on you."

Finally he spoke, and I listened carefully. "You ask, madam, what I intend to do," he said with deliberation. "Since you hold the cards, the essential question is—what is it that you want? You have obviously come here tonight to bargain with me. What will satisfy you? A share of Repose land? Jackson land? Will you hand Marietta Jackson over to me in exchange for her land? Yes, I will agree to that. Then we will both have gained our objective."

It took me a few seconds to grasp his meaning. If Hazard had not seized my hands in a painful grip, I would have screamed and run forward. Then, as I stood immobilized, it seemed that every drop of blood in my body was chilling, as though I had been encased in a block of ice. It did not matter that at last I recognized my enemy—no, that was not important. The noose was around my neck, the ancestral noose. "Always, always there is a noose which binds us more tightly into the Thaw fortunes—" My grandmother had escaped it, but now it was firmly fastened about my neck. If my hands had been free, I would have reached up to tear at it. Who will be the one to kill me? I cried out silently. Morris, straining for bloodshed, or cool, wily Hazard? Philip had said he would come back if the storm broke, but he would be too late.

"Mr. Thaw, you are blunt, very blunt indeed," said Anna quietly. "Give you the girl in exchange for land? Yes, what an interesting proposal. I can see how well that would solve your difficulty. But that was not what I had in mind. No, I'm afraid my bargain will not please you."

"More? You want more? For God's sake, madam—"

"Please. Pay attention, for the terms I am about to state are not what you expect, Mr. Thaw."

"You are to give back the document, the claim to the Jackson land which you now hold. The land will be returned to the Jacksons by process of law, with no discredit to the Thaw family. But if you refuse, Mr. Thaw, if you refuse, I shall go to George Shepheard with Miss Jackson. She will tell her story and I will corroborate it with evidence. The old scandal will be known, as well as the present one. It will be impossible for those in your family to hold up their heads, either here or in England. As for you and Morris and Cubba—I should prefer hanging in England to a trial on this island."

I had been so certain of my death that, for a few seconds, Anna's words had little meaning for me. Indeed, the faces of the participants in the room told the story far more clearly. James

Thaw's mouth had fallen open; he stared at Anna in disbelief. Morris had slowly risen from his crouching position; he moved several steps toward Anna, his fingers spread apart like claws.

"No, Mr. James. No need to give it away. She have no rights here—she have no rights—"

Anna stood up abruptly and confronted him with no sign of fear. "Rights?" she said in the peculiar cutting voice she reserved for Morris. "Who on earth are you to be talking of rights? My poor man, have you imagined all these years that you have rights at Repose? I knew your mother, Martha, most sinful woman I ever met. She'd have bled William dry. You think you're William's son, do you? You think you have the look of a Thaw? Faugh! There was a bookkeeper here the exact image of you. Rights? You have no more rights at Repose than a stray dog at the kitchen door." With a gesture of disgust, she deliberately turned her back on him.

It was a clear invitation to murder. My hands clutched at the railing as Hazard released me and moved swiftly across the verandah. It would be an unequal battle. I wanted to look away, anticipating the blood, Morris' scream. To my profound disbelief, Hazard took Morris gently by the shoulders. He spoke to him quietly and firmly, as one would speak to a child. Poor, crazy Morris. A moment before he had been poised to stab Anna Thaw in the back; now he stared at Hazard in a pitiful way. Then, without the least struggle, he allowed himself to be led from the house and out into the night. It was an unnerving spectacle, with a touch of finality about it. As I watched him go, I felt that Morris would not be seen again at Repose.

The room, after the darkness, seemed garishly bright. The two remaining figures did not move, James behind his desk, Anna standing.

"The document if you please, Mr. Thaw," she said pleasantly. "Marietta Jackson is waiting."

I came through the door uncertainly. The sight of me standing there must have been the final shock to James Thaw's overstrained heart. With a gesture of defiance that sent the wine glass crashing to the floor, he fell forward over his father's great desk.

CHAPTER 20

To enjoy true happiness we must travel into a very far country and even out of ourselves.

THOMAS BROWNE: *Christian Morals, c. 1680*

The dead must wait upon the living. I ran through the dark house to the nursery wing. "The boy is here," James had said, but nevertheless I lit the lamp with trembling hands. Nicholas was back, peacefully sleeping as though he had never been out of his bed. I shook him awake, calling his name until he finally opened his eyes and recognized me. The drug, combined with his grandmother's medicine, must have stupefied him: Jilly, too, was heavily asleep in her basket.

"Nicholas, where have you been?"

"Been?"

"When you were taken away. Where did you go?"

"Go? Let me sleep, Marietta. Don't bother me." I gave him a drink of water, pulled the nets tightly, and began to light the lamps throughout the house in a sudden urge to shut out the night. The rooms were glowing when Anna came into the living room.

"I have laid Mr. Thaw out on his bed. There is nothing more to be done. The doctor will come, no doubt, and make a report of cause of death."

I did not know what to say. Although James Thaw's heart had been bad, the events of the night had surely killed him. Anna Thaw regarded me with cold eyes. "You are not responsible,"

4o250

she continued, "and if you are sensible, you will say nothing about what has taken place here tonight."

"Nothing? But there will be questions; what about Morris— and Cubba?"

"Morris and Cubba have left Repose. Hazard has seen to it that there will be no trace of them. They are gone." I stared at Anna with horror.

"But that is impossible! People can't disappear. The law, the magistrate—there will be an investigation and then what shall I do?"

Anna moved closer, and in spite of the fact that she had saved my life, I stepped back.

"Ah, Miss Jackson. I see you have not quite learned your lesson. We have our own ways here; they may not be your ways, but if you take my advice you will save yourself much trouble. I am returning to my house and I shall never speak of these matters to anyone. You need not tell lies; Morris and Cubba have disappeared; James Thaw rode back through the storm and died of a heart attack."

For a moment I was silent. There was no evidence that I had come to Repose with a hidden motive; Mrs. Coulter need never know of the crimes that her father and brother had committed. There would be distress: "Poor James, he was so stubborn about not going in the carriage, and then to leave us and ride back—" But instead of scandal, there would be a well-attended funeral service and I would quietly return to my home.

Anna Thaw had crossed the room and stood under the portrait of William Thaw, studying it. Suddenly I remembered that she had never before set foot in this house. I realized, too, that I had not thanked her. When I tried to express my feelings, she stopped me with a gesture.

"There is no need to thank me. I did not help you because of any fondness for you, Miss Jackson. I wished to settle accounts with the Thaws for the humiliation they have caused me and mine. I hated William and James Thaw, it is true. But Nicholas need not fear me. There will be changes at Repose; much will depend on your judgment. You have risked a great deal for this document, Miss Jackson. See that it does not cause more harm."

She handed me the Jackson claim. Then, gathering up her cloak, she went to the verandah; I followed at a distance. In a moment there was the sound of the mule's feet below on the drive. She had not taken the lantern; it seemed that she did not need the light, this strange, bitter woman.

Beyond the cliffs the heavy fog had lifted and I could see the clouds move in shifting stripes across the sky. Tomorrow the sun would dispel the dampness that weighted the air; in time, the tree toads would sing, and the flowers sweeten the night. I returned and walked about the living room, touching the spinet, the rocking chair, moving about to keep myself from thinking either of the past or of the future. One thing was certain: I was not the untried girl who had arrived in the carriage, nervously twisting her gloves. My strength had been tested, and I had survived. I went to the door of James Thaw's bedroom, and then to the other wing to listen to Nicholas' breathing. For the last time, Repose was in my care.

When I heard the sound of footsteps outside, I felt an odd sense of regret. The old house had been at peace; now there would be upset, confusion.

It was Philip, but he did not look like the man who had gone off a few hours before. His face was white and drawn, his clothes wet through with mud and rain. When he saw me, an expression of profound relief came into his eyes; then he rubbed them wearily and leaned against the railing.

"I started back. I came as fast as I could, but the horse stepped in a hole and went lame. I had to lead him most of the way. You're all right? I never should have left you."

Always before, I had been the exhausted one. We stood, silently, seeing the other's need. Then he was holding me in his arms with a fierceness that startled me, but this was not like Stephen's frantic embrace. When he kissed me there was no fumbling haste. Indeed, my feeling at first was mainly one of discomfort; his wet clothes were soaking through my dress.

But as he held me, the memory of a favorite childhood pastime returned. I was lying in our orchard, warmed by the grass beneath me, and the hot sun above. I would close my eyes until the glow through the lids became too bright, and then open them for a second to the brilliance. Now, in Philip's arms, I began to feel the same intense warmth, knowing that it was only a shade of what it might become, a small discovery in our knowledge of each other. Philip was a giant of a man, but I, too, was strong. Together we would succeed in whatever we set out to do. And yet I clung to Philip, for it was he who must lead the way into this new and luminous dimension.

The horse, tethered in the courtyard, snorted impatiently. We drew apart, and I became aware of my damp clothes and the realization that I must begin my story. Should I take Anna's advice? In my confusion, I made a small sound of distress, and Philip stepped back.

"I'm sorry," he said, breathing hard. "After the other night, I shouldn't have—"

"No, it's not—that." Suddenly the long hours of waiting for him angered me irrationally. "If only you had come sooner; why didn't you come? It was so terrible—you can't imagine how terrible."

"It was an accident, the horse going lame, couldn't be helped. What was so terrible? Was Nicholas sick again?"

"No," I said, with an attempt to calm myself. "It's worse than that. Your uncle. The ride through the storm was too much for his heart. Philip, he's dead."

It was another endless night. The family arrived back, and then, some time later, Dr. Barrows came. After a few hours of fitful sleep, I rose and sat by the window, watching the gray lighten, and feeling the soft wind come from the water. I saw Philip leave the house, and soon the cutters were in the fields, taking up the rhythm as though there had been no interruption. It was comforting to see that Repose itself was the same; there might be new masters but the work of the land went forward.

As for myself, although the violence had vanished in a night which I would always associate with cold and blinding rain, my position at Repose had not changed. Should I depart with my grandmother's trinkets, or should I announce my claim? Philip

would despise me if I told him the story, for my August letter
had put in train the deaths of his brother, Nanny, and his uncle—
my burden of guilt could not be avoided. No, I decided. It
would be impossible to reveal my claim at this time.

Last night's encounter with Philip: what was its true meaning
this morning? Should I slip away to the Shepheards' without
meeting him again? Was the merging of souls simply the result
of fear and strain? I dreaded and longed to see him.

Nicholas bounced back from his day in bed with a shrill, mis-
directed energy; nothing held his attention, and soon Molly and
I were frantic with the effort of keeping him out of the way as
Agnes Shepheard and Elizabeth Coulter made arrangements for
the afternoon service. Pamela had taken over the direction of the
household; in its grief, the Coulter family had closed ranks. I felt
very much the outsider.

Late in the morning, Nicholas was dispatched with Molly to
ride for an hour. No one had asked me about my plans, and once
again I turned to the books to occupy my mind; I oiled, sorted,
and carried the heavy volumes about until my face was flushed,
and streaks of dirt soiled my dress. The sun shone down with
force and after a while I went out to the verandah to cool myself. I had not expected that Philip would be back before luncheon, but to my surprise he suddenly appeared on the steps. He
too was hot, his shirt clinging to him, his boots dusty.

"I wanted to talk to you," he said matter-of-factly, wiping his
face. "It must have been a busy morning up here. Shall we go
down to the cliffs?"

"To the cliffs?"

"Why not? Are you afraid of the cliffs? No one will bother us
there."

"Oh, very well." We walked down the path, and I tried to ignore the fact that my heart was beating wildly. He glanced
down at me; my hands and dress were a disgrace, and I had a
fleeting vision of Stephen and myself in the woods, delicately
sipping tea—dreamers, not builders.

"What on earth have you been doing?" he asked.

"Cleaning the books in the nursery hall. I can't bear to see
them so neglected, rotting away."

Today the sea was playful, tossing up bits of foam as though apologizing for its bad behavior. We sat on a grassy spot within the shadow of the great tree. I found, to my surprise, that I could enjoy the sweep of blue that Shelley had once described:

> . . . where the earth and ocean meet
> And all things seem only one
> In the universal sun.

"About last night," said Philip, and I jumped. The color rose to my face but he was not looking at me. "Morris has disappeared. I went down to his house early this morning; there's no sign of him and his things are gone. But that's not the half of it. The gold was in his house—the gold cups standing on the kitchen table as if they were nothing out of the ordinary. After I got over the shock, I thought about Gerald's murder; it all made sense. But last night, something must have happened for Morris to get the wind up and run off without them. I suppose we should be damn glad to be rid of him and have the gold, but I tell you, I hate the sight of it. As soon as I can, I'll have it locked up, away from Repose. When Nicholas comes of age, he can do what he likes. I never want to lay eyes on it again. By the way, should I tell Nicholas about the gold? Maybe we should have that treasure hunt after all, and let him find it! What I wanted to ask you, Marietta—did you hear anything last night that might account for Morris going off?"

In spite of the sun, I felt cold. Anna was wrong. I would have to tell Philip Coulter the truth. He might despise me—the Jackson intruder—but even that would be preferable to lying. I hesitated; he was looking out to the horizon and I glanced quickly at the profile that had reminded me of an emperor's. He must have interpreted my silence as a lack of anything to say.

"That is the dress you wore when I first saw you," he said reflectively. "Strange, when you think of it, how much has happened at the cliffs—Gerald, Nicholas, the gold—and our meeting. I knew that I loved you when we sang the carols, Christmas Eve. You were so beautiful, with the light on your hair—and then Nicholas gave us that bloody song."

I had to smile, remembering my relief when John Canoe's arrival spared us an outpouring of righteous wrath.

"When I carried you down from the hills, you were already falling in love with Stephen; I knew that very well, but still I had to warn you. You hated me, and I didn't blame you." He took my hand and turned it over gently, tracing the lines in the palm.

"Marietta, I've never been in love. I never thought I could love anyone as I love you—a miracle—strong, and beautiful and sweet."

Abruptly, I pulled my hand away. "No," I said bitterly. "No, I'm not like that. I've been trying to get up my courage; I've done you a great wrong."

"Stephen, you mean? But that's over, done with. You weren't to blame, whatever it was. He could charm the devil himself."

"I was never in love with Stephen, I know that now. It was the flattery, and maybe the life he leads—the excitement, and the travel." There was a long pause.

"Well," said Philip, and I could sense an effort to keep the tone light, "one of the great advantages of marrying a soldier is the excitement and the travel." He put his hands on my shoulders and turned me toward him. "Will you join forces with me, Marietta? With someone who wants to spend the rest of his life loving you, caring for you?"

I sat without speaking, and finally he let me go. "What is it?" he said quietly. "You'd better tell me."

The story went on endlessly. At times my voice faltered; I dared not look up and see the stern expression on his face. At the conclusion I stood and carefully brushed the bits of grass from my skirt. At least I could spare him embarrassment.

"I appreciate the honor you've done me, with your proposal." My voice was steady. "But you can see why I can't marry you, why I must leave Repose."

He was on his feet, pulling me to him, his shoulders broad against the sky. "I always thought bringing you here was an odd thing for James to do," he said softly, holding me close. "Marietta, believe me, it was my family that did the wrong, not you, my darling. Not you."

He said no more, for I was crying uncontrollably, as though to wash away the past few days. When the gasping and sobbing finally stopped, Philip lifted my chin gingerly.

"I must say, you do look a fright. Marietta, I've been thinking as you soaked my shirt that I first asked you to marry me because I loved you. Now I see there's a far more important reason —self-interest; it's certainly to my advantage to have Thaw and Jackson land joined, as soon as possible. What do you say to that, my dearest? Repose will be our home, when I'm on leave, until Nicholas can take over. Together we'll make it into the finest plantation in the Indies."

Suddenly the practical side of my nature asserted itself.

"Philip, can we have a swing under the poinciana tree? And songs and dancing at night? Oh, and I can finish the books and turn out those terrible old storerooms."

He let me go and stood back.

"Storerooms! Books! Good Lord, I thought a proposal was a sacred moment in a woman's life—and you begin to chatter about turning out the storerooms. Are you marrying me or Repose?" I caught at his arm.

"Philip, don't tease me, not yet. I was so terribly afraid that you would hate me, that I would go away without seeing you again—I really don't know what I'm saying."

He took me in his arms, then, his face serious. "I'm sorry. Let's start over. Marietta, I adore you. I want to care for you the rest of my life. Will you marry me?"

"Yes, Philip, I will marry you." I reached up and touched his face. The old evil had gone, and the new life was beginning. As we stood together, with the sea and sky at our backs, I knew that the ancestors had cried out. Their claim had been settled: with hatred, with violence—and with love.